I0538372

CONSTANT

ELIZABETH MUNRO

Blue Swell Books
Nanaimo, B.C.
Canada

First Print Edition: January 2015
ISBN: 978-0-9919759-2-1

www.elizabethmunro.ca

CHAPTER 1

"I love you, Rye."

Angel instantly regrets the words.

Her commander tenses in her arms. Moments before, she teased his ear with her teeth the way she knew drove him crazy. Unbridled bliss in the dirty and debris strewn room forced the words from her lips as he shook beneath her.

Now she confesses the one thing they shouldn't have.

"Damn it," she mutters, lips still pressed to his ear.

Angel wears nothing but standard-issue black socks and sweat sticks her breasts to his armour plated chest.

"I..." she tries as Rye pulls her away enough to look in her eyes.

"Angel," he breathes. This close she can easily tell the difference between the natural eye and the implant. His natural steel gray eye dilates with pleasure while the matching technical marvel closes tightly in deference to the room's weak light. Both are beautiful.

She can't hold his hard stare and turns away in shame.

This ransacked apartment once held a family. Scattered toys and furniture rest beneath dust dumped by two decades of abandonment. Angel used to be bothered by the broken remnants of life in places like this but now they are, more often than not, where she spends her two hours of rack a cycle.

1

"No," he forces her nose to his. "Never."

Never say it. Never think it.

Rye is a third generation soldier, his body far more modified than hers. His genetic alterations make his wetware implants more effective and eliminate the need for drugs and therapy to enhance his strength and speed. She joined the war ten years ago. First generation. Civilian parents.

She's not the kind of female chosen to pair with a specimen like him. Let off some steam during downtime, sure, but that's all it can ever be.

Angel nods since there's no point in arguing. They're in Aphid territory and her job is to get all the data she can while the rest of the team has her back.

Rye fingers the tender spots on her hips where they'd dug in with passion and hisses at the loss of contact as he helps her to her feet. With her back to him, she hides the burning in her cheeks and the flush of her chest.

"I'll grab rations," Rye fastens his trousers and weapons. Then he leaves Angel alone to dress. Ninety minutes remain off duty. More than enough for a tasteless meal and the hour of sleep she needs to stay alert and keep the shakes at bay. Rye can last a week before he needs to power down.

He returns with two small boxes as she adjusts her earpiece and tests the function of the zipper covering the data port embedded in her arm. Angel's own handgun seems small and impotent compared to Rye's weapons but she's not made for combat. Five foot nine isn't at the small end of things for a woman back on Earth but in Rye's unit she's a pixie.

Angel can't look at Rye when he shoves her rations in her hands. Once she takes her box he wraps his hands around hers to quiet her tremors.

"You need rest," he whispers.

Somehow his stating the obvious feels like an insult. Of course she needs to rest. She shakes every damn day as a reminder she's first gen and her position in his unit is temporary at best. Rye hasn't slept in three days and he's as still as the dead housing block surrounding them.

"We need to talk about us," he says as he drops to a squat then rocks onto his ass. A quick wiggle of his hips moves him against the wall and he crushes the corner of his box to activate the heater.

"Sure, Rye," Angel concedes. The colour code on her box contains a lot of red for protein. Rye's shows equal amounts of red, green, blue and white. Protein is for shakers but it stops her back end up like nobody's business and after two weeks she wonders if she'll ever function right.

She knows what's coming. Angel has been Rye's 'regular' for nearly six months since he came to her quarters dressed only in a towel. She was beautiful and very private, he explained, and someone he could trust to be discreet. Any intimacy shared wouldn't leave the room. Their time together would give them a chance to push the real world away for a while and nothing more.

He couldn't hide his emotion when he found out he was her first and after, he cried silently in her arms. He knew he could trust her, he said, if she trusted him with her innocence. It was strange to think of herself as innocent since she'd already taken hundreds of Aphid lives by sabotaging life support systems or overloading their weapons banks. Her physical demonstration of trust had triggered his.

"We got too close," she mumbles around a dry fibre bar. Like fibre will help with the protein cramps.

"Later," he insists and looks away when her hands become too unsteady to keep eating. "Sleep."

"Yeah."

Angel uses the ration box to keep her short blonde hair off the dirty floor and curls up. For a few minutes she watches Rye's face glow in the soft light of the palm-sized data tablet he pulled from his thigh pocket. His spiky brown hair and angular cheeks complement the three days stubble on his jaw as it works in thought.

"Sleep," he orders without looking up.

"Can't," she sits and goes through her pockets for something to help. Just as she breaks the seal on a small sleep-aid disk, a deep rumble no more than a block away jars the building, knocking dust into the steep light streaming in from the window.

"Tong?" Rye fingers his earpiece as he gets an update from his twin brother, his second in command. Tong's voice rattles in Angel's ear as well.

Town hall went up, Rye. A second blast jars the building and her earpiece shuts down to protect her hearing. *Greens everywhere. The school's gotta be empty. I'll keep the ... clear for Angel and follow ... in.*

"Need you solid for a couple more hours, Angel," Rye orders but she's already on her feet, pulling out a stim-tab. No sleep now but her hands shake so bad she can't get the packet open.

Rye grabs the tablet and pushes her against the wall. He opens the foil envelope containing a translucent thumbnail sized disk and presses it against her neck. Thousands of micro needles coated in stimulant penetrate her skin, not deep enough to hurt but enough to get the drug into her system. Shit, she usually takes it in the arm to slow the rush.

Nothing ever prepares her no matter how many times it happens. Rye turns, pinning her to the wall, his hip pressed hard into her lower belly as her heart lights up. With her head thrown back, she sucks her lungs full and Rye slaps a hand over her mouth to silence her involuntary screech.

Every nerve in her body immolates, triggering a fiery orgasm deep in her over-sensitive sex. It isn't good at all and tears burst from her eyes as she tries to bite her way free of Rye's hand.

As her sight fails, the building rocks through the biggest explosion yet and Rye's other hand shields her wide open eyes from a cascade of falling dust and ceiling tiles. Angel can't breathe and the dust thickens, sending her into a terrified primal reaction to Rye's big body and the hands over her face. Gun in hand, she strikes out.

4

"Angel," he growls as she recovers from the horrible jolt to her system. Rye holds his fist over hers on the pistol grip as he groans in her ear. "Easy."

"Rye," she wheezes but her legs tremble and she blinks as he brushes dirt from her eyes.

"You came hard," Rye sounds close himself as he shoves her pistol back in her holster and fastens the snap.

"You put it in my fucking neck, Rye."

"You're a big girl."

Angel shudders as her strength returns. When she holds her still hands over Rye's chest he rests his lips in her hair.

"Tong thinks the schoolhouse is empty. Their comm system is still blocking us up close so we can't be sure."

She nods. For two days they've been careful in the dead zone around the elementary school.

"I'll keep an eye on you then you're on your own until Tong gets there," Rye steps away, the lover in him shuts down as he checks his weapons. Angel does the same, thoroughly buzzing inside. For the moment, she forgets their intimacy and the stimulants take control.

"You're going to suck their data banks dry, Angel," Rye orders but his next words don't foreshadow the breakup she sees coming after her confession of love. "You're going to prove a first gen can pull her weight in my unit. You're going to prove you deserve to be here permanently, with me."

"I'll do my job."

She can barely acknowledge his words, the closest he's come to expressing he wants her and with his comm line open to Tong it isn't a private sentiment.

"Go."

The initial effects of the stimulant pass, allowing Angel to focus. Artificial endorphins and relaxation from sex combine to help her bring up models of Aphid computer systems and security protocols with unusual clarity.

Easy job, she tells herself. The chemicals in her system drive out random thoughts that might intrude on her orders.

5

Hack the Aphid comms, steal what she can and make Rye proud.

Be a good soldier, Angel. Show them you're not a pretty liability.

She's overheard the talk from some of Rye's men. After pulling off some minor miracles on previous assignments, she landed a temp spot with Rye's unit and it's just what she expected. She stays out of the way while the real soldiers work, moves faster than Scarlet the medic yells when things get hot and jacks herself into whatever Aphid data port they shove her at.

It doesn't take up all her time.

With access to the advanced and well appointed labs on Rye's home base on *The Barrington*, she spends her spare time duplicating Aphid tech and has several untested hybrid data blocks in her belly pack. Tech that may be able to draw Aphid data out and digest the mess of ones and zeros into something Core can use other than more mysterious ones and zeros. All without the constant babysitting of a biological interface like her.

When she steps from the building, the world outside no longer resembles the one she left half an hour before. The summer breeze moves toward the explosions, clearing the air and fist-sized chunks of demolished buildings dot the grass veined road. Fire and gunshots sound to the north where the town hall used to stand and she gets down behind a rusted truck. Even so far from Earth, humans built around them so it felt like they'd never left.

"Go, Angel," Rye shoulders his arc-rifle over the truck box, flips it to laser and squeezes off a couple of dirty, glowing rounds. The thick, two foot long sub-rifle doesn't recoil so the scent of hot plasteel is the only evidence it fired, other than the rounds themselves and the tight explosions three blocks away.

She doesn't question her orders.

Even with the humans gone, the air is redolent with their overgrown flowering trees. Transplanted lilac, magnolia and wisteria exceed three times the size of their earth grown

6

counterparts from over a century of alien nourishment. Midday sunlight, too bright for comfort, casts Angel's harsh, short shadow as she steps out on the main street of the small town six generations of colonists called Constant.

The schoolhouse stands two blocks south and Angel runs low and fast enough that a mis-step would put her flat on her face. Through her earpiece, she gathers what she can from Rye and Tong's chatter as Rye gets up to speed and takes command of the offensive around the burning town hall. Nobody knows what caused the explosions but it drew in the Aphids and in turn Rye's Core soldiers. As she nears the schoolhouse she's on her own. Aphid comm signals overwhelm her earpiece and over the last dozen meters she hears nothing but hiss.

Angel squats by the open school door, pressed flat against the wall. Smoke and the slow bend in the road hide the truck and Rye though the hisses and reports of the firefight still reach her.

Gun in hand, Angel crawls into the small two-story building. She knows the openings on the left and right lead to a couple of classrooms and the office. The heavy metal door at the end twists into charred chunks caused by an old battle. Not much remains of the ivory paint since the Aphids blew it open to slaughter the children and teachers who sought refuge on the second floor twenty years earlier.

Halfway down the hall, Angel spots what she came for and pulls her useless earpiece free so the buzzing doesn't distract her from any noises which would warn she's not alone.

The main computer station and thick rectangular keypad occupy the top of the only unbroken office desk. Like most Aphid tech, it accommodates a two handed grip. Finger control buttons and touch-pads on the sides in concert with pressure from the thumbs on the top send three dimensional data to the Aphid CPU.

In a few minutes, the three displays glow. The characters hide, indecipherable from the background and Angel pulls out special polarized glasses to filter the extra light. The data materializes before her in three dimensional arrays of angular text, the reason for the three dimensional grip on the keypad.

A small explosion to the north causes her to freeze until she's certain the rattle of falling debris doesn't conceal an Aphid. For a few seconds there's nothing then a minute rasp of boots against the dirty floor.

Angel releases the keypad and pushes herself against the wall to hide. Keeping her gun in reach, she pulls out a small silver tablet the size of a pack of cigarettes. With her eyes on the classroom door, she taps in an access code then another set of numbers which auto-program the unit. It warms quickly at her touch as it reads the comm frequencies and starts to produce a counter signal to partially mask the ones Core needs for scanning and comms. If the Aphids don't notice then they won't come to investigate the cause.

As she slides the tablet onto the desk beside her gun, she lets her lungs empty at the sight of Tong in the doorway. He blocks as much light from the hall as Rye can and if he wasn't facing her it would be impossible to tell which brother he is since his thin, sleazy moustache is the only way he's different from his twin. He steps in, back to the wall and scans around with his gun like he's clearing the room.

Bad news.

If Tong acts like she isn't there then he's been followed. He'll stay ahead of the Aphids, likely a small team of three, and set up an ambush. Before he steps out she stands at the keypad, well aware she's nearly out of time.

Angel draws a second silver customizable tablet from her pack and activates it. She doesn't program it for recording yet. Data storage is her job but she's been distracted by Tong. Rye and his brother couldn't behave more differently but the two are as close as Angel and her own brother had been. Instead of holding the Aphid data in the drives which share her ribcage with her lungs, she can use the tablet and help Tong.

If she can prove she can fight in close and get the data then she'll be a permanent addition to Rye's unit.

8

Once the zipper above her left jacket cuff opens, Angel grabs the thick tan mole on the inside of her wrist and pulls out her data tether then she rubs spit in the maintenance port on the keypad. During the two seconds it takes to reboot, she shoves the mole in the port and silently prays.

The display stays green when the Aphid keypad reconnects to the computer.

Angel programs the data cube while she overwhelms the Aphid system with maintenance protocols and watches as a single light starts to blink.

Holy shit, it works. She doesn't have to stand here like a target while her internal servers micro manage the data retrieval. Those internal computers, hardwired to her brain, take advantage of billions of neurons she doesn't use. No portable device has ever had the power to pull it off but this one does.

Angel squats out of sight as more footsteps enter the school. While the Aphids try hard to be quiet, they must still believe Core scanners are blocked and Tong doesn't know they're coming. Angel shoves her earpiece in place. The hiss remains but in the background she can make out the occasional syllable of human speech, each one stronger than the last. The clicky sounds of quiet Aphid talk reach her as she sends a signal to the Aphid computer to expel her tether. While she has an affinity for Aphid tech, she's never learned a word of their convoluted and subtle spoken language.

As the tether retracts, three Aphids pass down the hall. They don't look inside and stop talking as they reach the bottom of the stairs. Angel slips silently to the door and peeks out just in time to see their feet disappear up the landing to the second floor. A scuffle breaks out overhead. With her small pistol pointed at the ceiling, she unsnaps her dagger and follows.

CHAPTER 2

"Interference getting weak, Rye," Atom says. They hunker down half a block from the town hall in a shitty stand-off with a dozen Aphids. Atom brings his own type of class to the front lines. Smallish and wiry for a third gen, he comes off as nervous since he constantly licks his lips but he's really just annoyed at his still knife. Atom claims Aphid blood feels good on his skin and since the bright green stuff soaks his knife hand, Atom must be in heaven.

"Fucking A," Rye intones as he pulls out his tablet. Fifteen minutes earlier he sent Angel to the schoolhouse and five minutes after that he lost contact with Tong as he went after her.

"You think Angel did that?"

Rye's stomach rolls at the thought. His last Comms Officer tried to eat them a clear path through the Aphid interference and in doing so gave away his position. The Aphids caught on to him long before Rye could scan the area and by the time they got to him the man was dead, hanging by his feet with his skin pooled around his head.

"She wouldn't be that stupid," he allows, more to reassure himself than anything else.

"Shit," Atom breathes as he scratches his neck with his blade, smearing green all over his skin. Between the green

10

blood and a streak of red from a cut on his head he looks like an evil candy cane.

Rye hides his disgust.

"Two Core transmitters, one faint but I can't tell if it's Tong or Angel. Static too heavy." Rye smacks his tablet in a vain effort to improve the reception but this looks as good as it will get. Clever girl, Angel. She degraded their signal just enough and didn't get greedy. One of the humans is in bad shape and whether it's Tong or Angel it's going to be a very bad day. He needs them both in his life.

The rough pop of an explosion to the south knocks Rye to his ass and not due to the shock wave. One of the human life signs blinks out.

Only the injured human remains on his display. Whatever blew in the schoolhouse changed his life forever by taking either his brother or Angel.

"Scarlet," Rye calls and she looks up from Webber. The man has a round in his arm and isn't in any trouble but he's out until she stops fussing over him. "Now, south. Atom, you too."

The three break away at a run as the rest of the team tightens up the line to make up for their absence. Aphid gunfire peters off and stops and Rye looks back to see his soldiers prepare to advance.

A section of the schoolhouse second floor topples inward and black smoke curls thick around the hole. As Rye ducks behind another building, he takes a moment to run his hands over his face. They still smell of *her* and he can only hope the readout on the tablet is wrong and unreliable. He has no trouble going through fifty undetected Aphids if it means Angel and Tong are okay.

God, she loves him and she's braver than him for saying it. She's damn good for a first gen or even a second for that matter and came very highly recommended. Much of her record was sealed, of course, since most operations are classified but the legendary and very senior Comms Officer who signed off on her assignment with Rye took the time to escort her to *Barrington Station* himself.

Now, Rye has to face the very real possibility Angel is dead or dying alongside his dying or dead big brother.

"—oing on, Rye?" Scarlet asks. She doesn't even look up. Both arms sink elbows-deep in her med bag since she's always taking stock of her supplies. Each clamp, bandage and med-tab plays on her giant mental board game and she's a dozen moves ahead.

"Angel and Tong," Rye breathes as they run the last block to the schoolhouse. "Ambushed inside."

"Fuck," Scarlet mutters, articulate and colourful. Her long red hair dangles half out of the knot she keeps at the back of her head and the smokey wind snakes strands around her shoulders.

The main hallway lays empty and Rye and Atom check the rooms for Aphids as quickly as they can, keeping Scarlet in the rear. Second door on the left opens to the small Aphid mainframe. It only takes a second to see that Angel isn't there, only some of her hardware, and Rye signals to take the second floor.

Several smouldering chunks of debris litter the stairs but old damage marks the fire door at the bottom. Ivory enamel paint covers parts of the buckled and torn surface. Rye has seen it before in dozens of schools. Antibacterial and easy to keep clean. So much thought had gone into the properties but nobody ever made it another colour.

More charred bits cover the landing including an Aphid head. The three inch high pale green ridge running over the top lacks much of the flesh which once covered it and a small calibre round punched out one eye.

Angel.

Damn it, if she'd just stayed put...

There's nothing but silence from the top floor and Rye nudges the head aside with his boot.

Atom kicks it off the landing. The head makes a solid thunk as it hits the wall above the blown out door and bounces twice at the bottom of the stairs.

The ceiling above opens to the sky and the harsh sun reveals a garish mix of Aphid parts and rubble. Some property of the natural light makes the green blood glow vibrantly in spite of the dust and smoke trapped by what remains of the walls. Angel's knife rests hilt-deep in a green torso.

"One human life sign," Scarlet mutters to her tablet and Rye nods his permission for her to get to work. His own tablet shows no active explosives. With the sun in their eyes they can't see into the dark cavity ahead, the section of the second floor that still has a roof, but without Aphid life there's no danger.

"Enough gunk to account for three greens," Atom assesses. Rye thinks the same thing and as he strides after Scarlet he spots what's left of at least two more. Both appear to have been killed in close combat then smeared across the floor and over the body that has the medic's attention.

"Rye," Scarlet calls. "Tong."

Damn, where's Angel? Maybe she wasn't in the building when it went up.

Tong blinks as Rye kneels beside Scarlet and she assesses him. The panel on her medical tablet strobes green. Tong's heart beats strong and more bandages than even Scarlet could have done already bind his thigh.

"Whatever happened," Scarlet shrugs. The set of her mouth says she disapproves of the amateur dressing. "He'd have bled out by now without it."

Rye knows what that means. Brain death and no chance to get him in cryostasis until he could be repaired. Angel did that. If Rye has to guess, Tong was surprised by the two now dead Aphids and injured. Maybe he took care of a couple of the ones at the stairs but Angel had been there and shot the one in the head. Two had been dead before she got there and put her knife in the third and saved Tong's life or she wouldn't have reached him.

"Rye," Tong's voice grates through the thickness of pain meds and he grabs Rye's sleeve then points into the corner where the two dead Aphids lay. "Angel."

"Uh," air punches from Rye's lungs. He can't get on his feet and crawls to the pile of bodies. A camouflaged human knee sticks clear of the green, bloody mess.

"Scarlet," he gasps but she's ahead of him, pulling dead Aphids off Angel.

By the time Rye gets to her side, Scarlet has her tablet out. The display strobes an angry red and Rye's hope fades.

"Tong is stable," Scarlet mutters to herself and holds a hand over Angel like she's afraid to touch her. Angel's neck bends at a terrible angle and it's clear her head is close to severed. Her burnt off fatigues reveal black and red skin.

"Bag her," Rye chokes out.

"Rye," Scarlet shakes her head. "Wait."

The display flashes yellow then red again. Every few seconds another flash of yellow brings new hope.

"Lock her down for cryo, Scarlet."

"Shit," Tong moans behind them.

Scarlet rolls Angel to her stomach and snaps a thumb-sized black med-tab to what remains of the back of her neck. The lights flash on, green then red.

"Not enough circulation," Scarlet says but Rye knows that. He busts off Angel's chest armour and tears open the buttons of her shirt. Scarlet readies another med-tab and sticks it between Angel's exposed breasts.

The lights on this one turn blue and as they get clear, it jolts her with enough electricity to jump start her heart. Her lungs expand and a small trail of blood runs under the curve of one white breast. The device drove two spikes in through her ribs. It loads her up with drugs to dehydrate her body in order to supply enough fluid to her veins and arteries to distribute the other meds going in the back of her neck. Other drugs seal up the breaches in her circulatory system to stop the bleeding.

Once circulation resumes, the lights on the back of her neck turn blue. The med-tab on Angel's neck soaks her brain and internal organs in a massive dose of drugs to protect her tissues from the cold of cryo and oxygen deprivation until she gets there. Not a promise of life by any means but a chance. If her injuries are recoverable then she could be repaired.

"Nothing more I can do, Rye."

"I know."

Scarlet takes her tablet to Tong's side and brushes her fingers over his cheek. The two have always been close so he isn't surprised to see his medic comforting his brother.

To hell with it.

Rye takes Angel in his arms and cradles her between his legs. The unsettling grind in her lower back and pelvis adds to the pain in Rye's heart.

Her eyes flutter open but it's just the meds in her body and her brain reacting to the chemical preservatives. The blue light on her chest brightens with the beating of her heart and accelerates as the temporary fluids from her tissues leak out past the seals other meds made in her circulatory system but the light doesn't change colour. The preservatives have been in her long enough to do their job.

As the light flashes become irregular, a rough sob breaks from Rye's chest and Scarlet flinches at the sound. Her hand stays on Tong's cheek and when Rye looks up the breeze has cleared much of the smoke from the top floor.

Atom stands beside them holding one of Angel's silver data units.

"It's full," Atom reports but he can't look at Rye. He'd been fond of Angel, too. Not in the way Rye was but Atom was brotherly to all females in the unit. "Whatever she did… she got what we came for.

"Fuck, Angel," Atom stomps away and drops his ass on the top stair.

Rye rests his lips on Angel's cheek until the light fails.

"I love you, too."

CHAPTER 3

"You promised I'd get laid," Tong whines. At least he keeps his voice down so everyone in the coffee house isn't alerted to his unsatisfied state.

"That I did," Rye concedes. He isn't much into getting laid and hasn't been for six years. Not after Angel. Other than a single drunken, paid incident he hasn't given much attention to women and certainly not blondes. Drunken, yes. Paid, yes. Rye left the money on the bed and walked out without touching her.

Tong, on the other hand, is his usual insatiable self.

"But we're on Earth," Tong tries and Rye looks up from his black coffee to see Tong's grin. Milk foam from whatever the hell he ordered covers his moustache.

"And we're here to work."

"Awe, man."

There's always been a problem with Aphids finding their way to Earth but lately, sightings in high, cold places like the Whistler Dome have brought in Core surveillance. The ski resort was covered several decades ago and is a year round play place for humans. Aphids have a hard time with the cold and altitude but something changed. They are here and in other places humans once thought safe.

The assignment seemed like a waste of time at first but Rye's commander hinted the Aphids found a way to incorporate human DNA with their own. The Aphids had never been able to use tech implants like humans, too incompatible, but with human DNA it might be possible. There was only one place the Aphids could get a wide selection of human DNA and that was from humans. Word was DNA modifications made it possible for Aphids to live in places like Whistler.

Rye joked maybe they could put something in the water to make human DNA lethal for Aphids but the glare from his commander said he hit close to the mark.

Just get me a fucking body, Rye.

Some bullshit assignment it turned out to be. Nothing but humans and his horny brother.

"You've seen what the girls are wearing, right?" Tong demands.

Yeah, Rye has seen. Tong's radar goes off every time one passes in a snug one-piece ski suit. Tong's imagination needs no help and Rye can be sure because his big brother lacks the filter that would keep his lusty thoughts private.

They chose a window seat in this coffee bar for the good, elevated view it provides of pedestrian traffic among the shops and restaurants. Aphids prefer the tight cluster of bodies and where Rye and Tong would have kept out of sight on the Aphid home world, the green bastards get all out of sorts without the feel of overpopulation.

It doesn't hurt that Aphids walk a little funny. Rye's trained eye will easily pick it up even in a crowd. In spite of Tong's moaning for a woman, Rye is sure his brother is on task as well.

"What are you drinking?" Rye asks.

"Sweet latte," Tong mouths with a waggle of his eyebrows and a puckered kiss of his lips. Trust Tong to turn coffee into something dirty.

"Whatever."

A loud female laugh interrupts Tong's chuckle and sends a shiver down Rye's spine.

"Oh, hot Goddess," Tong breathes. He turns to the coffee counter and Rye's gaze follows. The woman's long blonde hair coils behind her head and a stray piece shakes with her laughter. Strong shoulders narrow into a tight waist and her feminine hips sway with the Christmas music from the overhead speakers. Hips were the first thing that got Rye's attention when Angel, the unwelcome first gen, was assigned to his unit. Third gen females don't have hips like that. They were the perfect fit in his big hands and along with her shorter stature he hadn't been able to resist the urge to protect her.

The blonde barista sounds just like Angel.

Dead Angel.

Rye had been reviewing the vids from Constant at Tong's bedside when the official report on Angel chimed its presence in his inbox. Estimated unrepairable past seventy percent efficiency and placed in permanent cryo storage. Any soldier below ninety-four wasn't good enough for service, even then resources were too scarce to put that kind of time into a first gen since it was less work to get a new one. Angel was as good as dead and Rye's heart froze with her.

"Angel, thanks for sticking around. I don't know where the crowd came from," a woman behind the counter calls and Rye's breath leaves him as his eyes lock with Tong's. His brother turns as white as Rye feels.

"Sure thing, boss," the blonde replies.

The open back of the blonde's shirt reveals a nest of tattooed flowers. Cherry blossom, jasmine and other exotics cover much of her skin and a vine climbs the back of her neck.

"Can't be," Tong whispers.

Rye's cybernetic eye focuses on the tattoo. Through all the ink, her skin shines with the gloss of heavy scarring. The blonde's back and neck have seen some serious repair.

"Nice hustle today, Angel," the other woman, a brunette, shouts and slaps Angel on the ass. She jumps.

"Wow," Tong recovers first. "Do you think the two of them…"

"And us?" Rye replies, flat and automatic.

The blonde turns and laughs and there's no mistaking who she is. Angel, the only woman to get hold of Rye's heart snaps a towel at the brunette. From across the room even Rye's human eye makes out the small, beautiful gap between her front teeth. Long gold earrings caress her neck and he's charged with memories and close to jumping the counter and taking her in his arms.

"You know, Tong, if you weren't my brother."

"And didn't leave the toilet seat up."

"Or the milk out," Rye's wooden voice replies as the rote exchange goes on.

"You'd marry me."

"In a heartbeat."

The pair falls silent as Rye realizes his eyes aren't the only ones on Angel. She's the centre of attention with most of the men in the coffee shop and Rye's both proud and angry about it.

Angel seems to know and glances around the room.

When her gaze reaches Rye and Tong, she pales then laughs again but it sounds more like a gag.

"Tall mocha extra shot," she calls and puts a cup and saucer on the counter before turning her back on the window seats, Tong and Rye.

"What the hell?"

Rye shakes his head.

"She back in Core?" Tong tries. "I mean, they still haven't figured out her data collectors after six years. You think they fixed her?"

"Then why is she serving coffee?" Rye can't help but feel bitter. If Angel is back in service he thought she would have contacted him.

"Not sure," Tong thinks. Both men avoid looking at the coffee counter and keep their eyes on the people pressed together in the square. "But she was brilliant. Maybe…"

"Then why is she serving coffee?" Rye asks again.

"Look, Aphids are here. We know it. That's our primary."

"And Angel just became our unofficial secondary priority," Rye finishes. The shock of seeing her wears off and now he's plain angry. Not so pissed to not hear her out but he's more than mad enough to need a moment alone with her.

"Let's get out of here," Rye knocks back the last of his coffee.

As he zips his bright blue ski jacket he shakes his head at his brother and remembers to maintain eye contact. Tong wears one of the skinny ski suits under his short jacket and if he didn't need a place to hide his weapon and gear, he'd toss the jacket to show off his muscled body. Rye is built the same, thick everywhere, all third gens are, but unlike Tong he never feels the need to advertise. Somehow it cheapens the man inside.

A glance at Angel shows she's regained her composure. She's involved in an animated conversation with an older man and woman who aren't dressed like skiers. Her bare arm points to the west wall of the building as she gives them directions.

The bell above the door rings as Rye and Tong step out. They stop two doors down and watch silently as the couple to whom Angel gave directions strolls past. The scent of fresh ground coffee follows them, leaving Rye inexplicably jealous of them for being so close to Angel.

Every ten minutes Rye and Tong move to another part of the square. Tong gets another coffee from a street vendor but Rye passes. His mood sours and he can't focus while he debates what he'll say to her.

"Over your left shoulder," Tong whispers. "Good makeup job on it."

Rye turns like he's bored and gets a look. The Aphid wears a lumpy knit hat and sunglasses to hide its oversized, pupil-less eyes. Its skin appears just like a humans and Rye knows it'll keep its mouth shut to hide the crop of short, pointy teeth. It stops to lean on a garbage can. Just behind it, Angel steps from the coffee shop and pulls her gloves on. Her bulky coat hides her shape and she rubs her palms together, oblivious to the Aphid two meters away.

Her military training is easy to see. Under the pretence of fussing with her hat she takes in the entire square. Rye steps sideways behind Tong to hide his distinctive blue coat and when he looks again, she hurries away.

The Aphid emulates a heavy sigh and heads off in the opposite direction.

"Thoughts?" Rye asks his brother. Even though he's in charge, Angel's presence is a huge complication and Tong will understand. Protocol dictates Tong has a say when it comes to modifying their orders on the fly. As long as they get the job done they can do whatever else they please.

"I got the primary," Tong stretches his head back and forth to loosen up. "Go see what's up with her."

"Yeah, Tong. You got me?"

They both pull out smaller civilian looking comm tablets and Rye verifies each can locate the other.

"Got you," Tong says. "But your date is better looking. Take your time."

Rye snorts. Tong is right. He's one of the few who saw how Rye suffered from Angel's death.

"You too," Rye says and enjoys his brother's laugh as he turns to follow Angel. "I'm sure it's got a lovely personality."

CHAPTER 4

Who am I? Angel wonders.

A woman with secrets, she's certain. Rye never knew why she got into Core and neither did Core for that matter. Not really, at least.

Now she's been dead for a year and with the support of the scientist who revived her and helped her walk again she's been alive for several more and has even more secrets. She's a mercenary of sorts. Without the near unlimited resources of Core, of course, but she's done more with what she has now than before she died.

Before she was reborn four and a half years ago in a quiet lab with the one thing she has left to fight for.

Angel doesn't bother looking behind her. Even if Rye isn't in sight he still follows.

It had been so easy. Go to Whistler and find out how the Aphids are able to survive. She shouldn't be surprised to find Core here but for Rye and Tong to show up where she works makes things messy.

Rye saw her and he's coming. Core protocol dictates she be turned in and forced to spill on those who gave her a second chance.

The cobblestone lanes of Whistler Village have been worn smooth like old European streets over the years but they are kept clear of snow. Her soft boots are no match for the cold. Angel hates Whistler. She hates the cold and days like this bring on the ache in her spine.

Once in her apartment, Angel pulls off her cold outer gear and strips out of her work clothes. Then she pulls on long underwear, a pair of heavy sweats, a long sleeved T and two pairs of thick socks. On top of all that goes a fleece lined hoodie zipped all the way to her chin and a green and red striped knit hat.

Todd, one of her roommates, snores loudly in the mens bedroom otherwise she has the place to herself. Three men and three women share the two bedroom apartment in order to make Whistler's high rent somewhat manageable. Her ski-addict roommates work in one touristy place or another to fund their love of the slopes. Angel claimed it was a car accident murder-suicide attempt at the hands of a psycho ex-boyfriend that messed up her back so she doesn't ski. Her roomies believe Angel loves Christmas and that's why she lives there.

It's always Christmas in Whistler.

Little Christmassy nicknacks Angel brought to Whistler to flesh out her cover story nestle amongst the poles, skis and snowboards. Her collection includes several additions from her roommates.

Angel gathers data on the Aphids because it's one of the few ways she can fight. Her intel leaks back into the Core data networks so it's her own hard work that landed Rye in Whistler. Something brought the Aphid's here and from what she can see they move perfectly well in sub-zero temperatures.

Angel checks the clock. Todd will be up soon for work and she doesn't expect anyone else back for hours. He only works out as a roommate since he snores when nobody else is home.

With her appetite illusive, Angel waits for Rye. Seeing him brought back so many things she thought died with her. One of the hardest to grasp, however, remains that last day on Constant. The doctor told her it was normal and was pleased not only with how much she recalled but that she also completely recovered all brain function following cryo.

Todd's snore stutters at Rye's heavy, double thud on the door before returning to a deep, regular buzz.

Angel hasn't had the shakes in years but they come back now. Nervous tremors make her rattle the lock so she steadies one hand on the jam and the other holds the door as she swings it open.

Rye's raised elbow rests on one side of the door and his hand holds the other. He owns the opening, both sealing it from the outside and blocking her in.

"Rye," she says, her voice more steady than she expects.

He doesn't say a word and she offers a smile but it falters at his steady frown.

"Hey," she tries but his fists clench. Knuckles whiten then relax.

Damn, she heard about his temper, mostly from soldiers outside of his unit who expressed smug alarm at her appointment to his team, but she never saw it. Perhaps this is what it looks like, silent and full with the promise of fury.

"It's me, Angel."

His eyes pick up the blue of his jacket, granting them a cheery colour and he takes a deep breath as some of the flush fades from his cheeks.

"Come in," she asks. "Please?"

Angel turns her back on the open door and moves to the small kitchen. Somewhere after the door opened Todd went silent and Angel hopes he just rolled over. The big skier acts like house mother for the five of them and takes an interest in any visitors.

"Do you want to split a beer? I have one we can share."

God, it sounds a little pathetic and humble to share a beer but every spare cent is saved. Over the sound of the fridge opening she hears the apartment door close.

Then as she takes out two glasses she nearly drops one. Cold fingers brush the back of her neck, giving her such a chill she has to grab the counter to steady her hands. Rye's gentle touch traces the scars on her neck and he peels back the bulky collar of her hoodie to look below her neck line.

With a hand on her shoulder, Rye turns Angel so he can follow the worst of the damage around the right side of her neck.

"I remember the smell, Rye, on Constant," she says. He startles at the sound of her voice, raising his eyes to hers before he fingers her earring. "The flowers. I had them put on my scars because I wanted to remember something good about that place. I don't remember much more than the glorious scents."

She didn't warm up after changing and takes a step back into the counter to avoid the cold from Rye's body but he follows. He nudges her chin up and places a hand on her hip then he pauses, just a wintery breath from kissing her.

Instead of placing his lips on hers, he puts them on her cheek.

Angel groans at the memory his touch triggers.

"There was so much blood," she whispers and his grip on her hip tightens to keep her up. "So much. Tong!"

The last minutes on Constant take her, steal her sight and leave her with only a shaky voice to release what she sees.

"He was bleeding so bad," she gasps. "I used my field kit and his. He didn't complain but it must have hurt. I'd only ever used the suture gun on smaller cuts but I got it closed and wrapped it up. Then he tried to push me aside but I wouldn't move and got meds in him. There was heat. And fire.

"Then there were lights and a soft voice told me I was safe and whole and…"

pregnant…

Angel drags in the stale apartment air to avoid the word.

"…alive," she finishes as the world goes black.

When she recovers, she's curled up on a corner of the couch.

"It's okay," Rye says when she comes to her senses. If he was at her end of the couch he'd loom over her but he's at the other end between her and the door.

"Angel?"

Oh crap, Todd.

"Um," she stumbles to her feet as Rye tenses. She's seen him strike too many times in combat and he'll go after Todd unless she does something. Todd matches Rye in size and can be a jerk about the girls' dates. Of all Angel's roomies, he's most protective of her. Todd wears nothing but plain, white shorts and doesn't seem intimidated by his own lack of clothing.

"Ex-boyfriend?" Todd's growl nearly sets Rye off and she holds on so she's not tossed to the floor. Behind her, she feels Rye's grip on his pistol.

"Yeah."

"You son of a bitch," Todd goes over a side chair to get at Rye and Angel puts a hand up to stop him while fighting to stay between them.

"No, Todd!"

"Ah," Todd stutters, coming to a stop over Angel. His mouth works for a moment then his face turns a furious shade of red of which Angel never thought he was capable.

"Shit, Angel. Wrong ex-boyfriend?"

"Yeah."

Rye doesn't relax until Todd retreats a couple of steps.

"Sorry, man," Todd tries. "Look, I'm gonna get a shower then off to work."

As the shower starts, Rye disarms the plasma gun in his pocket. The distinctive pop and soft whistle alarm her. The weapon will disintegrate half of whomever it hits and is completely illegal on Earth. The only thing it's good for is killing thick skulled Aphids and even then the weapon is more than sufficient for the job.

"Todd believes a crazy ex tried to kill us both in his lander," she points to her neck.

Rye looks up then glares around the room at the clutter of ski gear and Christmas decorations.

"He yours?"

26

"No," Angel whispers. "Todd looks out for the girls here and he's definitely not interested in me. I'm roommate, not female."

Rye scoffs. He's right. Todd came off as a jealous bastard, a little like Rye right now, except Todd knows he's on Rye's side and Rye doesn't see anything other than Angel, the first gen soldier who died on his watch.

"You don't shit where you eat," Angel says bluntly. "He works nights on the slopes with his girl."

Rye shrugs and she can see what really bothers him. Her old lover carries the merciless weight of six years of pain. To Angel, the lost time gives her a distance he doesn't have.

"You can't take me back to Core," she says. Rye's forearms stiffen under her hands and she rubs her thumbs over the smooth fabric of his jacket. The gray in his eyes deepens.

"Why not?"

"I know protocol, Rye, but you have to promise you won't say a word."

"You know I can't do that."

"You better."

The stern, firm line of his mouth refuses to engage the discussion further. Angel no longer knows the man beneath the shield. The creases around Rye's eyes and mouth slash his skin with grief as he tries to stare her down.

"What?" He asks.

"I didn't know my death would take so much from you, Rye. I was looking for something of the man I left behind."

Angel brought life back with her from the other side, a little dark haired child blessed with her father's moods but Rye spent the time pushing Angel's death before him as some kind of penance.

Damn, he's aware how much she sees in him and turns for the door to close it as tightly behind him as he's closed off inside.

27

"You're Intelligence now, aren't you?" Rye lurches to a stop but he won't face her. "Those Skunkworks assholes who make people disappear."

"You know I can't tell you that," Angel whispers. She isn't Intelligence or anything else, just a woman doing the same thing as him, fighting Aphids, but if he follows her scent down the wrong trail he might wind up far away from the right one. If Core gets wind of Angel's little girl, damn, Rye's little girl, then they'll see her as nothing more than property to be trained to fight. It's a fate Angel will do anything to protect her from even if that means guarding her secret from Rye.

"Son of a bitch. Six months after…" he hardens further as he goes on. "…after Constant, Intelligence took over *Barrington Station*. Most of us were locked down in our quarters, no contact with each other, computers shut down. They cleaned your lab out right down to the spare tool kit. The interviews about you and whatever the hell you were working on were long and nothing I'd wish on anyone."

Angel tries to remain unaffected but rumours of Skunkworks interrogators torturing anyone with a poor memory make her queasy.

"It was nearly three weeks when they let us out. Nobody knew if they got what they came for.

"Tong's contacts quietly learned you'd disappeared from cryo. I guess they called you back up."

"I can't talk about it," Angel insists.

A soft beep from inside Rye's jacket intrudes and he pulls a small data tablet from his pocket. Angel looks but can't make out anything on the display other than a red dot.

"Shit," he whispers. "We're not done here, Angel."

CHAPTER 5

The old building rocks beneath Rye as he descends the stairs three at a time. He doesn't bother with the handrails, steel wrapped in thick plastic. Both feet and each of his two hundred and fifty-one pounds punish every landing between flights.

Don't you dare run off, Angel.

He doesn't give a shit why she's back. Intelligence or whatever. He isn't letting her go unless she tells him to leave. Even then, she really has to mean it. Once she's back on *The Barrington*, Core will sort out where she goes anyway.

When she collapsed, he buried his nose in her neck, pushed that God-awful hat aside, and lost himself in the scent of her cool skin until he got her to the sofa. Then he backed off and stared like a fool until his temper returned. How could he be mad at someone he'd already completely forgiven?

Somehow, he pulled it off.

"Tong," Rye presses a finger just beneath his ear to activate his wetware mic and earpiece. They aren't as powerful or clear as an external but they offer discretion. For the moment, he pushes thoughts of Angel aside. "Report."

"Report your fucking self," Tong growls but Rye allows a grin. In spite of Angel's appearance and whatever the hell it means he can at least be happy his brother enjoys himself.

Rye gets his bearings after circling down the stairwell and takes a right toward Tong's red dot just two blocks north.

"Ah," Tong grunts as his mic pics up the ticky chatter of his Aphid opponent. The green must have its teeth close to Tong's damned throat. Maybe too close. Not good considering their spit will rot your balls off.

"Fights like a bitch," Tong continues.

Yeah, they suspected Aphids could cope with the Whistler environment but if they fight as hard as ever then they are doing much better than just coping.

"Hang in there," Rye whispers. Although Tong's breathing remains as even as Rye's, unaffected by their exertion, Rye can't fight the urgency in his heart. Another damned *issue* still plaguing him six years after Constant. Times like this, Rye swears the truth of a twins' mental link.

"Duck," he breathes.

"Got it."

Proof.

Seconds later, he forgets the uncanny exchange.

Tourists pack the streets and he hurries as much as he can while avoiding attention. Sun seems to set a little earlier in the Whistler Dome and the air fills with scents from restaurant kitchens and rowdy voices from the bars. Brilliant multi-coloured lights flash past in a festive blur.

"Miss me?" Rye skids on an icy patch as he rounds the last corner. His boots grip and he recovers his footing enough for a burst of speed into a deserted alley. Tong's heel appears as he steps back out of a recessed loading bay then disappears to be followed by a second pair of feet swinging out waist-high.

Tong grips the Aphid in a solid choke hold. Its trampled hat rests beneath one of Tong's boots and the makeup comes to an uneven halt part way up its forehead, below the distinctive pale green crest.

As Rye drops into a crouch, ready to assist, the Aphid struggles in Tong's grip and its last breaths whistle past the needle-sharp teeth. With a final squeeze, Tong lengthens the Aphid's neck and snaps its head over.

"Shit," Tong sighs as he probes his front teeth with his tongue. The Aphid blinks, completely unnerving since the now paralyzed thing lives. They take more than twenty minutes to drown so breaking the neck will only prevent it from fighting back as it dies of oxygen starvation. Even then, it bites.

Tong drags it aside before laying it face down behind a dumpster and jamming his dagger up into the base of its skull.

The Aphid doesn't blink again.

"With all my heart," Tong answers and pulls his top lip up, exposing his teeth and hiding the unforgivable pencil-thin moustache. "Ith ook iggly?"

"No," Rye answers but he doesn't look. Tong's lip swells but the skin remains intact so it won't be very spectacular. "Any sign of the others?"

"Naw," Tong drops to a crouch and they start going through the Aphid's side pockets. As expected, they don't hold much. An empty black wallet, some scraps of paper and a key. For the most part, nothing but props. The key could prove interesting but without a hint as to what it opens it isn't much. Tong pockets it anyway.

As they get the Aphid rolled over, Tong digs a hand deep in its front jeans pocket.

"Ooh, what you got for me, lover boy?"

Rye scowls as Tong pulls his hand out, fisting what passes for a personal hand-held data tablet. The unit is three inches by three inches and about eight inches long. No wonder the Aphid had the long coat.

The front has a square display but no sign of buttons anywhere on the outside. Tong wraps his hands around it and squeezes several times but nothing happens.

"You can play with its thing," Rye mumbles. "I'll pack this up."

"Okay," Tong agrees as Rye rolls the Aphid on its side and tucks it into a ball. Then he draws a thin bag from his back pocket and pushes the Aphid in head-first. He grunts as he shoves with his knees, rocks the body back and forth and tugs the bag down further. Once he seals the bag, he activates the vacuum and rolls the body into a corner. It doesn't look like any more than a shadow and can sit there until they come back with the lander.

"Oh, hey," Tong exclaims as he turns to show Rye the display. "I turned it on."

"I bet you did."

"Fuck you, look."

In the dim light, the little screen glows green. As Tong tilts the device, they can only make out a head, no details.

"'Sec," Rye mutters. "Filtering the light."

"Yeah."

Rye's artificial eye peels the background radiation away from the display and he knows Tong does the same. As the seconds pass, Rye's gut clenches a little more as the face becomes clear. The first feature he identifies is a gap between the woman's front teeth.

"Any sign of the other two?" Rye asks. Damn greens like to go around in threes.

"Awe, shit," Tong stuffs the unit in his pocket and takes off after Rye.

CHAPTER 6

Angel glares at the closed apartment door.

As much as she feels Rye's pull, she needs to be out of Whistler before he returns. She spins, steadying herself on one of the old chairs and marches into the women's bedroom. Other than confirming Aphids live in Whistler, there's nothing more she can do on her own. Maybe she could continue to keep an eye on them but Rye can manage that just fine.

Her battered metal suitcase hides in the closet behind layers of winter clothes and broken ski gear. She pops it open on her lower bunk and rifles through the contents. Several vacuum sealed packets amounting to eight pounds of ground coffee, gifts for her benefactors who have become her family and keep her daughter safe, a few little toys for her as well and thirteen thousand six hundred and twelve dollars in general currency fill the left side of the suitcase. She tosses a few toiletries, spare gloves and two one-piece thermal undersuits in the other side. Other than the contents of the suitcase, her wallet, a small, quiet charge gun and the clothes on her back will be enough to get her home.

"Angel?" Todd calls from the door. Only half dressed, his thermal long underwear thin enough to fit under his ski pants covers his bottom. A drop of water falls free from the blonde fringe around his face. Todd's big fingers scratch the wet trail it

33

leaves on his chest but all his attention focuses on Angel and her suitcase. "What the hell's going on?"

His eyes follow the corners of his mouth downward into a deep scowl and he nods toward the living room.

"You're leaving because of him?" Todd takes a deep breath and starts over. "He looked like he saw a ghost, Angel. You wanna take it from the top?"

"Todd," Angel sighs. "He did and it's too long and complicated. Look, I'm paid up until the end of next month and you won't have trouble renting my bed."

"Uh huh," he crosses his arms and shoulders the door open the rest of the way.

Angel approaches and stops before Todd, taking his warm, crossed arms in her cold hands. Anyone else would flinch from her icy touch but Todd knows how the cold affects her. She'll miss him more than anyone else in Whistler.

The front door clicks open. It's too early for their roommates to be home but Todd takes a step backward out of the forbidden females' bedroom just in case. Angel follows then pulls him in almost on top of her. Her automatic response surprises them both. It isn't until she kicks the door shut behind him that she realizes the single snick of the front door closing followed the quiet tick of Aphid chatter.

Damn. Skin crawling, she cocks an ear toward the front room and draws silent air in through her lips.

"Hey," Todd tries to pull back.

"Sshhh, listen."

His furled brow relaxes into open mouthed shock. The only Aphids Todd's ever seen would have been on the vid which can't be the case now because they don't have one.

"Gotta call security," he hisses as he turns to the door, forcing Angel behind him and placing himself between her and the Aphids. One hand grabs at his thigh and he curses the lack of pocket or phone.

"Nope." Angel draws her small, black pistol from her suitcase and slides a charged cartridge into the worn, rubberized handle. Todd's eyebrows pop up at the same time

34

the small click of the rounds snapping home touches her palm. Within seconds, the cartridge charges each round with enough juice to stun anyone, as long as it lodges in a body. Grazing an Aphid won't do any more than draw a little blood and annoy it.

"Give me that," Todd grabs at the weapon but she turns to keep his hands off.

"No," she lies, sort of. "This is what I do. I've been with Core for almost half my life, since I was seventeen. I'm here because they are. I'm betting there's three if we're in luck. Nine if we're not."

Todd's cool stare holds Angel still while she decides what, if anything, she can do with the big man to keep him out of the way. The Aphids in the living room don't try and hide their shuffle-walk as they move through the clutter and toward the hallway. The hall light shining in under the door flicks off.

"Craptastic," Todd sighs. "I know what they are and I don't think you'd give me a shit story like that at a time like this."

She shakes her head in agreement.

"Doesn't sound like nine," Todd offers.

Angel agrees.

He holds it together pretty well considering a two-on-three against Aphids isn't likely to go in Angel and Todd's favour. For a moment, Angel tightens her grip on the pistol and allows her forehead to rest on Todd's shoulder. She never felt fear facing the green humanoids before. Except once, before she joined Core, when they took the only person she had in the whole world and now she feels it again. All she had to do was go to Whistler, keep her distance and verify they were here.

It never occurred to her she wouldn't go home to her little girl. She'd been so careful. Had they figured out she was on to them? No other reason for them to be in her apartment.

The slow creak of the bathroom door swinging open leads to a few curt, Aphid syllables. Now they try to be quiet? Typical.

"I have a plan," Angel whispers, mouth tipped up to Todd's ear.

"Let's hear it."

"Wait until they get to the door. You charge it and knock them down. The gun will shock them like an old-school taser so if I'm quick, I can stun them all and we run for it."

"Yeah," a slow smile creeps across Todd's mouth. "I used to fight, you know. Pro. Then I got into illegal pit fighting and got busted, kicked from the pro league. Miss the action. Money was damn good."

Angel takes a step back. Human pit fighting? The disreputable sport stopped short of employing the recovering lion population but only because humans could be just as violent as the beasts. Rumors also told of sport hunters bringing live Aphid captives into the ring.

Todd wouldn't shit *her* about something like that at a time like this and she desperately believes him. Now she has a chance at getting home.

No further sound comes from the hall except for a rasp of fabric against the wall. Todd pivots his head and Angel does the same in an effort to place the sound but it's too brief. The Aphids could be near the door or right on the other side.

"Ready?" Todd breathes then he's gone. His two massive strides give Angel enough time to relive twisted memories of Constant. The fight with the Aphids on the schoolhouse top floor left her without her dagger and gun but she didn't need them any more. Nothing moved but her and Tong, a pool of blood growing beneath him. In her nightmares, the red stain covers half the room and her feet slip as she crawls through it, knee deep, never reaching Tong. Rye brought back the rest; her rush to close the hand-sized gash in Tong's thigh as he turned gray from the pain and his short moans as she wrapped the wound. The school room inhaled then, a silent breath before the deafening explosion and fire tore her up.

The small apartment bedroom does the same thing, waiting for Todd to hit the door. It gives, but unlike her last moment on Constant there's no explosion or shudder. One instant the door stands, their only protection from the Aphids, and the next it disappears taking Todd with it.

Move.

The door shattering on the opposite side of the hall cuts short a shrill Aphid shriek. Todd's absolute silence as he spins into the arms of an Aphid alarms her more. Made up, the thing looks like any other ski tourist until it opens its mouth.

Angel dives for the opening, brings her gun up and aims at the other side. A single round in the shoulder of Aphid number two puts the thing down as her hands vibrate with the recoil. She doesn't need to see the Aphid seize as its stiff body hits the floor.

Before she can get to Todd, who wrestles his Aphid down the hall and into the living room, she pulls the door away from the wall, ready to shoot whatever's under it but other than the hole the doorknob made there's no other Aphid.

"Todd," she calls. He faces her, back to the dark living room and presumably the third Aphid. Angel brings her gun up, both hands steady her aim and Todd freezes to hold the Aphid as still as he can. It struggles and trills in pain as bone snaps.

As she squeezes the trigger, Todd grimaces as if expecting her to zap him. The round jams in the chamber, far enough along to discharge into the metal. The rubber coated handle gives her some protection but the weapon isn't new and the rubber fails to keep the charge away. Angel's jaw snaps tight shut as her arms and legs lock up, at the mercy of the initial burst of fifty-thousand volts. She slides sideways and hits the wall shoulder first before the electric grip lets her go.

"Angel?" Todd gasps or she thinks he does. The charge short-circuits her hearing as well as everything else.

She can imagine the look of surprise on her face as she hits the floor. Todd's arms lock beneath the Aphid's, his hands behind its neck and a rough growl comes from his throat as he pushes down, nearly driving its pointy teeth into its own chest.

Damn, helpless sucks. She's the Core soldier and even at seventy percent of her pre-death performance level she should be doing better than laying limp on the floor while her nervous system recovers from the jolt. Todd has to deal with his lively opponent before the other comes to its senses or worse, before the third arrives. Even with the reduced charge Angel received, she won't be any help since Aphids bounce back from the stun so much faster. She meant it when she said shoot them and run. If she was lucky enough to hit something important it might not get up.

The Aphid's hands slash but Todd is so much larger it does little more than cut at the air in front of his face. A few seconds of blackness pass, how many she can't tell, and Todd's bare feet dig in closer to the apartment door. The Aphid in his arms still struggles as it did when the fight started but Todd's heavy breathing betrays his fatigue. Behind her, a muffled Aphid groan causes Todd's eyes to go wide. He takes another step back and his left moves to grasp the Aphid across the face, his fingers close to its snapping teeth.

As Angel hears the Aphid behind her get to its feet, Todd shouts, twisting his Aphid's head around nearly backwards. Had he hoped she'd get up and shoot it? No way she'll pull the trigger on her jammed gun unless she wants another ride to her ass.

"Stay down," he gasps, crouching to face off against the second Aphid.

Angel feels it move closer and it purrs in threat. Then it laces its fingers through her hair and pulls her head from the carpet. She can only see into the kitchen since her new position causes her to lose sight of Todd. A blade, as serrated as an Aphid's teeth, nestles in the juncture between her jaw and her throat.

Don't tense. Even a small movement could spook the Aphid, leaving her dead and Todd fighting the armed green alone. Better to remain limp when a single jerk of the knife at her neck will sink the jagged teeth deep, inflicting a wound nearly as severe as the one which killed her. The urge to swallow burns until she's ready to give in but the Aphid shifts position, shoving her face toward the floor and freeing a trickle of saliva from the corner of her mouth.

Shuffling. A door? Just as she readies herself to hear Todd fight the third Aphid, Rye's voice fills the small living room.

"Yeah, you know what this is, asshole."

CHAPTER 7

Tong remains motionless at Rye's side until the top of the Aphid holding Angel disappears.

Rye would be happy to shoot the half-naked roommate if he'd shown any sign of aggression toward the Aphid but the big blonde stands in perfect submission; eyes on the floor, lips shut tight and hands limp at his sides. The exact same posture as Tong. Either he's not an idiot or this isn't his first Aphid encounter.

Before Rye's finger relaxes from the plasma gun's pressure plate, Angel's head slumps to the floor with a thunk, carrying one gloved Aphid hand with it. The other, the one holding the knife, becomes nothing more than scorched, wet stink in the air along with the rest of the Aphid's torso, head and arms.

The Aphid's bottom squats behind her then with half its weight gone, the knees tilt into Angel's back before tipping over sideways. She groans as she bats at the hand tangled in her hair, hitting her forehead more often than not as Tong and the roommate get to her side.

"Furth," she slurs. "Fird."

"We got it, Angel," Tong reassures but Rye holds back. He'd only been gone a few minutes. Ten, tops. Enough for the green to get a knife to her throat. Before he can sink into

40

disappointment with himself, he locks down to focus on the job at hand. Tong and the roommate get Angel upright so Rye scans the room. The blinking Aphid Todd stepped over doesn't appear to have bled and other than a small line of dot-like punctures on the side of Angel's neck there's no blood in the living room. The Aphid Rye got with the plasma gun won't bleed.

The only light reaches the living room from a busted open doorway down the hall so Rye presses a couple of finger-wide buttons by the front door.

"You hurt?" Rye asks nobody in particular. Bitterness with his failure to protect her comes out loud and clear.

Todd scowls at him then tilts his head at a small black pistol on the floor.

"I think her gun shorted out," he says.

"Angel, that charger's antique," Tong scolds as she gets a shaky hand to his cheek.

"When I woke up, the first thing I asked about was you," she articulates. "They told me you were fine."

"Yeah," Tong sighs. Rye can't make out his mood but if he had to guess, Tong's grief at losing her is as close to the surface as his own. The whole unit, for that matter, underwent significant changes in the weeks and months following Constant.

"Angel," Todd says, pressing her hands in his. Something about the gesture shows they're familiar in a way Rye wants to understand. No jealousy, for the moment at least. Just sadness. "These two Core like you?"

Under other circumstances, Rye would tell her to zip it and discuss divulging details to civilians with her later but he lets this play out. If she talks then it isn't his mission details she shares and the information he gathers might spare her several days of interrogation. Todd won't remember any of this anyway.

She tightens her mouth and drops her jaw before lifting it again.

Your call, Angel, Rye thinks. If she chooses debriefing by Intelligence so be it though the idea doesn't sit well with him. If she's one of them she'll be in trouble enough for bringing a civilian and Core into her operation. If she isn't then she won't breathe the outside air until Intelligence knows all about whomever took her body.

Rye will have a few days in transit aboard *Titan* to encourage her to talk before she gets to the brig on *Barrington Station*.

"Tong," Rye nods toward the dying Aphid then pulls his data tablet out. Angel doesn't react to the crunch of Tong's knife entering the Aphid's brain. Neither does Todd.

Before he looks up, Rye taps in a quick communication to Atom in orbit aboard *Titan*. Location, situation. A memory wipe and some light repairs, job done. He doesn't mention Angel, their extra passenger.

"We'll have someone here in about sixteen minutes," Rye says after receiving confirmation from Atom. "Fix up the door."

"No," Angel says.

"I suggest you keep your mouth shut, Angel," he warns. "You'll be coming with us."

"No," Todd growls, turning to face Rye.

Her hand rests on Todd's bare shoulder, squeezing as she wobbles up onto her knees.

"Give him a choice, Rye, or I'm not going anywhere."

"Neither one of you has a choice," Rye answers. Tong finishes searching the intact Aphid, collecting its data unit and a few other things before pulling a vacuum bag from his pocket.

"What does he mean, Angel?" Todd asks.

"In sixteen minutes they're going to fix the door and wipe your memory like they were never here."

"Hell no," Todd gets to his feet, locking his knees in place as he stands protectively in front of Angel. Damn her for making this hard. All Rye wants is her on *Titan* so he can deal with everything he's carried with him since Constant. Or at

42

least start to. Or make sure she's locked up somewhere safe until he's ready.

"Why, Angel?" Rye says instead of the million other questions he has for her.

"Because I never got one, that's why."

She glares past Todd's thigh.

"What do you mean? Core recruited you, Angel. Tech skills like yours? That's nothing we can teach. No first gen can do what you can. Even Intelligence can't figure out what you did."

Each awkward passing second pushes Rye's chances at restarting as friends with her further out of reach. Why does he feel like such an asshole? Even when they were private about each other they always got along in public. Genuinely, too. She fit with the team as if she'd been there for years.

"Don't try and tell me they forced you."

Her frown deepens as a single tear runs past her nose and soaks a strand of hair stuck in the corner of her mouth. He'd do anything to take the words back. Something he said was cruel but he doesn't know what. Angel's breath hitches. She sniffles and looks away as Rye imagines brushing the hair free and tucking it behind her ear. Kissing the tear away. It should be his arm reaching around her, not Todd's.

"We don't," he insists but doesn't really know for sure. Core scouts first gens. Athletes, scientists, even little blonde girls who probably eat transistors for breakfast. Six years ago she didn't act like someone who didn't have a choice. She fought with as much heart as anyone, almost zealous, side by side with the third gens no matter what they were up against.

"Time you two left," Todd says. Though his voice flattens, Rye doesn't buy his resignation. In Todd's shoes, Rye would fight his way out with one arm while holding Angel with the other. He did that on Constant, Aphids coming from every direction as they retreated under heavy fire to their extraction point. Todd continues and though he doesn't plead, he makes a logical case. "This isn't the first Aphid I did bare handed. I took out five in the Pits. Running a tow rope's the only job I could get after I did my time."

"I thought those fights were all fixed," Tong interrupts. He pulls another bag from his pocket and passes Angel and Todd.

"Does it matter? Nobody's gonna throw a fight against a green. They'll kill you, not just make it look good. Give me a choice, man. I know what they can do."

"Shit," Rye mutters and stomps over to the cluttered kitchen to grab an old reclaimed plastic envelope and a pen. After scribbling a few words, he hands it to Todd.

"You want to do this for real, ask for Acquisitions. Not Recruiting. Don't ask for whoever's in charge or demand to see the boss. Be polite. Acquisitions. Quote the code on the envelope. Mess it up and you'll wake up with a headache and no clue where Angel's gone. If that's what you want though..."

"Bare hands?" Rye turns toward the larger bag as Tong dumps the smaller one beside it. "You'll be an asset to Core."

"Think about it, Todd," Angel whispers. "You have a few minutes. Your girl. Your life."

Todd shrugs. "Hasn't been a girl in nearly a month. I kept it up hoping she'd change her mind but she left Whistler a week ago."

Angel gives him a tight smile before disappearing down the hall and returning with a battered silver suitcase. She must have been just about out the door when the Aphids showed up. She sets it down before wrapping her arms around Todd, her face set in farewell.

"Stay warm, Angel," he whispers.

CHAPTER 8

"Give me that," Tong glances sideways at Rye's back and adjusts the intact Aphid on his shoulder so he can take Angel's suitcase. She holds the railing in one hand and extends the other arm at her side to catch her balance. The left side of her face still feels like it's at the tail end of a whopper dose of Novocain but at least she hasn't tried to stumble over her own feet since the top flight.

At the bottom of the stairs, Tong sets down the suitcase and drops the Aphid on top of Rye's bundle.

"Get the CN2 and pick up the other body," Rye orders. He leans away from Angel, pushing his shoulder into the wall as if the aged, gray concrete might oblige and let him get further from her.

Angel doesn't realize how annoyed she is with Rye's posture until Tong gives her an 'are you sure I can leave the two of you alone' look. Rye's remark about how she got into Core stings. Her only choice had been a memory wipe and she fought like hell for the other option to get in to Core. She didn't do any of the things Rye told Todd to do but she wasn't going to forget losing her brother. The memories of the tragedy back on her family farm aren't Rye's fault but it's easier to blame their resurfacing on him.

She gives Tong a nod Rye doesn't notice and he steps out, ushering in a nasty burst of winter air and evening snowflakes.

"Rye?" Angel opens her jacket and stuffs her mittened hands under her arms. A line of snow drifts up against his boots and she looks at her own small feet. Cold bleeds through the seams around the soles. Plain civilian winter boots. At least her old combat boots made her look and feel a lot taller. They weren't any better insulated but she wasn't susceptible to the cold then. Even a civilian does a better job of self-warming than her. "I couldn't get in touch with you. Can you understand that?"

Down the road, maybe, when her little girl is beyond Core's grasp, distanced by time and space, she would have reached out but not now. Her daughter is exceptional, far beyond even a third gen in her skills. A stranger would mistake the big four-year-old for a child two years older. Angel bites back her guilt. She'd give anything to have her family back and keeping quiet about their daughter feels two-faced. If Core finds her, she's gone and Angel won't put her through growing up alone.

"How much do you remember about Constant?" Rye blurts out as he spins to face her. Then he appears to lose himself in his data tab. "Cleanup crew is here. He asked for Acquisitions... confirming my code. Where the hell is Tong?"

"Not as much as I'd like," she explains, not sure if she's relieved Todd's enlisting or not. Acquisitions will be his first hurdle. He'll still endure a battery of psychological and physical testing followed by nearly two years of surgeries and drug therapy while he's expected to complete basic training. "Since I recovered, other than impressions of the bright summer and flowering trees, only dreams of Tong bleeding out. I never get to him fast enough. In the kitchen I got that back. I remembered I patched him up."

"You knew he was alive," Rye challenges, lips curling in anger. A single breath releases his tension and his next words are softer. "You said that upstairs."

"Knowing it and remembering, seeing him. Two different things."

Angel adjusts her mittened hands and pushes them a little lower seeking warmth since they've drawn the heat out from under her arms. She finds it in Rye's hands as they slide in her jacket and cover hers.

"You'll see the medic on *Titan*," he says then draws one hand out of her coat, pulls the mitten off and wraps her icy hand in his. Instant heat shocks her system but it doesn't spread far from where he touches her. Her hungry skin soaks it in. "That charger threw off your nervous system. You're not getting that piece of shit gun back."

She shrugs, letting him think electricity decreased the circulation to her extremities. At least she doesn't have to spend half her money getting it smuggled off-planet. Rye will do it for her.

"Other one," Rye continues, stuffing one of her hands in his coat then the other and sandwiching them between his big arms and his body. Her mittens go in her pocket. With her hands restrained and his free he moves on to see the knife marks on her neck and though his hold isn't enough to prevent her from pulling away, she doesn't.

He strokes her jaw with a warm thumb while he tilts her head aside to inspect the knife wounds.

"Just scratches," she tries to push her chin down but he keeps it up. They sting and probably need a good disinfecting but the old Angel, the soldier, rises to the surface to ignore the injury.

"You're still bleeding. Medic. You single?"

"Seriously?" she gripes. A come-on? Now? She fell for him hard before she died and the slippery road to completely giving him her heart again steepens before her. A crazy thought about giving their daughter a real family shakes her. Core soldiers live for nothing but Core. Raised by surrogates and in full service by the time he was sixteen, Rye wouldn't even have a basic idea of what a little girl needs from her family.

"That's a no?"

She finds his eyes. Deep gray pierced with old pain stares back. It isn't his fault she died or anything else for that matter.

"It's a yes, Rye."

"Okay."

He never used to stoop to kiss her, instead choosing to pick her up and press her hard into whatever he found available. This time he does, touching chaste warm lips to the corner of her mouth.

"Now the answer is no," he breathes then straightens, shaking off surprise at his own words and she understands how fragile he is around her. It comes off him in restless waves. Maybe it wasn't only her who let feelings go too far. Rye doesn't act like a man who saw being her 'regular' as just sex and after six long years his words are just as possessive as when they used to be alone. She thought it was play though she fell for it just the same. He acts like he meant it.

No, Angel chastises herself for letting him continue. For not arguing. For not forcing him away.

Rye leans to her again. His lips open as they seal around the other corner of her mouth and she quivers inside, fisting his shirt in her cool hands. The concrete floor beneath their boots seems to tilt as she remembers exactly what she told him the last day on Constant.

I love you, Rye.

She surrenders her mouth to him to stop the words from pouring out. His hands settle under her jaw, one thumb dueling with her tongue as he licks his way to her ear and pulls the lobe in. Their bodies remain inches apart, fused only where their lips make contact. She pulls, desperate to close the gap when his tablet buzzes and he releases her, stepping back and leaving her cold and alone in a stairwell with nothing but her suitcase, two Aphid bodies and the side of his face.

"In the transport, Angel," he mutters. Like pushing a button, the heat from him shuts off.

"Rye," she tries to think through her confusion. For a moment he does nothing as she gets back to reality. There's no room for anything between them now, not anymore.

"I get it," Angel snaps as Rye pushes the door open to let Tong in. "I'm property."

"Cool it, you two," Tong whispers, turns his back to Angel and pushes past Rye.

Rye straightens his coat, grabs the intact Aphid and stomps out, looking both ways to make sure he isn't seen. At least Tong steadies her before grabbing the other body. Angel waves him off when he goes for her suitcase.

The CN2 sits a few meters from the building with the back panel already open for their cargo. Rye doesn't look at her as he dumps the body in and slams the panel down after Tong adds the other dead Aphid. The transport looks as she remembers. Resembling a civilian family air-car on the outside, the inside contains extra shielding, computers and of course, weapons useful both in atmosphere and in space.

"New racing stripe?" Angel asks Tong. Rye can go piss up a rope, using his damn mouth to try and make her talk. She knows exactly what she said to him on Constant and now he's going to use it to find out where she's been.

CHAPTER 9

"Sure is," Tong grins. Rye looks away before the skinny moustache splits in the middle. "My work, of course. That and half a dozen modifications Denman doesn't know about."

The crooked stripe ripples, marred by bubbles from the roller but could be worse considering how drunk they were when they staggered out of The Gin Palace, *Barrington's* off duty lounge, and got into the white paint.

"Denman still run Blue Team?" Angel asks. Blue team includes Rye's unit and several others.

"Not only Blue. Everything on *The Barrington* as of two years ago. We expected it to go to a third gen but for a second gen the old man is about as good as they get."

"It's really good, Tong," Angel nods at the hood and squeezes his elbow. He gives her a pathetic awe shucks like she hasn't been unforgivably dead for six years. Rye's probably the only one on *Titan* who will do the right thing and turn her over, as hard as it will be. He's shaken to see her alive, grateful even, but that doesn't excuse whomever stole her. Bad enough she was dead; five years of believing her body to be lost as well left the hole in him jammed up tight.

Denman always rubbed Angel the wrong way. At least he'll squash any for old times feelings until Angel's benefactors have been dealt with and she's back on duty. Seventy percent efficiency isn't enough for his unit but there's always work on *The Barrington* if Intelligence doesn't take her.

Rye's mouth still tingles from Angel's chilled skin and he resists running his hands over his face to discreetly smell her. All he's done is make her madder. She should have put the brakes on, Rye decides. A slap, he can understand and even expected. Damn, hoped for and deserved as reward for kissing her. It would be so much simpler if she hated him but the way she glares his way just makes him want her more.

With a shrug, Rye pulls open the passenger door.

"Get in," he grumbles. "In the back."

"Whatever," Angel replies, then hesitates as she gets ready to climb over the passenger seat. "There's not a lot of room."

"Whatever," Rye pushes the door into her butt, shoving her in but not because he meant to. His eyes on her ass left him with little attention on where the door was. Her hair, loose from the knot it was in at the coffee shop, sways to the side.

"Asshole," she whispers.

"Pardon?"

"I said ass and I said hole," she shouts but gets moving before he shoves the door at her again.

Rye ignores Tong's puzzled look and strides around to the pilot seat. By the time he gets in, Angel has wedged herself in behind him making use of the only available space and Tong plots their route. Once he seats his data tablet in the dash, the CN2 hums and starts up, elevating high enough from the ground for him to crawl under if he chose to. The wheels fold up beneath them then the covers snap shut. Environmental controls light up, verifying they run on internal systems and the hull integrity check indicates a space-worthy seal.

"Heat?" Angel asks.

"No," Rye replies. The first Aphid they caught chilled enough sitting in the alley but he has to get the temperature down on the other two. Still half an hour from *Titan*, he needs the bodies preserved before any deterioration sets in.

She mutters something he doesn't try and make out though he can count the two syllables.

Whistler streets and sidewalks fill with tourists and locals as Rye negotiates the CN2 out of the lower rent residential sector. Avoiding the main commercial centre, they head for the southern dome entrance as Tong contacts local departures for a vector and clearance.

"YVR vertical departures, this is CN2 designated Oscar Alpha Nine Seven dash Tango. Requesting clearance for discreet orbital exit."

"Oscar Alpha Nine Seven dash Tango," a smooth female voice fills the cabin. "Transmit identity. Maintain current vector and stand by."

"YVR, Oscar Alpha Nine Seven dash Tango transmitting, maintaining and standing by," Tong finishes with a sigh. No getting laid for Rye's slightly older brother.

The aerial corridor south to the Vancouver Airport carries light traffic toward the city. Heavier traffic approaches from the opposite direction, toward Whistler. They bank east, out over the water to follow invisible beacons displayed as a three dimensional path of purple lights on the nav board. Black ocean, only visible in reflections of the city towers, carries surface ships toward the Pacific. Tong and Rye arrived in Whistler during the day, just a week before, after descending to YVR and taking the same corridor to the Dome. That day, clouds sat low and heavy with wetness from the ocean. The towers in the downtown core and beyond hid behind layers of fog and icy drops of autumn drizzle.

Rye hadn't taken time to look at the scenery. Preliminary intel on the Aphid sighting in Whistler scrolled past on Tong's display as Rye listened to his brother read it out. Not that they hadn't gone over it already. Preparation and simplicity describes life in Core but there was no damned way to plan ahead for the immense complication riding with the dead Aphids behind them in cargo.

"Heat?" the complication asks again.

Instead of answering, Rye activates the air curtain. An intense downdraft knifes the compartment in two and keeps the cold with the bodies where it belongs.

"Asshole," she mutters again then starts pumping her palms up and down over her jacket covered arms. The display must be meant to annoy him since there's no way she hasn't shaken off the effects of the stun.

Risking a look in the rear view mirror, he catches her angry glare as she shakes in time with the wisp of her hands over her nylon jacket. Without breaking eye contact, Rye pushes the button to retract the mirror.

"YVR vertical departures, Oscar Alpha Nine Seven dash Tango acknowledges receipt of discreet exit code and departure vector," Tong speaks. Rye missed the chirp of the code arriving and adjusts his vision to concentrate on their route. Half a minute later, they leave the civilian air corridor and head further east toward the vertical path reserved for smaller transports leaving for orbit. Once there, he only has to put up with twelve minutes to orbit and another ten to *Titan* which is about all he can take of Angel in the back seat.

Even the air curtain doesn't prevent her scent from traveling forward, invading his nostrils and stirring up memories of their first night together aboard *The Barrington*. Granted, it had only been a couple of hours. When she confessed she'd never been with a man he knew, absolutely knew, it was already too late for him to ever need any other woman. Without knowing what made him worthy of her innocence he choked up and thanked her. Looking in her eyes, he used every ounce of control and patience he had to wait out her nervousness and was rewarded with—

"Starboard, jerk," Tong smacks Rye in the back of the head with one hand and changes course with the other. "Keep that up and you'll have to explain the deviation fine to Denman."

"Yeah," Rye pushes Tong away and finishes the maneuver himself, grateful to the darkness and his long coat for hiding his arousal.

"Yeah is right," Tong pulls the Aphid data tablets from his pockets, securing two in the small storage compartment between the front seats and examining the other. It lights up in his hands then dims in deference to the dark cockpit.

CHAPTER 10

In spite of the airtight bags, the dry, burning smell of Aphid scratches at Angel's throat. The scent lingers in her hair and clothes, staining everything she touches with the smooth, dry slippery feel of their skin. She lost the feeling in her fingers before they were out of the Dome and the friction of her coat on her mittened palms does little to bring heat to her numb hands. Several niches near *Titan's* main engine heat exchanges should be warm enough to help her shake off the cold but she has to get aboard the bigger ship first.

If she's already hypothermic then she's in trouble and really will need the medic Rye threatened. She feels the same whether she's dropped half a degree or five and hasn't been in the cold back seat all that long.

She can't see Tong's breath in the Aphid tablet light but she can see her own in the faint, green glare.

"Hey, Rye," the front speakers crackle to life with Atom's voice and she can't help but smile. The man was everyone's buddy back when she was in the unit. The social glue who eased the team through misunderstandings and kept up morale on long trips. "You're reading a little heavy. You smuggle me something in a g-string?"

Their delta-A, ascension readout in front of Tong agrees in bold, warning yellow. It will take a full fifteen to achieve orbit.

"Yeah," Rye answers. "Three and a half bodies heavy."

His answer makes it clear she's nothing more than cargo.

Atom laughs. "Which half?"

"Bottom, my friend. Right up your alley."

"You ain't leaving that shit in my bunk," he answers. "Tong's quarters, right next to mine."

"Fuck you, Atom," Tong spits though he doesn't mean it. Nothing bigger than a pencil would fit in an Aphid's orifice and no human who knew better would even try to get their dick that close to an Aphid's back end, dead or alive.

"We'll see. Light a fire under it. Denman wants us home now."

Tong kills the comms and gets his attention back on the tablet. Angel's face appears on the screen and she shudders. The Aphids damned well knew she was on to them. Just like she suspected, they came to the apartment looking for her. It took three weeks from her confirmation they were in Whistler for Rye to show up at the coffee shop and she used everything she'd been taught about surveillance. Not her best work, not by a long shot and she used to be a Comms Officer, not a tracker like Atom or Rye. Even Tong, with his disposition for getting hands on and dirty was decent at eyes on in the field.

As the CN2 strains to hasten their ascent, Tong squeezes the Aphid data unit in both hands then shakes it, bashing it several times against the storage compartment between the seats. He rearranges his fingers and manages to get the thing beeping.

"Tong," she warns though the beeping only means it runs a diagnostic protocol as a result of the blows.

"Oh, shit," he breathes then turns to Angel, eyes wide in panic. She's too frozen to show humour at his honest alarm and to be fair, chances to put one over on Tong are few and far between. Or they used to be.

"What did you touch? I think you turned on the self destruct."

"I don't know," Tong's voice rises as she leans forward.

"Well, shut it off."

"How?" He thrusts the unit at her and she backs up as far as she can, getting her butt up on some part of a dead Aphid to get away from the beeping tablet. Damn, grunts can be so gullible when it comes to tech. Tong's brute force carelessness with the thing is going to get her into the heated front seat.

From her perch, Angel holds her hands out and tries to demonstrate what to do but Tong's panic escalates. His knuckles whiten as he tries to repair the unit by crushing it. The tablet responds with a double beep.

"Fix it, fix it," he whines.

"Tong, she's busting your balls, man," Rye says from the pilot seat but he doesn't sound convinced. He even leans into the door and pushes Tong's hands away.

"Damn it, Tong," Angel lectures and pretends she holds the unit in both hands to demonstrate, wiggling her fingers. "Haven't you ever watched an Aphid masturbate?"

Tong, eyes wide, shakes his head while the beeping rises in tone and speeds up.

"Shit, Tong," Rye growls though he goes from worried to amused. At least he doesn't miss a chance to prank Tong. Maybe there is something human inside him after all. "They're fucking androgynous."

But his older brother passes beyond listening and Angel has her chance to get out of Aphid cold storage. He shakes his head.

"Hold on," Angel climbs into the front and shivers in spite of what feels like warm air. The temperature sits a few degrees below how she liked the apartment but in contrast to the refrigerated cargo hold it's a day in the sun to her hands and face. The rest of her is too well insulated to let the heat in.

She sits down on Tong's knee, her back to the passenger door, while he clutches the tablet to his chest. Ignoring the glare from Rye, she rests a hand under the tablet and digs her feet in to avoid sliding off the smooth finish of Tong's skinny ski suit.

The screen flickers then strobes in time with the shrill beeping and brightness rolls brilliant, green, vertical bands up the screen and reflects in the whites of Tong's big eyes.

"You'll need a third hand," she explains, not hiding her annoyance with Rye.

"Are their dicks that big?" Tong asks, completely serious.

Oh, Lord.

"No, hands are that small."

Tong nods as if he understands though if he wasn't preparing himself to blow up all over the Salish Sea, he'd remember an Aphid hand is about the size of a woman's and an Aphid has no obvious genitalia. At least Rye stopped interfering and plays along. With her left hand, she pretends to adjust Tong's grip while she uses her teeth to push up her sleeve and pull out her data tether. The smooth cord extends just fine though the retractor near her elbow complains with a tight cramp.

"Oh, hurry," Tong moans. "I don't want them picking my guts out of the Aphids' blown up parts."

The beeping escalates, increasing in pitch and speed then he yelps as it starts to buzz.

"I am," she snaps and rubs spit in the data port on the end closest to Tong. When the screen goes black, as it should while it reacts to the fluid coating the port's sensor, she jams the tether in and floods its CPU with protocols to unlock the device and disable the real self destruct, just in case.

For a moment, there's nothing but Tong's heavy breathing and Angel silently counts down.

Three, two, one...

"Boom," she shouts as the screen lights up. Tong kicks in surprise, shooting them both up off the seat and bashing her head on the ceiling. Through the stars behind her eyes she keeps a grip on the Aphid tablet so Tong doesn't put it through the windshield and get them all shot out into orbit.

Rye laughs, hand on his mouth to hide it from Angel.

"Mother fucker, Angel," Tong gasps, still in the grips of shock. Every muscle jolts before he comes down, relaxing a little at a time as Angel pries the Aphid tablet from his fingers. "Damn it, so good to have you back, girl."

What does she say to that? Tong hasn't thought through what the implications of Angel back in Core will be for her. Since they found her, things moved fast. He didn't have much of a chance to speak with her until now.

To hide her sadness, she winks then turns to the window. Daytime Earth fills the lower windshield, only partly hidden by the hood. Hot, white, unblinking stars fill the black wash above it. To port, YVR's orbital counterpart hangs suspended and waits to inspect inbound and outbound vehicles for customs violations. Their discreet departure allows them to keep their Aphid cargo, Rye's plasma gun, her charger and whatever else they have stashed aboard from landing them in jail. Core has its privileges when one carries a valid transit code.

"You didn't trigger anything, Tong," she explains, avoiding looking at her image on the front of the rebooted data unit. Pain near her elbow worsens as she massages the retractor with her thumb. It obliges though it will take days to work the tether back in. "You must have disabled the mute and activated the vibrator then you bashed it on the console and triggered a self-test so the thing could make sure it's okay. The beeps, buzzing, and light display are a simple diagnostic.

"I also disabled the real self-destruct."

No point telling him that any of her data units should be able to download the data and translate it into something a Core mainframe might be able to churn into something useful. From what she's learned, she's still far ahead of Intelligence when it comes to Aphid tech.

"Mother fucker, Angel," Tong says again. "You won't see me coming when I pay you back for this. I think I pissed."

Angel moves away, a little closer to his knee and he laughs.

"I just," Tong sighs, his voice harsh with emotion. "Didn't feel right surviving Constant with you in a bag. There's no fucking justice. You saved my life and paid for it with yours."

Tong pulls his top lip in and works his moustache with his bottom teeth.

"So what the hell were you doing in Whistler, anyway?"

"Selling coffee," she shrugs but Rye shoots her a glare. He doesn't need to say it. Lying to Tong after his admission is a bitch thing to do. She continues. "Needed a cover. Been there a while gathering intel on the Aphids. I guess I wasn't as discreet as I thought if they had me on their tablet. I think there were only three. Hard to tell because they swap outfits like a bunch of teenage girls.

"Anyway, if you found a key on one of them I have the address."

"Sure did," Tong leans past her and flicks the comm on as Rye gives her an approving nod. For what? Coming clean with Tong or coming clean, period? She's sure Rye won't be satisfied with what she told Tong. "*Titan*, this is CN2. Open your ass-end up, Atom, and let us in."

The expedition class ship faces away from Earth, engines pointed down at the Atlantic and top-side solar surfaces toward the sun. Six levels amidships at the thickest point, the aft narrows to five for engines and access and the bow to two levels in a rounded curve. The spartan, light gray exterior matches the interior and includes the Core symbol painted three meters tall on both sides. A simple circle, black on the left and green on the right. A blue line for Earth dividing the two. Centuries earlier, Earth politicians decided the design was symbolic on many levels, most irrelevant today. Green was for life, for protecting the environment humans fought so hard to cure of twenty-first century contamination. Now, with human colonies spread far and wide, the current government wants the green removed because of the Aphid threat. Angel hadn't had an opinion until she died. The symbol means Core and one way or another, Core still defines her path.

Titan doesn't reply but as Rye brings them around to the starboard side near the aft section, two panels retract, one up and one down, revealing the lower cargo bay. Soft, red light brighter than the red lights inside surrounds the opening. Angel doesn't feel the vibration of the cargo bay doors closing until they make contact with the deck. Once the doors slam shut, Rye remotely brings the bay lights up.

Angel gives Tong's hand a squeeze as he rubs her back. Maybe he figured out she's in a heap of trouble.

CHAPTER 11

Angel waits, suitcase dangling from one arm, as Rye and Tong drag the bodies into a storage locker off the main bay. Her other hand clenches as she flexes at the elbow, wincing when her fist reaches her shoulder. As Tong sets the environmental controls to preserve the bagged remains, Rye turns to Angel.

The last time he saw her, the long blond hair around her shoulders barely reached her ears.

When he kissed her in the stairwell, he moved to her ear to feel those long, soft waves against his lips and there's nothing he wants more than to touch it again. To feel it fall over him as she looks into his eyes from above, offers her wide smile and gives herself to him.

Never going to happen.

Not in this or any other lifetime.

"Let's go," Rye orders.

Tong opens the hatch into *Titan's* system of narrow halls and ladders and Rye waits until Angel follows. He watches her from behind, as if she could go anywhere. *Titan* only flies for the men and women on this particular mission and she won't be able to even palm open a door for herself.

Two decks up, they reach the bridge. Scarlet dozes, boots up on the weapons console and Atom sits in the command chair, back to the door. Otherwise, everything appears as he left it. Environmental controls on low, main viewports open and the soft hum of electronics welcome them to space. The star field ahead moves across *Titan's* bow.

"Rye?" Atom asks.

"Who else?"

"I've already cleared us for departure," Atom slumps sideways and casts his arm over one arm rest. His leg flops over the other revealing the meticulous shine on his boot, glowing in spite of time spent crawling around the engines. "Ten years, Rye. Been stuck on this bird keeping her in orbit while you get to go to the surface. Passed up on shore leave to come here for ski buns and bunnies but what the fuck, stuck using flattery and my sexy touch to keep the engines alive so we don't burn up waiting for you."

Everyone ignores Atom's complaints as he leans forward and reaches for the command console to start the drives up for departure. Atom spends as much time on the surface as anyone else but the unfounded complaints reassure Rye. Hell, they reassure the whole team. If those remaining on board have nothing better to do than bitch then they have nothing negative to report either.

"Never so much as a thank you but this time you brought me a souvenir. I think I might actually un-tamper the shitter in your head."

Rye laughs though not without worry. More than once Atom fouled up the facilities in Denman's private head without arousing any suspicion what so ever. "I didn't get you anything, Atom. Engineering is your assignment this run and your thanks is a clean uniform and me not knocking you on your ass for messing up."

"Sure," Atom smiles. "Nice try, but you got me real coffee you bastard and if I didn't have a personal rule of no flirting within my unit I might just make a pass at you."

Rye rolls his eyes. Though Atom's tastes vary, within the unit it's nothing more than banter.

"Rye didn't get you coffee, Atom," Angel interrupts. "I did."

Atom pauses, half out of his seat and Scarlet wakes with a phlegmy gasp. Her legs straighten against the weapons console and she rolls out of her seat, landing face first on the cross marked metal floor. Klutzes don't get to be medics, even third gen klutzes, so the graceless tumble surprises Rye but Tong snickers at her uncharacteristic lack of coordination. She gets her cheek from the floor and freezes, eyes locked on Angel.

"Pardon?" Atom whispers, refusing to move.

"I brought you coffee," Angel tries again and shoves her suitcase in Tong's hands before popping the lid. From the awkward angle over her shoulder, Rye spots cash and vacuum sealed foil packets. She pulls two out and snaps the lid down, casting a wary glance back over her shoulder. Was that all she brought besides the confiscated charger in his pocket? Money and coffee? Her blush tells him it is.

"Hi, Atom. Scarlet," she says.

Atom turns, hands out for balance before gripping the back of the command seat in his left and palming his eyes with the other.

"See?"

The same wide eyes and gaping mouth Rye saw mirrored on Tong in the coffee shop appear on Atom. His lips snap shut before he looks at Rye then Tong. With a finger pointed at Angel, his mouth opens again to silently ask if they see her too.

Get over it, Rye wishes. The sooner they move past their shock and land on his side the better. Welcome back, Angel. Enjoy the brig. He doesn't feel the least bit shitty for being angry and blaming her for the past six years of hurt. He should but he doesn't. It won't take long for the others to feel the same way but for now he has to keep his gorge down as they get through being soppy.

Without another word, Atom embraces the little blonde. In spite of standing four inches shorter than Rye and Tong, he rests his chin on the top of her head and sways like a contented fool.

"It's you, Angel," he whispers into her hair. "You smell like coffee."

She still holds the coffee packets and hugs him. "I smell like Aphid."

"Nope. Coffee, girl," he laughs then draws back to cradle her face in his hands, holding tight like she might just disappear. "Damn, you're freezing."

"C... cold?" Scarlet sputters to life on the floor before getting to her feet. She nearly knocks Angel and Atom sideways with her embrace. "Bleeding? What the fuck, Rye?"

She casts him an angry glare then an angrier one at Tong. "I'm sure this is your fault."

Tong shrugs, not hiding his exasperation. If he opens his mouth Scarlet will only get madder and Atom does nothing to step in with an easy comment to divert them.

"Hypothermic, Rye," she growls as she inspects the wound to Angel's neck. "Come on down to Med, Angel. I have a nice cocktail to warm you up."

"Won't help," Angel replies, eyes to the floor. "My big muscles won't respond to the stimulants to make heat and when the other drugs boost my circulation all that cold blood in my extremities—"

"Means you'll arrest," Scarlet nods. Her surprise now buried under professionalism and training. "Not uncommon after cryo."

Rye flinches inside. Had he known he wouldn't have been such an ass about making her sit in the back seat or at least been just as big an ass about letting her sit up front. The stun from the charger threw off her internal temperature and the effects of cryo only made it worse. He doesn't allow any more than a cool stare for Scarlet. If he encourages sympathy for Angel it will be all the more difficult to turn her in.

"I'll need the thermal bag from stores," Scarlet says then reaches for Angel's suitcase. She pulls it a few inches from Tong before shoving it into his chest. The move surprises him

65

and he steps back, out of her reach, as he lets it go. "Come on, Angel."

With her arm around Angel's shoulders she hustles the other woman off the command deck and down the hall.

"I'll get it," Atom announces and tucks his coffee in his pockets before disappearing after them.

Rye doesn't ask Tong what's up with Scarlet. His brother has never said, but their friendship fell apart fast after Constant. Scarlet and Tong go through phases of civility and open war and it appears the current period of amicability ended a minute earlier.

"Lock up the Aphid data units and the charger," he pulls Angel's gun from his pocket and hands it over. The thin rubber coating on the handle appears melted. Although Rye didn't notice a burn to her hands he steels himself for the responsibility even though it wasn't his fault. "And get back in uniform. I'll get us out of orbit and on course to Jupiter before I clean up."

"Yeah," Tong sighs. Renewed hostilities with Scarlet appear to exhaust him already. Although both rested well on Whistler, his eyes hollow and darken.

As Rye takes his seat, the command console flashes green, indicating the jump drive has enough juice to shoot them to *The Barrington* in its home orbit around Jupiter. At least they won't be traveling for weeks to another system to drop off their cargo.

All of it, Angel included.

Damned Atom. Maybe Rye should take him aside and have a talk about keeping the next two days from becoming completely intolerable. Between the obvious, growing division between Tong and Scarlet and keeping the reunion with Angel from getting out of hand the next forty-eight hours and thirty-one minutes won't be pleasant. Atom never takes sides, but in this case, he took Scarlet's which means Rye either has to shit on everyone to mind their attitudes or come down on Tong's side which could just inflame things even more.

Titan slips from orbit and as the stars ahead freeze in place, the computer adjusts their heading for a straight shot to the big planet. If he sets his implanted eye just right he could make out Jupiter but he doesn't bother.

After making sure the nav computer has all the instructions it needs to keep them on course, Rye leaves for his quarters. Helm control travels with him and his tablet. He undresses, putting the civilian clothes away and lays out his uniform. The trousers and long sleeved shirt sport a similar though slightly darker gray than the walls around him and the front pocket bears Core's round insignia. No other symbol of rank. A first gen squad would need it since they understand the chain of command of civilian armies.

Steam surrounds him in his small cleansing bay then the sonics kick in, knocking dirt and sweat from his skin. Atom didn't pick Scarlet's side, Rye realizes with a jolt then slaps his angry palms against the wall. He chose Angel's and so has Scarlet.

Tensions on *Titan* are about to get a whole lot worse.

CHAPTER 12

"What you mooching for, Atom?" Scarlet asks as she maneuvers Angel toward one of the two beds in the Med Bay. "You want to rig up a coffee brewer from the medical supplies?"

"I was hoping," Atom grins, lips wide with genuine anticipation.

"Trade you, then. All I want is a cup."

"Deal," Atom drops the thermal body bag on the surgical bed and starts going through the cupboards. "Not going to move anything I don't need."

Scarlet gives a tight nod though Angel knows the big redhead stresses about having her Med Bay rearranged.

"Now you," Scarlet says with a warmth she didn't give the brothers one floor down on the command deck. If Angel wasn't so overwhelmed by her current predicament she might have the nerve to ask what went south between Tong and the medic. They'd been regular like her and Rye and not entirely discrete about it. More than once Angel caught them having sex in parts of *The Barrington* they shouldn't have assumed were private, the CN2 included. "Let's start warming you up then I have to close a couple of those marks on your neck."

"'kay," Angel surrenders, feeling no awkwardness at undressing in front of the pair. Scarlet takes the hoodie collar

68

and eases it over Angel's ears before grabbing the shoulders and lifting, pulling Angel's arms up. Angel would have tugged the hem over her head and tossed it aside but this is Scarlet's domain and if she learned anything in her previous life Scarlet's order permeates all.

Behind Angel, the quiet whoosh and crackle of a flameless burner coincides with the soft exhale of a coffee packet opening. Atom inhales with a lusty groan and Scarlet chuckles. Her hands don't slow as she folds the hoodie though she studies Angel's scars.

"Anything else I need to know about your recovery from cryo?"

"I don't tolerate most drugs so it's safer to not give me anything and my data tether doesn't retract like when it was new. Otherwise I need a solid six hours every night since I can't handle anything I used to have to boost my stamina. The implants that stimulated my production of those compounds are gone and since then I've stopped seizing."

Scarlet nods as she folds Angel's sweats and moves on to the thermal long underwear. Boots and socks already sit tucked beneath the bed with the silver suitcase.

"No way I can get you a spare tether unit. Hardware like that is even more controlled than when you got yours. I might be able to do some light surgery to make adjustments depending on how much scar tissue I find around it. Core could swap it out, scarring and all, but I might just make things worse. We'll see. Into the bag," she instructs as she spreads it on the bed, peeling the side open enough for Angel to climb in.

As Angel makes herself comfortable, Scarlet activates the heater and sets it to forty percent.

"Good?" she asks.

"Yeah, I wouldn't set it any higher."

"Hold still," Scarlet presses a thumb-sized med tab to Angel's neck and she winces as the metal sensor enters her artery. After a moment, the monitor built into Scarlet's data tablet displays Angel's vitals. "Hypothermic. Can you tolerate a local anesthetic?"

"Yeah, but don't worry about it."

"I'll just say Atom cut himself in the engine room to account for all the supplies."

"Do it," Atom agrees.

"No," Angel doesn't want to be a wimp.

"Chin up," Scarlet's tone brokers no argument as the fine syringe pricks Angel's skin. "All my data on you is going into my private log. Nobody will see it but me."

"Okay," Angel mouths as Scarlet gets to work with the sutures.

"I know what Rye's planning. We all do. He's commander because he so damned anal about the rules. He'll get over it. I could see it written all over him. Turning you in to Denman," she scoffs. "Please. None of us will leave any sort of detail about you in our official logs and I'm damned sure Rye won't either unless he's certain he's handing you over then he'll get in a big fit about making it look like he didn't fail to promptly document you."

"Got that right," Atom agrees but to Angel, relief remains out of reach.

Scarlet swabs the line of cuts until the pads come away clean then eases Angel's arm out of the bag. She hyper-extends the elbow and probes the implant with her thumb.

"You might be stuck with this busted-ass retractor," she admits. "Tissue's grown nearly solid around it. I can hardly feel the implant."

"I figured," Angel agrees as she draws her arm back into the bag. "The tether will sort itself out."

As Scarlet accepts a beaker of fresh coffee from Atom, she pulls her desk chair over to sit near Angel. The fragrance from the dark brew doesn't stand out for Angel since her eyes still burn from the fresh scent of antiseptic but the bliss on Scarlet's face makes her wish she wasn't so immune. In Whistler, coffee didn't do any more than keep a roof over her head and allow her to save enough for the smuggler to get her charger off planet and for fuel for the small, personal transport she left parked in the Moon's main business district. No way to get it home now and the storage charge will only get bigger.

For several minutes, contented sips and coffee cooling breaths fill their silence.

"Was your pregnancy normal?" Scarlet asks.

"Pardon?" Atom sputters his coffee and waves an 'I'm shutting up' hand at the medic.

Angel closes her eyes, hoping to disappear. One thing to be caught but to have them find out about her daughter means it's all over. If Scarlet can't keep her a secret then Core will do all they can to find the little girl.

"This is between us, Angel," Scarlet reassures. "I saw your stretch marks."

"Normal," Angel answers.

"How long ago were you brought out of cryo?"

"Almost five years."

"And the child?" Scarlet asks.

"Four and a half."

Let Scarlet do the math. Angel woke up pregnant.

Scarlet swirls her coffee around inside the clear beaker, mesmerizing Angel with the rhythmic simplicity of the movement.

"Has he been tested?" She finally asks, genuine curiosity in her eyes. "I mean, I don't want to get too personal but you know how we're raised. Even though we had surrogate parents to see us through our early training they were loving and nurturing, for our emotional stability, you know.

"It rubs off," Scarlet shrugs. "Even though it shouldn't. Third gens are still human after all and my mother was a great role model and I guess I'm just..."

"It's okay," Angel lowers her voice. "I woke up five months along with the major spinal reconstruction behind me. I started walking without help just before I delivered."

Angel keeps her child's gender private. Somehow, even that bit of anonymity acts as a shield.

"I guess, what I meant, how has he tested?"

"Third gen in some areas," Angel allows although third gen is extremely conservative. Wanting to trust Scarlet and needing the confidence of another woman, she continues. "More advanced in others."

Scarlet's brows rise. A true fourth generation soldier remains more an ideal than a set of specifications.

"So the father?"

Angel wiggles a hand out of the thermal bag and gestures Scarlet near.

"Rye," she whispers when Scarlet's ear touches her lips.

"Wow, shit," the medic exclaims. "I mean, on Constant when... I mean we all took it pretty hard."

"What about the father?" Rye's voice booms from the doorway.

In a flurry, Atom and Scarlet move to get between Rye and the bed.

"Later, Rye," Scarlet orders and straightens up to her full six foot three. Behind Rye, Tong appears and places a hand on his brother's shoulder. In uniform and nearly identically armed, the pair usually get their way without argument. In this case, Scarlet holds her ground. Nobody messes with her in her Med Bay.

"Who is the father?" Rye repeats, the calmness in his voice juxtaposes the tension in his body. Set to explode into the room, he uses his own white knuckled hands to hold himself back. "I'm not saving this for later, Scarlet."

Atom's hand on Angel's shoulder makes her aware of how hard she breathes, wheezing and gasping, as light headedness threatens to let panic overwhelm her. A steady, warning tone issues from Scarlet's tablet as Angel's heart rate rises then the tablet beeps with urgency.

"Get the fuck out," Scarlet growls and turns her back on Rye. "Irregular, fast heart beat, cold from her limbs..."

Here we go again, Angel forces deep, even breaths and tries to induce a trance-like state sufficient to slow her own heart but all she can think of is Core descending on the quiet farming community hiding her daughter.

"Atom," Scarlet orders something Angel can't hear clearly then plastic covers her nose and mouth. Fresh, cold air invades and she fights the rhythm as she looks up at Atom. "Could we have any more broken shit around here? The thermal bag quit and you got her so agitated the cold in her arms and legs is putting the chill on her heart."

"Scarlet, I..." Rye says. "What do you need?"

As Angel drifts away, two thick pads stick to her chest.

Cardiac defibrillator, she thinks. *Yeah, a nice big jolt will hit the spot. You know what you're doing, Scarlet. I'll be back in a few.*

CHAPTER 13

"What do you need?" Rye demands as he and Tong move to Angel's bedside. Nothing hides the surgical scars around her pelvis, deep puckered dents where metal rods held bone together from the outside as her inside healed. Silvery webs of feathered stretch marks scar more lightly below her navel. A tattooed vine around her neck and shoulders bulges with clusters of small, purple flowers and dangles down the center of her chest. One cluster shares her bra with her left breast. Core wouldn't have let her get pregnant but then it must have happened before she died. Too many conflicting details race through Rye's mind and for the moment, none matter. Arrhythmia and the accompanying lack of circulation will kill her just as quick as if her heart stopped. Regulation white panties and bra appear to have colour against Angel's pallid skin and the tattoos stand out in oddly hued vibrance. She strains to breathe though her hands lay limp at her sides.

As Atom continues forcing air into her lungs, Scarlet pastes the defibrillator pads to Angel's chest. A thick white wire connects the pads and Scarlet activates them from her tablet then silences the klaxon.

"Orders?" Tong asks. As Rye stares, unable to do more than witness the devastation a six year old explosion did to Angel's body, his brother moves to the drug dispenser.

74

"Nothing," Scarlet murmurs. "She said most of it will make her worse."

"Damn," Rye rakes a hand through his hair then clutches the foot of Angel's bed. He should have left her in Whistler like she wanted. If she doesn't perk up he'll be saying goodbye again anyway.

"Charging," Scarlet calls out. Her tone modulates to overcome any emergency conditions and Tong startles at Rye's side. The small room echoes with only their breathing. "Hands off."

Angel lies still, the center of a heavy pause. Her heart flatlined seconds earlier and Rye turns away, pressing his face into Tong's shoulder. In the corner of his eye, she jerks. A tightening of her shoulders and abdomen, a slight bend of her back lifts her spine from the mattress and her jaw tightens while her cheeks draw back in a pained grin.

Nothing.

"Atom," Scarlet orders. He resumes respirations incase her heart starts to function and manages three before the defibrillator recharges. "Hands off."

Angel jerks again and Scarlet holds a hand out to forbid comment. Apparently she likes what she sees on the display and after an agonizing second, her tablet reads a regular heart rate.

"Atom," she whispers. He starts breathing for Angel again. "I need a couple of warm saline I.V.'s. Heat packs."

"On it," Tong says, moving for the cabinet. He pauses to rest a hand on Scarlet's shoulder. Without meeting his eyes, she puts her own over top and squeezes then their moment passes. Rye removes two I.V. kits from the shelf and takes station by Atom, willing his hands still to start the first line as Tong activates a couple of heat packs and tapes them around the suspended bag. He gets the second ready as Scarlet starts the second line.

"I should have noticed her temp hadn't come up but we were taking it slow and the thermal bag said it was working," Scarlet sighs but Rye waves her off.

"Scarlet," Atom says and pulls the air bag away from Angel. His pressure to keep the seal left a red ring around her mouth and nose and her lips part to allow a soft breath.

"Good," Scarlet doesn't bother pulling the torn open thermal bag around Angel. Instead she gets a plain sheet to cover her. "Couple more of those thermal packs, Tong."

He complies without looking up. Scarlet packs them around Angel. Once satisfied each heat pack functions, she adds a light blanket and several remote temperature sensors to make sure everything under the blanket warms. She pries one of Angel's eyes open and her own eye implant flares up, shining a beam of white light in to trigger dilation.

"Very good," she sighs after testing the other. "She's not leaving my Med Bay, Rye. Not for several days and if you think you're handing her over to Denman you've got another thing coming. We've hid plenty of even worse shit from him over the years."

Rye doesn't answer though he's close to agreeing. Keeping Angel hidden on *Titan* will be the least of his worries. Getting away untracked to take her home will be next to impossible.

"Fill me in on my patient, Rye," Scarlet insists. Tong and Atom make scarce and judging by the thumping in the strategy room next door they've gone for chairs.

"Her charger misfired during a confrontation with a couple of Aphids. When Tong and I got there, her roommate had killed one and the other had the knife on her. I erased half of it, recruited the roommate to Core and brought her here."

"And you didn't think to be cautious? A charger, those old ones in particular, causes a drop in temperature. Seventeen percent of those who've been in cryo lack the ability to efficiently recover body heat."

"I didn't know about that, Scarlet. I swear. You know I wouldn't risk anyone that way or any other."

"Yeah," she sighs as Tong shoves a metal chair behind Rye then moves his next to Atom on the opposite side of the bed.

"I got Navs," Tong takes up his tablet and runs through system checks. Atom stays near Angel's head and works the air bag in his hands though it isn't likely he'll need it again. Rye doesn't sit as Scarlet makes another physical check of Angel, probing under the blanket and rearranging the heat packs.

He remains standing when Scarlet settles in her chair.

"She said it was me, I heard it," Rye says though he isn't sure what he heard. He's certain it can only be him. "It's impossible. I couldn't have, I mean. How can I be?"

"Sit," Scarlet kicks the back of Rye's knee to start his drop and he eases into the chair. "There's a lot you don't know. Until ten minutes ago I didn't know you'd ever been with her and neither did Atom. He knows everything and makes sure I do."

"Yup," Atom mumbles and slides a hand under the blanket to hold one of Angel's. "Medically necessary, Scarlet told me. She has to know."

"You're both nosy bastards."

Angel stirs, turning to her side and triggering another round of fussing from Scarlet. Resting and with some colour to her, she gives no outward sign her heart stopped.

"When someone warms from cryo," Scarlet explains. "They're pumped with a nasty mix of drugs to cleanse their system of everything including their birth control implants. Any remaining storage of hormones is neutralized. Other drugs kick start their body's systems, thyroid, heart, kidneys, reproductive organs. Truth is, she would have ovulated within half an hour. My guess is you had sex shortly before she died."

Rye turns to Scarlet, his only reaction, then looks at Angel.

"If I'm ever going to be fertile," his flat voice echoes off the walls. "It's when I've been called to make my contribution to the genetic bank. Then it's off again."

"This does not leave the room," Scarlet looks around, holding each of their stares in turn until she gets a nod of consent from all three. "Contraception implants in Core females are fool proof and we've discussed the effects of cryo.

"It's true. A third gen male cannot impregnate a civilian female. Too much changed in them. Male contraception is certain in first gens and second gens but only about forty percent effective in third gens. Since Core females won't get pregnant and civilian females can't there's no harm in saying you third gens have nothing to worry about."

"Well, fuck," Rye breathes, surprised to hear no denial or anger in his own voice. Resignation to the facts and a small amount of awe, sure, but everything he feels now trumps anything he's ever feared before. He doesn't have to say it. He was raised to be a soldier like the other third gens sitting around Angel's bed. No parenthood, no family, just plain respectable service. In spite of the things he was made for, the appeal of family is undeniable.

He slumps down in his chair and looks at Angel again. Her eyes have opened and she stares back, heart steady.

"She wasn't even on Genetics radar before," Scarlet admits. "There's a triage order. You don't know about it, not even Denman but as your medic I must adhere to it. I have no choice."

"What do you mean?"

Scarlet remains silent and Rye recognizes the conflict in her.

"We'll be in a lot more trouble than you think if we let her go."

"Tell us everything," Tong whispers. "Not that it will make any difference to me, she's not going to be turned over unless it's what she wants. I'm sure the *analyst*," he nods at Rye, "will need all the details."

Rye can't even manage a comeback.

"In spite of whatever Angel pulled off to make it to our unit, there was no cryo order for her. If treating her meant further harm to a third gen I was to let her suffer, even die. She has second rate implants, her surgeries were probably contracted out. I don't think a Core doctor ever had a hand in her modifications."

"Shit," Rye stands. Angel was expected to make the same sacrifices as him but in the end Core treated her as an expendable body with a gun.

"I broke the rules," Scarlet admits. "I got her ready for cryo and took a lot of shit for it. Those resources should have been saved for a third gen. I should have let her go and was told if I ever wasted resources like that again I'd be busted down to teaching first gen medics how to treat toe fungus.

"I did it again anyway, just now. She has a child and it was the right thing to do.

"When Intelligence took over *Barrington* they backed down on their threats to me. They got a hold of her toys in the electronics lab and suddenly they wanted her more than anything and I received a citation for saving her. You think they wanted her bad then? Consider she's the mother of a very advanced third gen without the assistance of Genetics. This gets out, they'll take her and your son. They'll be split up and you'll never see either of them again."

Rye sinks back into his seat, mind made up.

"A girl," Angel whispers as her lids fall. "Quinn is a girl."

"Leave us," Rye pulls his chair closer to Angel. Scarlet nods and takes a moment to verify her tablet displays everything she needs to know. "Wait."

The three stop at the door.

"I need a Med Bay set up under the aft thrusters. It'll be loud but there's no way *Barrington* will pick up her heat or anything else. We've hid things there before."

"On it," Tong says. Scarlet and Atom nod assent as the three leave, already discussing plans.

When did Rye become such a rule breaker? Every moment up until now was thought out, planned and executed with the most exacting precision. Thoroughness kept him and his full unit of twenty-five alive with the exception of Angel, the last loss to hit his team.

Hiding Angel, arguably a huge asset to Core, would get him kicked from *The Barrington* and reassigned to the most meaningless first gen unit Core could find regardless of how remarkable his child is. He'll make his contribution to Genetics, a given, but the rest of his life will be spent with the knowledge he brought shame on himself.

Angel sighs when he pushes her hair from her cheek.

His punishment if they're caught doesn't change anything.

This little female means more to him than she'll ever mean to Core.

CHAPTER 14

"Where are we going?" Angel jolts from the nightmare of gunpowder and green blood but not the nightmare of Constant. In this one, she one-shots Aphids on her family farm in the Fraser Valley east of Vancouver. By the time the trio of greens is dead, her brother's cries have disappeared with the second trio who took him.

Rye carries her, the thud of his boots marks their swaying steps through an echoing hallway. The past few hours? Days? Nothing but the bliss of warmth and sleep and the steady throb of a rocket going off in her chest from the defibrillator. She takes every conscious breath with silent gratitude and releases it with thanks.

"Alternate Med Bay," Rye says. "And relax. Don't get all worked up again."

"Where?" She can't tell if they are still on *Titan*.

He was there whenever she woke, sometimes holding Scarlet's medical tablet and sometimes his own. When he caught her looking, he stood, pressed his lips to her ear and whispered until she fell asleep. Each time he apologized though he never said for what. She suspected his perceived transgressions were many, some old and some new.

Her left hand rests on Rye's shoulder, extending from the sleeve of her gown and exposing a bandage where her I.V. had been. The patch of tape stands out on her pale skin, otherwise she's bundled so tight in several layers of blankets she couldn't squirm if she tried.

"I have enough on my mind," he grumbles. Stubble tangles in her hair and she shivers with the warmth of his breath on her skin. If she turned her head even a little she might catch his lips with hers. "You're not leaving *Titan*. Scarlet's orders."

"So?"

"I'm not asking for your approval, Angel. It's all been thought out and has the best chance of success."

A second set of boots catches up as Atom skips once to fall in step.

"Hustle," he hisses. "We're almost in sensor range."

"Of what?" Angel demands and makes a disgusted click as Atom messes her hair.

"Breathe deep, coffee girl," Atom whispers. "It's all under control."

Rye turns them sideways and doesn't lose speed as he carries her down a narrow flight of stairs so steep it feels like a ladder.

The room they enter looks more like spare storage and less like a Med Bay. Rye stoops to avoid the low ceiling and puts her down on a mattress that could have been taken from any of the personnel quarters above. *Titan* can support over seventy crew and passengers with individual bunks, many more when they take turns sleeping, though it runs just fine with one person and a tablet.

Scarlet's cool hands check Angel's vitals again.

"Just try and sleep," she urges though it won't be hard. After her big chill, anything warm makes Angel dozy and this room boasts air six degrees warmer than Scarlet's Med Bay.

"Where the hell is Tong?" Rye asks.

"Here," Tong drops to a squat, joining the circle surrounding Angel's bed. Overhead, the drives whine though not so much as she recalls. The ceiling was never this low either. Maybe they got some insulation in.

"Atom?"

"We leave. Make it look like we're home to stay."

"Wait," Angel yawns, twining her fingers with Rye's. He doesn't notice though he squeezes her palm to his. "How long will I fend for myself down here?"

"Not long," Tong says but Rye finishes.

"Denman got our logs more than twenty-four hours ago. I know what he likes and he'll tell us to turn right around and go back to Earth."

"Then what?" Angel asks.

"I want to meet Quinn," he insists. "But not at the expense of exposing her or you. Your transport is on the Moon. We'll get you there. Just tell me where to find you."

"Twenty minutes," Atom looks up from his tablet. "We better get to the command deck for pre-checks and docking."

"Go," Angel sighs and Scarlet dims the lights before disconnecting her tablet from all the sensors still stuck to Angel.

"Anything needs my attention, Atom will get a fake buzz from Rye bitching him for leaving a mess in *Titan's* galley," she explains.

"Nice," Atom mutters.

After docking with *The Barrington*, Rye and his unit wait at the main hatch for final confirmation of a proper seal at both ends of the low-g gangway. They left Angel alone in her compartment more than an hour ago and it could be much longer before they return. Even a quick turn around waits for the dock master to provision rations and water.

The four of them collaborated, falsifying logs and what they claimed to have found on Earth until satisfied it not only looked routine, but irresistible to Denman. Their boss likes keeping the same team in place until a job is done, in fact Rye suspects the older man stays awake at night fantasizing about it.

Nope, this will be easy. Rye will act inconvenienced, admit he really wants to finish the job himself in spite of his men missing out on the last few days of leave on Saturn then stand straighter and promise to tie up all the loose ends on Earth.

As the control panel lights up, signaling a complete seal, Tong palms it open and takes his place beside Rye for the thirty foot walk through the translucent tube. Jupiter glows to their right, dayside lit by the Sun and half concealed by *The Barrington's* bulk. The station houses a dozen expedition class ships like *Titan* and over seven thousand soldiers and civilian support staff.

Three ships currently share this docking hub, *Titan* being the largest, and judging by the crush of anti-grav sleds and uniformed station crew, all just arrived.

"See you at the bar," Atom announces, unscripted but a damned good idea. Not only could they all use a couple of drinks but Rye doesn't have to paste on a fake scowl.

"Don't be in too much of a hurry," he says.

"You kidding?" Atom skids to a stop, nearly knocked flat by Scarlet who follows too close behind.

"No, he isn't," Arthurs, today's dock master, appears from behind as if he stepped off *Titan* with them. He doesn't look up, eyes on his tablet. "Leave your gear. From what I hear you're back out again, departure in sixty minutes."

"So I have time for one drink?" Atom asks, hopeful.

"Not if you're crossing my flight deck," Arthurs warns. The middle aged first gen rules his small domain more firmly than Scarlet's hold on her Med Bay and can issue demerits for simply crossing the hub after drinking.

Atom shrugs his bag from his shoulder, shoving it hard to the deck before picking it up and stalking back onto *Titan*. "No point in even getting off, was there?"

Rye drops his bag to the side so he doesn't have to endure the dock master's anger for blocking access.

"You," Arthurs points toward Rye. "Are late for your meeting with Denman which puts me behind schedule since I can't finish loading *Titan* until I get his final sign off which he won't give until you've had your meeting."

Long sentence, asshole, Rye thinks as he heads for the lift. He doesn't argue with Arthurs about who's to blame for the dock master running late. Whatever Tong and Scarlet will do to fill their small amount of spare time better keep them both out of trouble or their departure will only be delayed further.

Rye crowds into the lift with several maintenance personnel, their bright uniforms denote their tasks aboard. This close to the docking hub, most wear brilliant orange and yellow for visibility. As the door closes, he spots Scarlet returning to *Titan*, leaving Tong clenching his fists and working his jaw. That didn't take long, but at least Angel would have Scarlet nearby.

Six stops, three hallways and another lift later, Rye shoulders to the front and steps out sideways just before the door closes. *Barrington's* command bridge takes up as much space as the entire middle deck of *Titan*. Clusters of gray-clad command crew attend displays and consoles while Jupiter turns lazily overhead. Rye had only been up here a few times before Denman took over the base. Denman once reported to the previous commander but Rye's unit remained at Denman's direct disposal in spite of Denman's promotion. A new sub-commander took over the three other units that had once been Denman's.

That means Rye still comes to his old boss whenever he gets the word.

"Soldier," Denman extends a hand toward his office. Once seated, Rye waits for him to round his desk and get comfortable. *Barrington's* commander stands six-four, a couple of inches shorter than Rye, though he's no less sturdy and broad. Gray hair graces his temples, claiming nearly half his dark hair, and would fill most of his beard if he let it grow.

"How was Earth?" Denman asks then holds up a hand to stop Rye's answer. With his other he pulls two short glasses from his desk and pours an inch of good whiskey in each before standing enough to pass one to Rye. The two raise in toast before taking the drinks down in a single swallow. The booze must be at least eighty proof and for a moment Rye swears the stars shine inside Denman's office and not outside it. Before Rye puts his glass down, Denman fills both and gives a grin Rye wants to knock off his face.

Tong gives the very same look when trying to convince Rye that some demerit worthy prank is in the best interest of their careers and Rye knows Denman is about to put a shine on a turd.

In spite of Denman's waiting question, they knock back their second shot then the bottle goes away.

"About that," Rye shifts in his seat. Damn, the man has a way of making anyone squirm. He looks too normal with his relaxed fingers laced together, whiskey induced smile and smug tilt of his head.

I don't think I'm gonna like this. Rye clears his throat to knock loose the last of the whiskey and squash his misgivings. This isn't Tong and it won't end with Rye bruised, hung over and stuck with some sort of double duty.

They've been working for Denman far too long if the boss can pull Rye's strings as quickly as Tong.

"I read your report," Denman says and waits.

Damn, the old man wants Rye to try and twist his way out of returning to Earth. Well, that he can do.

"I wrapped it up as quick as I could," he sighs to make it look good; part surrender and part standing up for his men. "The rest of my unit is on leave on the casino barge orbiting Saturn and I hoped the four of us could..."

Denman quirks a brow. "Tell me what you know about Toll."

"Sir?" What do the Tollians have to do with going back to Earth?

"Humour me, Rye," Denman produces the bottle and pours but this time he doesn't reach for his glass and neither does Rye. He doesn't drop his gaze as his smile parts ways with his lips. "My second gen memory might have some gaps in it."

"The Tollians were one of the first clusters of colony ships to leave earth," Rye dusts off a rarely used corner of his brain. "Five hundred years ago?"

Denman nods to continue.

"Found a system rich in minerals then seceded from Earth a hundred years later. We were too busy dealing with sabotage shutting down reactors, the absence of fossil fuels and too much pollution for solar panels to work to notice they were gone."

"And that's how things stayed, until recently."

"Sir?"

Denman takes his drink and Rye does the same. Any confidence Rye had in their plan to get Angel home dwindles as Denman relaxes. The old man can only be pleased with himself and it doesn't bode well at all.

"I have less than forty minutes to get prepped for departure," Rye hints then puts his glass down, still full.

"Right," Denman agrees.

"And I realize how important it is to follow up on the leads from Earth."

"It is and you don't have a lot of time before you leave. Your Aphid cargo will have been unloaded and placed in storage. Investigator Sesia from Intelligence will arrive in a few hours to take personal charge of them."

Rye's nuts pinch at the mention of the bitch's name. She personally saw to his questioning when they took over *Barrington* to clean out Angel's lab. The only one who seemed to get along with her was Atom, but then he gets along with everyone.

"We couldn't wait for you to return, Rye," Denman continues. "Once your report was received I dispatched another small unit to act on your information. They should have access to the Whistler residence the greens used in a day."

Rye swallows and stares at his knees. No Earth and Angel could be trapped aboard *Titan* indefinitely. Try explaining frequent visits to *Titan* to Arthurs.

"I have something far more important for you," Denman confides. "Diplomatic parcel. You're going to deliver it to Toll."

"With all due respect, Sir," Rye starts but Denman gets to his feet, signaling their meeting over.

"Listen to me," Denman lowers his voice enough to force Rye's temper down. His fisted hands rest on his desk and Rye stands, feet apart and hands together at ease behind his back. "I appreciate how you feel about finishing things on Earth yourself in spite of the fact you and your three best people got the shit end for shore leave.

"The Aphid situation is worse than you have been made aware. We have manpower, but are dangerously low on some materials essential to our war effort. We can only hope Investigator Sesia can quickly make sense of what those Aphids were doing playing ski tourist. Toll has started to feel the sting of the Aphid presence as well. They've grown peaceful during the past four hundred years. With an inexhaustible supply of mineral wealth they can buy whatever friends they want but now their friends don't feel the currency is worth the risk.

"Now, Toll has Aphids at the airlock.

"You, Tong, Scarlet and Atom will report to Toll. You will be there for the next several months along with a team from Genetics to show them what we can offer in exchange for what we need from their asteroid belt."

Hell, letting Angel down again. This time maybe for good. But if things are as bad as Denman suggests then they have to get to Toll and still find a way to get her to the Moon.

"Sir," Rye pivots on his heel and leaves.

CHAPTER 15

"Eat up," Scarlet orders. "I need you on the command deck."

"Me?" Angel asks. She may be eating a ration pack but it has all four colours on the box and it was all Scarlet could get together on short notice. Real food, Scarlet promised, would come later during evening quarters.

"Uh huh," the redhead answers, not looking up from her task of gathering up bits too small for the naked eye. If Angel didn't know her better, she'd say something troubles Scarlet. "I'm moving you to regular quarters. No permanent damage to your heart and your temperature remains stable without any intervention on my part."

Angel chews the last of some kind of chocolate flavoured veggie dessert bar. It doesn't taste all that bad, certainly better than any of the bachelor fare she cooked for herself back in Whistler. She didn't splurge on dessert there.

Angel raises her chin and hisses as Scarlet deactivates her central line, the med tab still stuck to her neck. The retraction of the metal sensor burns then she hears a small pop as the device detaches from her skin.

"Sec," Scarlet says. "Almost done."

Cool alcohol cleans her skin and a colder burst of silicone spray seals the hole. "The dressing will be gone in a few days."

"Why do you need me on the command deck?"

"I'm keeping the thermal and cardiac monitors on you," Scarlet doesn't answer her question. "That's all the leash you'll have but you know best how to keep warm. You and Rye. I'm still getting used to that one."

"I fell for him, Scarlet," Angel admits. The only thing she dreams about more often than the Aphid nightmares is Rye. Some days the difference between the dream hangover and waking reality doesn't amount to much. "I don't know what he feels now."

"Hands up," Scarlet pulls Angel's disposable gown off and gives Angel her clothes. "I know what that's like, loving one of those boys. Tong and I, we must have fallen in love because we hate each other so much. If anyone found out, one of us would have been shipped out to another unit. Maybe it's for the best though some days I'd give anything to hear him say the words. Just once."

"What happened?" Angel clips her bra behind her back and slides the straps over her shoulders then leans forward to shake, settling the weight of her breasts in the cups.

"He changed," shrug. "After Constant. Shut me out. I guess I changed, too. We all did. Glass, the new Comms Officer, he's okay but after six years he's still the new guy. We stopped thinking of you that way after a couple of weeks. Now it's like you never left.

"Anyway, there's a situation on the command deck I need you to sort out."

"Me?"

"Yeah, one of those Comms Officer things," Scarlet pats Angel's cheek and pulls her to her feet. "See you up there."

The air temperature drops as Angel leaves the space below the thruster bay and makes her way up two flights to the command deck. Crew quarters line the intersecting hallways, each door marked by a number. One door rests half open, Angel's silver suitcase stands at the threshold. Voices echo ahead. Tong and Rye argue and judging by their tone neither one will back down.

"Tell me again?" One of them demands. "I'm not letting you at the controls, deviating our course will get us all in shit."

Angel hurries, unable to figure out the dispute ahead. The voice of reason sounds more like Tong than Rye, the one she'd expect to keep rash decisions at bay. Then the voices stop, replaced with the echo of shuffling boots and grunts of a scuffle. Someone hits the ground hard, another drops and Angel bursts in to find Rye flat on his back under Tong and catching his brother's fist in his own before it connects with his chin. Doesn't look like Tong meant to miss. Rye plants his feet and boosts his hips up, sliding Tong up onto Rye's stomach then with a shove, Rye pushes Tong back as a leg comes up. Rye's boot catches Tong under the chin and he goes over, grazing the back of the command chair on the way down.

They don't fight as they've been trained, more the way brothers learn to wrestle each other when they're small; grappling for who's on top to display dominance and not with any sincere effort to injure.

Tong gets an elbow to the side of Rye's head then he's face down on the deck, pinned beneath his brother.

"Whoa," Angel shouts. "You're acting like a couple of children."

And judging by the sweat on their faces and soaking their gray shirts they have been for a while.

"That's what I told them," Atom chimes in from the command chair, unconcerned with the wrestling match behind him.

Tong continues to struggle but Rye has him pinned.

"You won't get to the controls," Tong gasps.

"Get up, you two," Angel orders then she lies. "Scarlet said I gotta take it easy."

"Doesn't concern you," Rye glares at her. "Go take it easy in the Med Bay."

"Like hell it doesn't. I thought we're going to the Moon but now you're arguing about our course," she takes Rye by

91

the collar and tugs. He doesn't budge so she digs a thumb into a nerve by his neck. A cheap shot, to be sure, but when you're nearly a foot shorter than your opponent you don't worry about honour. She got a broken jaw learning that lesson in basic training. Her weakened hands take longer than she expects to hit the sweet spot considering he's muscled and everything flexes to hold Tong down.

When she hits the nerve, Rye's right side goes numb. He grabs at her hand but it's all the opportunity Tong needs to slide out and scoot away.

"Speak," Angel orders as she lets Rye go. He flexes his hand and shakes his arm to get the feeling back.

"We're going out of system," Tong explains, eyes on Rye.

Rye eyes the control panel.

"Oh?" Angel steps between them and places her hands on their damp chests.

"The boss here wants to disobey Denman's orders and take us on a four day detour to the Moon before we go."

"You can't, Rye," Angel sides with Tong. "You've risked too much for me already."

Rye leans back against the bulkhead, eyes closed.

"Any decision to disobey Denman is up to the four of us," Tong insists.

"So why don't you tell us why we're even considering it?" Rye finishes. "You're keeping Quinn from Core, I get that. We all do. But there's more to it. How far do we need to go?"

Angel takes the seat next to Atom. At least Rye isn't focused on changing course or charging the nav console.

"Private transport?" Angel suggests. "I have enough currency for third class. Drop me off."

"Not an option," Rye growls. "Tell us where you're headed. If you were Intelligence you wouldn't be with Quinn. If we're shielding a criminal I damned well want to know."

Scarlet slips onto the command deck and doesn't spare Rye and Tong a glance. Her smug grin says she's pleased Angel stopped the fight.

"They're," Angel starts. It's time she trusted these four since they can't get into much more trouble than they already are, if they're caught. "For the most part, deserters and Core believes some of them long dead. They find people like me, abandoned to long term cold storage and give us a second chance. I'm still willing to fight even though Core says seventy percent efficiency isn't enough. I still believe in Core and what it stands for. Seventy percent isn't good enough for them but it's good enough for me to keep fighting.

"We trade intel on the Aphids for favours. People look the other way."

"What kind of intel?" Rye asks.

"We heard about the Aphids in cold places on Earth. I volunteered to go to Whistler. When I found them, we leaked it to Core."

"And they sent us," Rye sighs. "You could all be up on charges of treason. Out the nearest airlock."

"Really?" Angel doesn't hide her anger. "An old woman and a four-year-old girl, people with missing arms and legs and worse who were abandoned by Core? I was garbage, Rye. Desperately grateful for getting frozen and even more so for my second chance but still Core garbage.

"Just drop me off when it won't get you in more trouble."

Angel turns her back, the burning in her cheeks could warm the whole room and her arms knot to keep from lashing out. Then she uses her sleeve to wipe spittle from her chin, wishing it was venom and she got it on his skin. When she tucks her head under Scarlet's chin, the medic wraps an arm around her shoulders.

"No," Rye whispers. "I'm not handing you over to pirates and smugglers."

"Then what?" she demands. "I will not let you take me to the Moon."

"Thank you," Tong breathes.

"Where are we going?" Heavy defeat sinks into her muscles. A few weeks from going home has turned into an intolerable, indefinite wait.

"We've been assigned as demo models for the Tollians," Rye explains with distaste. "Seems they want to contribute to the war effort."

"Toll?" Angel thinks. She remembers the general location of the system and tugs at Scarlet's shirt.

"What are you thinking, Angel?" Scarlet gets a second arm around Angel as if sensing her excitement.

"Can you bring up a star map? I have an idea."

The room goes dim then the three dimensional map appears around them in soft blues and golds.

"We're here," Atom says. "And Toll is here."

A green line traces a graceful, curved path through the clusters and nebulae between them and their destination. Angel touches a point near their route while remaining near Scarlet.

"Here," she points to home, the system where Quinn and her new family support themselves off the land.

"Helm-Dent?" Atom asks. "Nothing there."

"Can you divert enough to get me there?"

"Angel," Rye brings up the system on his tablet. "The system gets surveyed every six months for Aphid activity. There's no human activity either."

"I know," she says. "We watch the drones circle. Sit out at night under the stars. The fourth planet has no natural satellites so it's a big deal. Unless they knew what to look for, they'd never find us. Even then…"

She trails off before she says too much. Not only are they well hidden, they have a very discreet escape plan. Atom moves from the command chair to make room for Rye.

"I think there's a lot more to your friends than you let on," Rye muses. "But then if they're former Core officers then I guess they know how to avoid attention.

"Atom, can you get enough out of the engines to give us seventy-two hours? I figure that much time to get to Helm-Dent, take Angel to the surface and get back on track?"

"You'll need more than that," Atom's eyes lose focus then he blinks, returning his gaze to the star map. "It will take time to decelerate from jump and change direction if you want a minimum disruption to our course."

"So?" Rye cuts him off.

"It'll be done."

Angel turns to Scarlet for a final hug and to hide her relieved tears. The worst of the burn in her eyes fades as she rushes from the room and down the corridor. Just before the turn to her quarters, a big gray shadow slides in place before her. Rye waits but Angel doesn't look up.

"You're going the wrong way."

CHAPTER 16

"What do you want?" Angel's soft voice leaks out from behind her hands. With her sleeves drawn over her palms, she wipes her eyes and sniffles.

How can she be so upset by the prospect of going home? Rye wonders. It doesn't make sense she'd be unhappy about it. Wouldn't her way have taken longer? Her small transport parked on the Moon might take weeks to get to Helm-Dent. Could she be upset about the damned ship?

"Privacy," Rye measures each syllable to ensure he sounds confident, calm and most of all, kind. "I think you could use it."

"That's where I was headed."

"Nope, other way."

She looks up, revealing red eyes, and doesn't seem to like what she sees in his. How the hell can she see so far inside him with just a look? Rye feels like a kid again, busted for one thing or another, and facing his surrogate mother. No matter how hard he and Tong tried to get away with things she always knew. Sometimes he counted on it. Rye forces his jaw loose before he can break a tooth.

Angel steps sideways. There's plenty of room to go around and though Rye doesn't move, she thinks twice about slipping past.

"My quarters," he says, voice softer than her sniffles. "My ship, my risk, my orders. Move."

She never would have tried defiance with him six years ago but today she does. Just before he has to repeat himself, she turns around and stomps off in the other direction. With her arms crossed tight, the middle of her oversized hooded sweat shirt pulls in close, revealing her small waist and exaggerating the curve of her hips.

He didn't have her ass in mind when he went after her but every step she takes and every sway of her hips does its damnedest to make him forget what really bothers him. It took a while to figure it out and now he's likely to forget before he can make his point.

She stops, a foot and a half from his door and forces him to lean into her to palm the lock. A bright flash of white light reads the creases on his hand and the door slides into a wall pocket. Rye follows her in and she stops to look around. It isn't the first time they've been alone here, in his quarters, but they aren't here for intimacy today.

"Sit," Rye puts a hand on her shoulder and presses her toward his bunk. She shrugs him off, instead choosing the chair next to his desk. "Your choice."

After pulling off the shoulder holster securing his double-edged eight inch blade to a spot nestled in the centre of his back, he tosses it on his bed. Rye unsnaps the buckles holding his hand guns to his thighs, then the belt. Those weapons join the knife.

Angel keeps her eyes on the floor, hands pressed together between her knees.

"I don't think you understand me," Rye opens the buttons on his shirt. In the field, he puts up with the stick of sweat between his clothes and his skin but aboard *Titan* where he can change, he'd rather not. "I want to make sure you do. This isn't what it started out as a few days ago."

The shirt lands on the floor and Rye starts the steam in his cleanser, letting it warm as he kicks off his boots.

"You mean when you arrested me?" Angel demands. She swings the chair around and yelps when her knee makes abrupt contact with the desk leg.

"And why did you kiss me in the stairs?" She asks and he hides a smile. If she's angry then she won't hold anything back. He tosses his pants aside and steps in the shower and she raises her voice so it reaches into the small cubicle. "Was it the mood? Taking my charger and the dead Aphids on the floor? And I'm not single anymore? What the hell does that mean?"

After a pause she continues. "I knew it, thought you'd soften me up for questioning."

"I'm going to let that go, Angel," Rye steps out and she turns away.

"What do you think I am?" He rubs a thin towel over his short hair before wrapping it around his hips. "More machine than you? I'd say we're about equal in that department. Do you think because I grew up with surrogate parents I don't know what a family is?"

Angel raises her eyes and her brows knit though in anger or confusion, Rye can't tell. He doesn't want to sound like he's telling her off but in this case there is no avoiding it.

"Do you think Quinn wouldn't be safer on Earth with your family than on a colony in the middle of nowhere?"

"Quinn is my only living family," Angel flushes with the admission.

Okay, so much for getting her to Earth. At least keeping in touch with her there would be a whole lot easier than having to sneak off to Helm-Dent.

"My parents," Rye starts as he pulls out a clean uniform. "And I do call them parents, are bio-engineers. Textiles, materials. Half the things Core soldiers wear were developed by my mother's family. They couldn't have children of their own and wanted to do more for the war effort than hunker down in the lab so they applied to be surrogates and moved to Vix Three to wait for me and Tong. We were only a few hours old when we went home with them.

"My father worked in the labs on Vix Two, shuttling home every few days for a few days off with us. My mother taught and lectured online as Tong and I permitted.

"I know what it's like, Angel, to see how much joy we brought them. To feel loved. Just because that life was never in the cards for me doesn't mean I don't know it."

When Rye looks up, his desk chair stands empty. Angel no longer sits. Instead she steps closer, mouth open and intent on his story. Without interrupting, she takes a seat on the other end of his bed.

"I know what you fear for Quinn, to have her taken by strangers," he continues. "When we were fifteen Tong and I were supposed to leave for basic. Two days before, he dared me to jump out a third floor window. I landed safely but he broke his leg in three places and was still in medical.

"I left, alone. Said goodbye to Tong but he was out of it and didn't notice. My mother cried and my father tried not to. I was a foot taller than both of them and for a moment, as I held them, I used everything they taught me to give them comfort. To tell them how much I loved them. It was important to show I'd learned as much from them as I had from all my Core teachers.

"Then I boarded the transport, went to the quarters I was supposed to share with Tong and fell apart. I know exactly what happens inside when someone says goodbye to everything they know. And to do it alone."

"Rye," Angel takes his hand. "I..."

"We go back to Vix every couple of years. We're big brothers to a second gen female they named Amber, gives them as much trouble as Tong and I put together. She's twelve now, gonna be a Comms Officer like you.

"I just wanted you to know I have a damned good idea about family."

She keeps quiet while Rye dresses and replaces his weapons, then he crouches before her, balancing on the balls of his feet. When she reaches for him, his right hand tremors. Just a small amount, only the tips of the outer fingers, but he feels looseness in all the joints right up to his shoulder. The muscles tingle and though he doesn't yet experience any loss of coordination, those symptoms will steal the use of his hands in a few hours.

Rye doesn't want anyone to see him like this.

"I slept a couple of days ago," he says, in denial of his exhaustion.

"A couple of stressful days ago," Angel adds and folds his hand in hers. With her smaller, warm fingers, she starts with the muscles in his palm. Rye rocks forward onto his knees, his whole body relaxing at her touch. She never touched him like this before Constant, when they'd been lovers. This touch wakens more than the lust that mercilessly filled their brief hours alone together. She doesn't hurry or tease. Only her fingers move. "Not battle stress, I know you're on top of that. Regular stress."

By the time she reaches the tips of his fingers, the shudder in his muscles subsides.

"That won't hold it off for long," Angel tilts her head, smiling with only one corner of her mouth. "I'm an expert on the shakes."

"Just don't think because of this," Rye touches the Core crest on his pocket to move her attention away from his embarrassing weakness. "I don't understand anything else. If I screw up, it's because I'm learning how to do it myself."

Angel nods and releases his hand but Rye slips his hands around her butt and pulls her closer.

"Tong is my only living relative, like Quinn is yours," he stares into her eyes, not letting go. Thank you doesn't convey Rye's gratitude for her part in keeping Tong alive. "I cannot imagine not having him."

"I know," she says, then her lips part and her tongue peeks at him from the corner of her mouth. "Going up the stairs and facing two pissed off Aphids? I didn't see him hurt until I took them out. I mean, Holy shit, I thought. I'm doing my job and took out two.

"Then I saw him and the blood and I didn't think about anything but stopping it. Me? Fighting like a second gen grunt? It meant nothing when one of my friends was a couple of minutes from bleeding out."

"I know, Angel," Rye softens his tone, awed to see her warm and alive again as he as in so many other moments during the past few days. "And I kissed you because I needed to know you're real."

"And am I?"

Rye seals his mouth around hers and finds lips as warm as her hands.

"Mm, and you taste like my new favourite flavour."

Angel giggles, triggering another round of shaking in his arm. He ignores it, instead he decides he'll never eat one of those damned dessert bars again without thinking of Angel.

"Oh," she slides her hand up his arm and rotates it, palm up, before working the nerve in his elbow. His hand steadies again and he cups her cheek as she massages around the joint, teasing the nerve just enough to calm the spasms.

The new steadiness allows Rye to put a hand on her hip, just below the hem of her sweatshirt and seek warmth inside.

Titan shudders, shifting his balance sideways and by the time he compensates, he drifts. Angel tilts with him. She doesn't have a choice as Rye circles her with his arms to keep her steady until he knows what happened to his ship.

"What the hell?" Rye growls and kicks off toward his tablet. The device floats toward the cleansing unit, bounces off the closed translucent door and tumbles toward the head. As he tries to grab it, his hand shakes worse than before. Angel takes his arm and works his shoulder.

"Atom?" Rye thumbs the tablet with his left.

"Sorry, boss," the display shows part of the engine room and the top of Atom's shiny boot as the view moves up his shin. "Figure if we shut off the artificial grav and life support to all decks but the main I can get you sixteen hours in orbit around Helm-Dent without arriving on Toll suspiciously short of fuel. That accounts for solar recharge while in orbit. Good sun there. We're sealing off the other decks as soon as Tong brings up sufficient rations for the trip."

"Could have warned me," Rye says.

"Whatever. Oh, and Scarlet says Angel's heart rate suddenly jumped eighteen percent and her temp is climbing and if you know where she is get her to the command deck."

"Hi, Atom," Angel laughs.

"Oh, sorry," Atom chokes out then the comm feed goes dead.

"You need sleep, Rye," Angel's voice invites no discussion. Rye gives orders the same way and ten minutes ago he wouldn't have taken it from anyone but now, from her, he listens. "I'll go give Tong a hand and run interference between him and Scarlet for a couple of hours. I think Atom has his hands full."

"My ship, Angel," Rye scowls as he palms the door open for her. Then he kicks to his bunk and pulls out the low-g straps so he doesn't float away while he sleeps. "My rules, my orders. I'm getting some rack and you're going to help Tong."

"Got it, boss."

CHAPTER 17

"You're wearing that?"

Angel looks Rye over, alarmed by nearly seven feet of full battle gear. In addition to his medium gray uniform, or more on top of it, Rye's boots, thigh plates, body armour, bracers and gloves cover everything but his head. The health status lights centered on his chest glow green, shielded behind special lenses so they are invisible except up close and in front. In one hand he carries his arc-rifle, in addition to two projectile weapons strapped to his thighs. The other holds his full-face combat helmet. His body armour doesn't reflect light, instead, it draws in enough to darken half the landing bay.

"My daughter is down there," Rye explains and lifts his arm, pointing his heavy helmet at the CN2. "I'm not going to be ambushed and unable to protect her."

Angel purses her lips, unsure what to say. The residents of her small colony on Helm-Dent live peacefully, unbothered for five decades. If anyone were to cause them trouble, it would be Core. In any case, the sight of Rye dressed to kill will scare the colonists more than anything else.

It's also the first time Rye uses the word daughter to describe his relationship with Quinn.

Angel unzips her warm jacket and pulls the sides open to show she isn't carrying any weapons. Scarlet stole her charger out of lockup and secreted it in her suitcase. "My daughter is there too and well protected by what's already on the planet."

Rye drops the helmet to his side. The plasteel face plate smacks against his thigh.

"What are you saying, Angel?"

"The last time some of them down there saw Core combat gear, they died," she explains. "I promise, not even Atom will be able to track us once we're within five hundred klicks of the village."

"Watch me," Atom says from where he floats between Scarlet and Tong, though he says it more in defence of his abilities than in acceptance of a challenge.

Angel secures her suitcase in the back of the CN2 and hooks her toes under the floor rungs so she doesn't shoot herself into the gray plate metal ceiling as she closes the rear storage cover. The floor rungs and rows of similar handles came out of all surfaces nine days ago when Atom shut down the gravity.

"I'll wait," she hints. "But the clock is ticking."

"For fuck sakes," Rye kicks off for the stairs.

"I tried to tell him to dress appropriately," Tong says once Rye is out of earshot. "We all did. He's a little loose around the edges right now."

"No kidding," Scarlet agrees.

Not only did Atom have to shut down five decks on *Titan*, he left them confined to the bridge and one small anteroom where he installed a couple of zero-g sleeping bags on the walls. Scarlet and Tong's tension subsided to a slow simmer before it disappeared nearly completely.

For now.

Rye would have put them in the brig if their issues interfered with running *Titan*. Life support or no.

The close quarters also meant Angel hasn't had a private moment with Rye. No time to explore their new lives, maybe together and maybe not, or find out if Rye can even make his way back to Helm-Dent.

When Rye floats back in, he's dropped the armour but kept some of his weapons. Instead of the gray Core uniform shirt, he changed into a white, long sleeved dress shirt. It looks like silk, a little puffy around the wrists, but the weave didn't come from an expensive Earth based factory. The fire resistant fabric also gives radiation protection and prevents penetration from all but the most direct knife attacks. Over top, he wears a hip length leather vest.

Much better. Angel can't help but let her gaze linger. She's never seen much of any of them in civilian clothes and on Rye, they look good. Angel wears the same thick sweats she wore when they left Whistler.

"Thank you," Angel waves good-bye to the others as she moves to the pilot door, beating Rye there by seconds. "You don't know the route."

"You'll tell me."

"Nope," Angel gets in and waits.

"Damn it," Rye mutters but he concedes without argument. Taking the controls herself will prevent negotiation over every non-standard maneuver. She pre-arranged her re-entry path so everyone would know it's her. Even in her own transport, it would verify her identity which is much more important in the CN2, a vehicle the people below won't expect and will stink of Core.

"Angel?"

Allowing her to sit in *his* command seat verges on dumb. Angel's flight certification expired half a decade ago and now her descent to the small planet borders on reckless. She doesn't answer and Rye's hands turn to fists beneath his thighs.

"Angel? Watch your approach."

She doesn't bring the CN2's nose down. Rather, she brings it up even further and adjusts the yaw another six degrees, turning his side window toward their descent path. Not that he can see it with their nose so high. Red flame, charged pink by the polarized windows, licks another inch up the glass.

Hers remains somewhat clear of fire.

"You don't understand," she gets an excited knee bouncing on the floor. Could be a trick of the light but the pink flames nibble higher with each nervous jump of her leg. "I haven't seen Quinn in almost ten weeks. We never spent a night apart before I left and they don't expect me for another month."

"Straighten our course."

"Uh uh, can't."

"I'll do it for you if you've forgotten how," he grinds out from behind his clenched teeth. Such a plan involves tying her down in the back so she can't endanger him further. The angry red in her cheeks would be priceless. And irresistible.

Angel rolls her eyes and turns toward Rye, taking her attention off the controls as the bouncing ceases. An uneasy vibration caused by their asymmetrical descent takes its place accented by the rattle of her suitcase against the inside of the small cargo compartment in the rear. The high-pitched wump, wump, wump goes unnoticed by his so-called pilot.

"This is the pre-arranged attitude for re-entry so they know it's me and isn't outside of operating spec for this old bus."

At least her answer is reasonable.

"So we get shot down if you get it wrong?"

"No," she mutters as she turns back to the controls. Blonde waves fall forward, hiding her face, and light up in the glow of re-entry.

"They won't open their protective shield?"

"Rye," she laughs, shaking more golden-soft hair free. "They don't have one. Think about it. A Core runabout dropping into orbit from a ship capable of carrying a small invasion force is going to scare the bits out of them. I hope by maintaining my pre-arranged entry they'll know it's me and won't freak out."

The ache in his fingers from forcing them straight rewards him for at least unknotting his hands. Besides, getting the circulation back is a good thing.

"So they're watching us?"

"Undoubtedly."

Twenty seconds later all forward windows show nothing but flames. Maybe this orientation met spec fifty years earlier when the CN2 rolled out of assembly but now it's been roughed up and put together so many times anything could happen.

Rye forces a deep breath. The CN2 has been recertified enough it's twice the ship it was when it was new but he doesn't feel any better.

"What are you afraid of, Rye?"

"Pardon?"

"You. Afraid," she shrugs as she begins to correct their orientation. "My flying or meeting Quinn?"

"Neither," he tries to sound calm but his own ears pick up the tight answer. "I just don't like letting anyone else at the controls when my life is in the runabout."

"She's just a four-year-old," Angel says. Her voice takes on the tone his surrogate mother used when either Rye's patience or his temper needed a bit of soothing. "Remember what you and Tong were like as kids?"

Rye snorts, quite certain he and his twin were nothing like a four-year-old girl raised on a farm by civilians.

When he looks at her next, her hands cradle the yoke between her knees as she switches to manual flight. Several minutes pass as they fly north, a thousand meters high between blue skies and bluer seas. The display before his navigator's chair shows them cross the equator.

"Halloween was my favourite when I was growing up. I didn't think I'd make it back for this one," Angel says. Her smile comes through in her light tone and the way she drags out her words. "Did you have Halloween?"

"Sure," he remembers something about it from Civilian Studies, more appropriately titled Blending In. He'd taken courses on blending in on all Core allied planets.

"Grandma would spend weeks with me on my costume," Angel says. "Then everyone would get up early to make sure our chores were done. We'd go into the city and knock on a few doors before going to a dress-up party."

Sounds a lot like what he learned in the ten minutes they spent on the subject when he was eleven. Civilian Studies was more a lesson on how frivolous civilians were than anything else. A Core soldier needed no more than for their basic needs to be met and often got by with a lot less. Luxury and vanity were things civilians did best.

"What did you do?"

"Tong and I," Rye laughs. The pair had decided to scare some younger third gens, nothing to do with Halloween but it meets the criteria of dressing up and going out so he shares the story. "He got hold of some green paste from somewhere and we stripped down to our shorts and covered every inch of us in it then left our quarters and went looking for a pair of smart asses a couple of years younger."

"Uh huh," Angel says. She doesn't sound as entertained as he feels but her question brought the memory back and he'll have to remind Tong of the story.

"We got down a couple of flights of stairs and into the hall to their quarters and I'm getting itchy but I don't want to say anything. Tong scratches at his thigh and I'll be damned if I'm going to admit the itch is turning into a burn before he does.

"The last turn in the corridor, just a couple of doors away, Tong gets on this really good Aphid walk. You know, not bending at the knees properly because they got those fucked up hips. I figure I better get my Aphid walk on too because he *can't* be better than me at anything.

"I say 'teeth' because I realize we forgot something to make our teeth look sharp. He wanted to file them and almost talked me into it before we ran out of time and had to get going.

"He says this weird ticking thing that doesn't sound like Aphid at all and I hear this yelp. He turns around and I realize it's me. I don't know what the green shit was he swiped for our skin but at that moment it started to burn through the backs of our knees and under our arms.

"I don't know which one of us was screaming louder when we got home," Rye laughs and turns to Angel expecting she'll be as amused as he is.

"It, um," she frowns at the console. "Sounds awful."

"It was great," Rye snorts. How can she not understand how hard they laughed about it after their burns healed. "We —"

"Hey, Rye?" Atom barks from the console. His choppy voice breaks up, misses syllables and competes with a high pitched whine of background noise. "All okay? You disappeared from my display."

"Good here," Rye says and eyes the nav display to see most of their location and heading information has reverted to random clusters of lit and unlit characters. When he reaches for the controls, the display shuts off.

"I prefer you keep an eye on our route so you can find us again," Angel says as she banks starboard, leaning in to a steep roll. The CN2 comes about but not back the way they came. Instead, Angel settles into a deep recess in the broken, scrub covered ground. In places, short bushy trees gather otherwise nothing higher than his elbows marks the surface.

"You don't trust me enough to tell me why my ship is malfunctioning?" Rye asks.

"Truth is, I'm not sure why."

Rye believes her. She sounds as baffled by the flickering display as he is.

"Atom?" Angel calls. "Rye will be back on time."

Whatever messed with navigation also turned Atom's reply to static.

"Hm," she says as she descends to within four meters of a wide river. Seconds later, the flowing water drops away beneath them and Angel chases a rainbow in the mist before bringing them about to face the massive falls.

"Oh no way," Rye growls and grabs for the dash. His only thought to prevent himself from slamming into the front window as they enter the waterfall. For a moment, the crush of water on the roof rattles everything inside the CN2 then they break through into a roomy stone chamber. Daylight filtered by cascading water fades behind them and Angel slows to hover.

"Letting my eyes adjust," Angel explains.

"Can I take it from here?" Rye offers. He ignores the light blind input to his natural eye. The implant doesn't need time to adjust and shows him a narrow tunnel leading off over a quiet, underground creek.

"Yeah," Angel sounds relieved. "I didn't realize how rusty my flying is. Watch out for tight quarters ahead. I had no trouble in my own runabout but it's a single seater and a lot smaller than the CN2. Follow the passage about seven hundred meters. It opens to a larger cave where we can land. We go on foot from there."

"Got it."

Rye reaches over to the main controls and switches piloting to his copilot seat. Even with his enhanced vision and the CN2's array of sensors, the tunnel challenges his piloting. Part way through, they stop to check their harnesses so he can turn the CN2 on its side to pass safely through a narrow twenty meter section. The last half of the trip takes them up more than forward until they must be nearly level with the river they passed over above.

Angel points toward the broadening of the tunnel and light ahead. Before they make their final turn into the larger cave, Rye can see the chamber isn't empty. A single human waits at the far side near a narrow set of stone stairs leading to a door sized opening in the rock.

"Giselle," Angel says. "She's been on Helm-Dent since the colony was founded."

Giselle looks to be in her mid to late seventies and wears the matching neutral tone slacks and short-sleeved cotton shirt Rye associates more with a lab coat than spelunking. She pushes back her long white hair then clutches her hands in obvious excitement when the CN2 enters the chamber.

CHAPTER 18

Giselle remains at the stairs as Rye brings the CN2 down to rest on the broken rock floor.

"Rye? You can have Quinn without me but not me without Quinn," Angel turns and waits for his hands to stop moving. "Do you understand?"

All the way through their descent she considered how to tell him and couldn't decide on the exact words until he took control of the CN2 and she didn't have to concentrate on keeping them from hitting the cave wall. Maybe she shouldn't have said anything, at least not right now.

"I get that."

Damn, what is he thinking? If only she had more than a few seconds to set the ground rules. She can't get her hopes up. She can only protect Quinn and if that means she can't have Rye then so be it.

"I'm sorry, Rye. I didn't mean for it to sound like that. I don't know what will happen between us. I just want you to know her."

Rye's lips tighten then he tilts his head toward her and squeezes her hand before turning to the CN2's console.

"We don't need to wait for the hull to cool," Rye keeps his attention on the lights and continuous scroll of updates and alerts. "Looks like the waterfall took care of the re-entry heat for us."

"Okay," Angel doesn't wait any longer to climb out of the CN2 and rush to Giselle. Although the hull isn't hot, it's still warm enough to feel through her clothes.

Finally, home.

Giselle's sun-aged skin and startling green eyes were the first things Angel saw when she shook off the haze of cryo. Angel's stiff fingers relaxed in Giselle's smooth, warm hands and the old woman's hair surrounded a crop of proud wrinkles. Angel studied her for a long time before she tried to speak; long enough to know there wasn't a single strand of blonde, brown or black left on Giselle's head.

"It's been so long," Giselle steps into Angel's arms. "I couldn't let myself hope until I was sure it was you descending from the orbiting ship."

"I felt the same way," Angel hugs Giselle even tighter.

Behind them, the CN2's passenger door servos whine until the hinges lock fully extended. Until the CN2 cools completely, the servos ensure no damage to the vehicle or its passengers.

"Ah," Giselle fists the back of Angel's sweatshirt and turns her toward Rye. "You told me how much Quinn looks like him but until I saw it with my own eyes I didn't understand what you meant."

Rye scowls, even more than he had in the CN2, and Giselle's throaty laugh echoes among them in the cave. He moves to the rear hatch and pulls out Angel's silver suitcase then slings his own bag over his shoulder.

"Yes, that's the look I saw just an hour ago when she negotiated an acceptable outfit."

"Well," Angel agrees. "If you doubled her height, dressed her like a man and cut off most of her hair then I suppose you're right."

"Not the hair," Giselle argues and pulls her own thigh length silver and white over her shoulder. "Introduce me, Angela."

Angel doesn't bother to correct Giselle, the only person to use her given name since Acquisitions first took her in to Core. She tried. It didn't help.

"Rye," Giselle says. She doesn't wait for the introduction she just demanded and it doesn't surprise Angel. "My name is Giselle Keller."

"Giselle," Rye nods and accepts her hand. He doesn't seem troubled when Giselle looks him over, eyes hesitating on his weapons.

"Are you with us long?"

"No, I can't stay past midday tomorrow," his voice lowers in deference to her commanding posture and tone. Then he takes Angel's elbow in hand while Giselle motions them towards the stairs.

"We must hurry then," Giselle says. "Quinn will be back shortly. She's berry picking with Max and we gather for dinner within the hour."

Angel stumbles on the top step in surprise. Before she can ask what on earth got Max on his feet, Rye voices his own concern with Giselle's remark.

"Wait, you let Quinn leave your compound with an unknown expedition class starship in orbit?"

Angel decides there is plenty of time to find out about Max and how they not only got him off his ass but berry picking as well. Better for Rye to understand how well hidden they are before he becomes any more alarmed. His grip on Angel's elbow tightens and not just from catching her stumble.

"Did you honestly believe this planet was occupied when you settled into orbit and found nothing on your sensors?" Giselle steps ahead into the tunnel to lead the way single file. Rye takes up the rear, moving his hand to keep his fingertips on Angel's other elbow.

"Honestly? No."

"But you came anyway, right? Even though all your Core resources saw nothing?"

Nobody speaks again for several seconds. Rye made Giselle's point for her.

Phosphorescent stones mixed in the pea gravel at their feet provide enough light for safe passage.

"Nearly two decades ago, more than a thousand first and second gen soldiers set up three camps only ten kilometers from here. They spent the next month playing wargames both on the surface and in the air. Other than keeping the outdoor lights off at night, we did nothing special to stay hidden.

"I assure you, Rye, we are invisible. If they detect our life signs at all we look identical to the seven and a half million medium sized herbivores occupying this part of the continent. We live below ground and release any excess heat generated by our activities into the river just below the falls."

They step from the tunnel into a sunken street. Dwellings and all facilities exist in hollows cut from the meters-deep stone towering above. Overhanging tree branches, vines and low, broad, short-leafed shrubs allow plenty of light while camouflaging the narrow streets below.

Low voices echo through the rock faces and ahead, in the main courtyard, two middle-aged women rest in a patch of late day sun. One sits on a low rock, knitting needle in one hand. Her other, and artificial hand, currently sports the second needle. The other woman, in a nearby hover chair, tucks the end of a half completed knit afghan around her legs. One ends just above the knee the other ends just below. She leans forward, nearly tangling her fingers in the other's work as she points.

Both look up and lean closer together as their eyes settle on Rye.

"Look who's here," Giselle calls.

They pause their work to wave, knocking a large ball of deep red yarn into the short yellowed grass.

"Come," Giselle offers and leads Angel and Rye through the courtyard. Again, the women look Rye over, this time with less worry.

"Neither speaks," Angel explains once far enough away she won't be heard. "Dara, in the hover chair, can't and Carrie won't. Giselle couldn't restore Dara's balance enough to be safe on prosthetics. Most of what we wear to keep warm was made by their hands. Wait."

Giselle nods in understanding as Angel disappears up a trail. Rock walls still flank her and she stops at the entrance to a large garden where she kneels on a smooth stone. She whispers a near silent greeting to the dozens of markers clustered around the space. At the sound of footsteps, she speaks to Rye.

"Sixteen graves for our founders," Angel says. Rye's fingers brush the side of her neck. "Giselle's parents and the others. The rest are people like me who lived out peaceful lives here. Only one suicide, the year after I woke. Giselle does her best to screen us, to make sure her gift is something we want but..."

Rye says nothing and when she turns, he's already gone.

"Denn," Giselle says when Rye returns to her side. "He and Angel both moved to their own homes at the same time, well enough to meet most of their own needs. She found him the next day, went with Quinn to help him come to breakfast.

"He hung himself the night before. They were good friends and took a lot of support from each other."

Giselle sighs and leans against the stone wall.

"Truth is, it was Angel we worried about. If she didn't have Quinn she never would have been left alone. She got up for Quinn, walked for Quinn, learned to love living again for your daughter. She has other ghosts in her past I'm certain but nothing she's spoken of, at least not to me. Something drove her to go to Whistler."

She looks up at Rye but he shrugs, unable to give any answer to her unspoken question.

116

"I only knew her six months before she died," Rye offers. "If you're from Core then you know it never could have been serious."

"That's a pile of shit, soldier," Giselle says and rests a hand on his elbow. "Things can be far more serious than you admit."

Angel's smile returns as she makes her way down the trail.

More serious doesn't even begin to describe how Rye has changed in the past two weeks. What began as a minor complication, turning Angel in, escalated into conspiring to conceal her from Denman and from Core. Adding to that, as each minute passes without seeing Quinn, Rye's mood takes another leap past serious.

Angel takes a deep breath. Her lashes still clump with drying tears. Rye refuses jealousy, deciding to loath himself for it later. She mourns a friend, nothing more.

"Better?" Rye tilts her chin higher, aware of Giselle's scrutiny. Late afternoon sun catches the gold in her hair; the same warm silvery-yellow as the fat clumps of grain waving over the stone ledge above.

The colony differs from any other place he's been with Angel. Compassion lingers in the air here. Peace. He last felt it in the apartment he called home with his surrogate parents. They never told him to leave Core outside but he and Tong did it anyway.

"Max," a child's voice shouts, still out of sight up the trail. "If you don't move it I'll tell Opal I picked all those flowers for her."

"C'mon, Quinn," the man replies, almost whining but Rye can hear his amusement. "Please don't."

"Dear Lord, Giselle," Angel asks. "How did you get Max walking?"

"I'm not so sure, Angela," Giselle's eyes widen with wonder as she tries to explain. "It all seemed to happen at once. When you left, Quinn started spending time with Opal in the infirmary and forced Max to help. She started bringing in the baby faux-mink she found and made Opal help feed the little thing. Then she started forgetting the bottle or demanding another blanket and before I knew it Max was on his feet running errands.

"I suspect there has been a lot more four-year-old blackmail like you just heard than I've caught wind of but it does the trick. Even Opal will get out of bed to help and now I think Quinn loses that damned faux-mink on purpose just to get Opal and Max looking."

"I missed so much," Angel sighs.

"I've done all I can for Opal," Giselle lowers her voice further. "The jaw and inner ear will be expensive but if she can speak and eat…"

"I have about thirteen and a half thousand credits, I didn't have to pay the smuggler or fuel but the transport's stuck back on Earth's Moon."

"I'll worry about your transport," Rye's voice fades as Max approaches and a head full of long, dark curls appears beside him. Rye doesn't pay any mind to the mistrust on the other man's face. Then Max's jaw drops and his head snaps back and forth from Rye to Quinn.

"Holy shit," Max breathes, eliciting another round of reprimands from Quinn before she lets him get a word in. "Your mom is home."

Rye rocks, clinging to Angel and Giselle as his daughter skids to a stop halfway from Max. Quinn stands nearly half his height, as Angel said. Even her thick dark ponytail doesn't hold her waves and curls against her scalp. She wears a simple blue dress, barely long enough to cover her ankles. The dirty hem isn't worn in fact the mud along its edge appears fresh.

One fist holds the skirt up high enough to reveal a too-big pair of black boots while her other carries an old small pail.

"Giselle," Quinn calls, shaking the pail. "Sie sagte meine Mutter nicht zu Hause ist heute gekommen."

"Wirst du sie zu begrüßen," Giselle replies. "Oder wirst du dort stehen Gießen unser Frühstück auf der Straße?"

"What are they saying?" Rye whispers.

"Quinn learned German from Giselle," Angel and Giselle exchange a glance. "Quinn thinks it's their secret language. Best to not bring it up."

"Quinn didn't expect her today," Giselle says.

"And Giselle said to stop dumping out the berries," Angel finishes.

Perhaps this is what Angel meant when she said Quinn is more advanced than a third gen. She sounds just as fluent as Giselle, whose English still hints at her German background.

"Come here," Angel takes a couple of steps forward as Quinn sets off running again. She almost doesn't get to her knees in time for Quinn to wrap her arms around her neck, swinging the berry bucket around without spilling a single thumbnail sized pink fruit.

"Mama," Quinn giggles as Angel gets a finger in the child's ribs. Then she pushes Angel away and looks at her, eyebrows pressed together in a look Rye's seen all to often on himself and Tong. "Are you hurt?"

"No, baby. See?" Angel tips her head from side to side. "I spent more time in zero-g than Giselle would like but she'll make sure I'm fine, okay?"

"Okay," Quinn lets out a shaky sigh and falls back into Angel's arms. Only then does she look at Rye, eyes popping wide as they go up, up, up. "You promised, Mama. You promised my father would come one day and he did."

"I did, didn't I?" Angel agrees.

"You did, and I love him so much," Quinn finishes the sentence with an excited squeak as she lets Angel go, circles Rye twice as fast as her skirt and heavy boots will let her. She skids to a stop just in time to avoid running right in to Angel.

"I love him," she whispers.

She's mine, Rye decides. At first in pure astonishment. He never disbelieved Angel but now he feels the simple truth. As Quinn's words sink in, he decides he feels possessive as well. Not as much as he knows he will later but that will come. The more often he can show it to others, the stronger the feeling will grow but in the end it doesn't matter. As long as Quinn says she loves him, it's all he needs.

"Hi, Quinn," Rye kneels beside Angel.

"No, no, no," the girl proclaims. "Up. I've never been tallest and I want to be tallest."

"Quinn," Angel whispers, about to jump in but Rye gives his head a quick shake. It's been a long time since he played, not since he and Tong were a lot younger. His surrogate parents play with them as young boys involved a lot of cheerful giving in to whatever they were doing and Rye is pretty sure he can do the same.

"Turn around," Rye smiles. When Quinn faces around, Rye takes her under the arms and pulls her up over his head to settle her on his shoulders. The blue skirt falls, covering his eyes. "Where did you go?"

"Here," Quinn laughs and pulls the dress back, jamming it behind Rye's neck.

"Where? I see your mom and Max and Giselle," he tries. He doesn't even mind the little hug Angel gives Max as she looks him over and he can't help but notice the ancient prosthetics. Max sways slightly, adjusting his weight on their stiff balance.

"Thank you for doing so much for Quinn," Angel says. "You and Opal."

"Here," Quinn leans over Rye's head and pulls his brows up so she can see his eyes.

"There you are," Rye says. Quinn puts the berry pail on his head as he grabs her ankles. "I thought I might have tossed you up too high but there you are."

CHAPTER 19

"Let me look at you," Giselle says. Behind Angel, the older woman fusses with the inside of her hood before bringing her hands up and pushing Angel's hair aside. "How long were you in zero-g?"

"I know gravity's good for me. A week and a half," Angel admits as Giselle's smooth fingertips probe her neck. There's no point in explaining the culmination of circumstances that put her through ten days of weightlessness. Opposite them, on the other side of the small, central square, Quinn sits on Rye's knee. Her little legs swing, thumping into his calf. In response to her yawn, he pulls her closer then leans over to gather her fallen boots and put them under his chair. They disappear into the deep, purple shadows of violet light cast by natural fungi clinging to recesses in the tall, stone walls.

Opal and Max sit beside them. She doesn't take her eyes from Max, peering out above an opaque veil hemmed in Max's distinctive, clumsy blanket stitch. Hidden beneath, Opal's jawless mouth sags to one side. Once enough to cause her to hide under her sheet, the young woman seems content outside the infirmary at least when she's near Max. The brown and white speckled faux-mink sleeps in her lap next to her hand, her fingers tangled with Max's.

121

"Rye's data unit is transmitting," Giselle whispers then clicks her tongue in distaste. "I don't think those things turn off. His ship is moving toward a geostationary orbit and will likely wind up right on top of us."

"Mm," Angel closes her eyes. Between her palms, she cradles a cup of warm coffee flavoured with a heavy shot of Giselle's spicy home brewed liquor. Giselle calls it Kirsch like the traditional German liquor but the only thing cherry about it is the colour of the fruit from which it's made.

"I pinned one of my father's trinkets in your hood. Whoever's up there is damned good if they've found him through the radiation diffusion net. I boosted the signal when you came down. The piece in your hood should be enough to block him completely. I just need you within five meters of him. Closer the better."

"'kay."

"Do you think Rye suspects Quinn's facility with German is unnatural?"

"No." Although she's just four, her grasp of English matches that of a teen. Rye already knows she's more advanced than a third gen and Angel let him think she's just gifted with languages.

"He's good with her."

"I want to hog her so much right now but who knows when he'll be back."

"What about you and Rye?" Giselle eases into the low seat next to Angel.

"I'm not sure. It really doesn't matter what I want as long as Quinn gets enough of him."

"If I said two meters apart could you figure it out?"

Angel laughs, drawing Rye's attention. He pauses, mid sentence, and Max takes the opportunity to put his mouth to Opal's temple. Ten weeks ago the two barely spoke.

"It's not just for the three of you. I need you in his head because I have everyone here to consider."

"So do I," Angel agrees but Quinn, more than anyone, has her heart. If that means taking her daughter and leaving

Helm-Dent to protect Giselle and her charges then she will, as hard as it will be to say good-bye. "Time to turn in, I think."

Most of the residents retired for the night over an hour ago and while Quinn settled in with Rye, Angel and Giselle took care of the cleanup.

Quinn draws her knees up under her skirt and curls into a little, sleepy ball, arms folded over her knees. She still sleeps in the same position she took when she shared Angel's cramped infirmary bed, slightly smaller than her bed in their quarters. It was only in the past year Quinn moved to her own room and an adult bed though she still takes up a tiny portion of it.

"'til morning, then," Giselle rises with her.

"Gute Nacht, Giselle," Angel crosses the courtyard and rests a hand on Rye's shoulder. "I need to take her to bed."

"I got you, baby girl," Rye stands, his shoulder hidden in Quinn's loose curls and gets an arm under her bottom. "Nice to meet you, Max. Opal."

"G'night," Max yawns, tucking the little, brown faux-mink under his arm and helping Opal to her feet with the other. The younger woman fits perfectly under his arm and the two disappear from the courtyard before Angel picks up her suitcase and Rye's pack.

"Here," Rye slings his bag over his shoulder and gestures for Quinn's boots. Her arms come up over his shoulders and she gives a contented sigh. "Which way?"

Angel takes a moment to rub Quinn's back before leading them toward the tunnel where they left the CN2. The second to last door leads to her quarters.

After using the old fashioned knob to open the door, Angel ushers Rye in and activates the lights. They flash on in a brilliant surge before she dims them to a more comfortable level.

"Come," she whispers then relieves Rye of his bag and the boots before leading them to the bathroom. Once he sits Quinn on the counter, Angel starts her brushing her teeth before disappearing for clean pajamas. "Bath in the morning, my little berry picker."

"'kay, Mama," Quinn spits then Angel waves Rye out so Quinn can change and dress. By the time she emerges from the bathroom, holding Quinn's hand, Rye has his vest over the back of her tattered sofa and his weapons are gone.

"Night," Quinn palm waves.

As Angel tucks her in, she senses Rye in the bedroom door. She kisses Quinn then squeezes Rye's elbow on the way out, leaving him to say his good nights.

A single steam shower four days before, the same day she borrowed Scarlet's clothes so she could wash her own, is a distant memory. Atom kept environmental controls set to save energy and where one would expect the cold of space to leave them chilled, a quirk of ducting and internal power transfers left the command deck a little too warm. With life support off everywhere else, it seemed all the excess engine heat followed them into their limited accommodations aboard *Titan*.

By the time she steps from her own real water shower and pulls on her robe, there's nothing left but fatigue.

"You can have a shower," she offers, peering around into the main living area. "Gonna have to stoop though, ceiling's a little low. I can carve the rock out and make it higher—"

Rye stands with his back to her as he folds his shirt. Several scars she doesn't remember mark the left side of his back as well as another up by the crest of his shoulder. Otherwise, his sides taper just as she remembers; tanned though he spends most of his time in space and every inch displays his physical third gen power.

The shelf before him holds dozens of holos and stills of Quinn scattered amongst her collection of pinned insects, fossil rubbings and dinner plate shaped antlers.

"We all left Constant scarred in one way or another," Rye puts down a picture of Angel and Quinn curled up in Giselle's make-shift delivery room. "Tong was already on his way out of orbit when the Aphids came at us. I carried you, took some shrapnel but at least they didn't hurt you again."

"Rye, I—"

124

"I'll take you up on the shower," he interrupts before she can finish but he doesn't move until she steps into her bedroom and closes the door.

Angel didn't exaggerate about the confining stone shower. After bumping his head on the wall while avoiding the ceiling, Rye dropped to his knees to finish washing up. The very hot water hinted at sulphur and enough had filled the porous tub over the years to stain it in graduated layers of yellow, darkest on the bottom and around the drain. Even with the absence of any heating or cooling system, Angel's apartment stays a uniform temperature throughout.

When Rye steps from the shower, his warm skin detects a small movement of air close to the floor and toward the vanity. A thin gap between the base and the floor must be responsible. Giselle said excess heat vented out under the waterfall so he figures natural air currents draw the steam out.

Wearing nothing but a towel, Rye folds his clothes up and turns off the light. The only brightness in the hall comes from under Angel's bedroom door and inside she makes quiet movements, shuffling objects on a dresser or desk then the gentle closing of a drawer.

He doesn't bother with the light in her living room, instead relying on the implant to make use of the faint glow from her room. Her sofa has been folded down and a pillow and blankets sit at one end.

Rye drops his clothes next to them before checking his tablet once more for any communication from Atom. Again, nothing. For a few minutes before they turned in, it showed a two-way link with *Titan* but no data came or went. Then the link disappeared.

Dinner started out strange, at least from his point of view. Nearly twenty residents curled into corners and sat on rocks to eat a simple meal of boiled vegetables and roasted meat. It seemed most couldn't manage serving, moving to the courtyard and eating completely on their own. At first, Rye felt inadequate after spending so many years surrounded exclusively by people in peak condition. After watching everyone chip in when they could without waiting for help when they couldn't, he came to understand how much each small effort contributed to the success of the whole.

Conversations grew and ebbed; how the big moose-like herbivores averaged four percent larger than a decade earlier, how Max discovered a deep brown root he charred, ground, and soaked in cold water to make a brilliant pink dye (a favorite of Quinn's) and several stories of childhood pets came up when Quinn excused herself to feed the faux-mink.

Rye's daughter is the kind of bright, helpful child his surrogate parents would have pointed out to Rye and Tong as a good example. Core teachers would feed her mind with knowledge as well since she had no trouble keeping up with any scientific talk, even contributing on a few topics Rye would have to read up on to follow. She'd make a great analyst, like him, since her mind already operates at a level he only reaches with a heavy dose of cognitive booster and a solid six of sleep.

At first, they'd been subdued around Rye but everyone relaxed as the evening wore on.

Now Rye stands facing the shelf of pictures and mementos as he did only twenty minutes earlier.

Once Quinn turned in, he opened his mouth and said the wrong thing. He made it sound like everyone's injuries on Constant, both physical and emotional, were a result of what happened to Angel. Then he dismissed her and wouldn't turn around until she was gone.

Other than when his surrogate father was away on Vix Two, he never spent a night away from his wife. When he was home it was rare to see them in different rooms. Their relationship flourished with their love for their surrogate sons. Angel certainly isn't Rye's wife but after six years thinking of nobody else there is no way in hell he'll spend the night on her couch.

Rye lifts his fist to knock but before he brings it down on the wood door, he stops as he realizes this isn't a blast proof, metal door like aboard *Titan*. Instead, he taps three times with his knuckles rather than the two solid thuds he planned.

After a few seconds of silence from Angel's room, she draws the door open and releases the same soft gasp she made when he came to her quarters six and a half years earlier. Has it really been that long? Just like then, he knew what he wanted. He even had most of the words planned but the moment he realized Angel saw him as a half naked man and not her commander, all his planning froze in his throat.

Just like now.

And just like then, she raises an eyebrow and waits for him to speak.

"I'm coming in," Rye announces, disappointed he fell back on the same arrogant words.

"Alright," Angel answers and steps clear, closing the door behind him. "I need to say this. I'm not okay with being something casual, Rye. If that's what waits for you back on *The Barrington,* I can't be the same for you here."

She doesn't need to move a muscle to tell him she's not done speaking. Standing there in a hip-length, button-up night shirt and long underwear, she holds him quiet with only her words.

"I just," she tries, looking again at the towel. Rye makes sure the rough, homespun fabric hasn't moved from where he put it and her eyes snap back up. She knows he caught her looking. "I'd rather not, if you know what I mean, make things awkward for Quinn because I'm jealous as shit."

"Ah."

She's not so hard to understand.

"I swear," Rye raises a hand and wiggles his fingers. "It's just been us. Since you, I mean."

"Jesus," she slaps a hand over her mouth then one over each cheek to hide the heat. "Here, too."

Then she turns away, shoulders shaking.

"Look at me, Angel," Rye waits. Even the tips of her ears blush. When she faces him, she snorts in laughter. Then she has to sit down.

Rye rubs a knuckle under his nose to stop himself from joining her. As Angel peeks from between her fingers, he drops to his knees and rests his hands on hers to help settle the subtle tremors of her laughter. She carries on another few seconds, before reigning in the lack of control he would expect in someone who hasn't had a good laugh in years.

Maybe she hasn't.

"Better?" He wraps his palms over her knuckles to ease her fingers down. Her freshly dried hair sticks in her teary eyes and he pushes the damp strands away. "Sshhh, I'm trying not to fuck this up, Angel. Honest, I'm giving it my best."

Desperate to prove his sincerity, Rye plants his lips on one teary eye then the other. She mumbles through her hands in protest but he doesn't stop. Once his arms tighten around her, folding hers between them, she has no choice.

"I didn't even know I died," Angel sniffs. "Giselle woke me. I thought I survived the explosion. The last thing I remembered was Tong's bloody leg. Core was my life, Rye. All I had to work for and without it I didn't want to live."

"Hey," Rye tugs her chin up, pinched between his thumb and folded first finger. Then he eases his grip. "I want to say I don't ever want to hear words like that from you again but until a couple of weeks ago I didn't have anything outside of Core to live for, either."

She turns away, closing her eyes though it doesn't take away from the intimacy of the moment.

"This place is good, Rye. For the rest of them, it's enough, but for me there has to be more. I know you lost me. You all did, but I woke up here alone. I lost everyone and everything. All I had was a baby in me and a wrecked body that would never be whole. Never."

"I didn't think about that," Rye says. All his selfish anger she'd been alive for four and a half years. A time through which his grief was as fresh as the day he fled Constant with her body in his arms and strips of flaming steel in his back. She lost a year and a half to the cold of cryo plus everything her life had been.

Rye doesn't realize he's closed his eyes to hold back the burning until her cool palm touches his cheek.

"I told you something, the day I died. And I lost that too. I don't even remember your answer."

CHAPTER 20

Rye's breath hardens, shaping his jaw into the firm line she only sees when he's all business. Damn, he couldn't handle it then and he can't now. Up until she saw him with Quinn, Angel denied she still felt the same way she did on Constant and every day for weeks before.

His rough stubble presses to her cheek and for a moment she hopes he's past the urge to bolt from intimacy but he stands, turns his back and storms from the room. From her living room, the solid click of the sofa tuning back into a sofa startles her upright before she slumps in the chair. Rye can only be leaving if he's folding up the bed. He promised to stay until morning, to say goodbye to Quinn but maybe it's for the best she remembers the good night she had with her father and not the anger Angel won't be able to hide.

She ignores the other sounds from her living room until she hears him in the bedroom doorway. Maybe if she didn't fall apart every time she had his complete attention he'd see her the way he used to. She isn't the hardcore soldier she once was. Instead, her physical and emotional recovery from death left her softer in every way possible.

"How are we going to do this, Angel?" Rye asks.

130

"How do you think?" She replies. He's walking out. Time to shore up the defences since it's too late to prove she's every bit as tough as he remembers.

"Okay," he answers then she looks his way as his bare feet pad across her stone floor onto the thick throw rug. Not boots.

Rye drops his packed bag at the foot of her bed and wraps his weapons in the belts he uses to hold them on before placing them on her bedside table, taking up nearly all its surface. He still wears nothing but her good towel.

"Have some patience with me, please," he says. "I can't remember the things I want without remembering the things I don't."

Her bed groans as he sits in the centre, leaning back against the wall. Rye looks left and right and furrows his brow then shrugs and spreads his knees. The gap in the towel opens, granting a view high inside his thigh and a hint of thickening short, dark curls.

He'd dress if he planned on leaving.

"Come closer," Rye closes his eyes and pats the mattress between his legs. "Please?"

Brave enough to hope, Angel kneels on the mattress. His hands close around her thighs then he reaches further out and takes her elbows before making his way to her shoulders.

"We didn't see you at first," he says as he opens enough buttons to push her nightshirt off her shoulders and expose the full extent of her scars and their covering tattoos. Warm hands run over her collar bones as his calloused palms catch on the thin fabric covering her breasts. With a shiver strong enough to chase away the goose flesh on her arms, Angel relaxes letting him ease years of stress from her body. "After we found Tong, he showed us where you were. The blast picked up a couple of dead Aphids, threw them into you. Without them as a shield, it would have left you in pieces."

One hand drops, cupping her breast through her shirt as the other cradles the back of her neck. His rough skin grabs at the pilled fabric. The vibration forces a tight moan from her lips as everything slows down; his fingers kneading her scars and the way their weight shifts the bed as he leans forward to lick at her throat. Even the silence offered by the stone surrounding them becomes thick and patient.

Angel brings a hand up to cover his, to feel his movement as he thumbs her responsive nipple.

"No, not yet. I need to do this."

She drops her hand, not daring a word past her lips. A glance at the drape of his towel shows he doesn't share her arousal. Instead, he uses touch to rewrite the tragedy he sees whenever he closes his eyes. He must have something else in mind other than their usual position where he was a gentleman keeping her off whatever dirt floor they found themselves on. Other than their first night, they hadn't been together in a real bed.

Another button opens, releasing the pressure of her shirt around her shoulders. Then two more. Rye pulls the nightshirt up over her shoulders, holding in the heat from his hands as he lifts her to full kneeling and traces a warm, wet line down the center of her chest to the two circular scars made by the device used to secure her circulatory system back on Constant.

Rye's hands shake as he turns her in his arms then his breath hitches as he holds her close.

"Broken," he whispers. "I couldn't move you without feeling the grind of bone on bone. The sound filled the room. It disappeared into the dust and smoke and stink of burned flesh and bounced off the walls. I held you so still but the sound of bone on bone kept coming to me no matter how hard I tried.

"When the lights failed," Rye places a hand between her breasts so she knows which ones then rests his lips on her cheek as he has so many times since he found her in Whistler. "I kissed you."

He tries to speak but his voice breaks free as a bitter choke. After clearing his throat, he tries again.

"'I love you, too,' I said. I thought it would be enough. You'd be okay."

Angel can't help but smile. He says the words she needed to hear. Words she dreamed over and over when she wasn't washed in visions of blood and death. In spite of the pain Rye wrestles inside, her smile widens and she presses her cheek more firmly against his mouth.

Angel gasps in surprise as Rye twists to the side, pressing her down beneath him and tearing the remaining buttons open in a single, impulsive move. The towel releases from his hips undoing six years of restraint and Rye gets his toes tangled in her long underwear. It only takes a few kicks to pull one leg to her ankle and the other clear of her foot.

"Please, Angel," he breathes, nose to nose, desperate for the memory of her lifeless body to end with anything other than the rough, tearing of a zipper sealing her in black plastic. "Be okay. Open your eyes."

Despondence and guilt falter and fade as she does what he says, blinking twice to focus. Her pale blue eyes stare into his.

"Yes," he clutches her chin in one hand and strokes her hair from her eyes with the other. "Look at me. God, don't stop looking."

She nods and he lets her lift her chin to kiss him, a chaste meeting of their lips. Rye doesn't yet trust this vision of life and covers her with his warm skin. Suppressing a shiver, he concentrates on warming to trigger his third gen ability to quickly turn stored energy into heat. In spite of her layers of clothing and recent shower, the air cools her faster than he'd like.

"Need you, Angel," he whispers, nipping his way down her jaw. She shakes but not from lack of sleep. Her deep sigh starts in the center of her chest then grows to a moan as it passes her lips. "I..."

Rye stops, stupid and tongue tied. He's never engaged in this kind of conversation with a woman. His soul needs cleansing and nothing short of spending his years of grief inside her will do it though putting the urge on hold to discuss contraception engages his logical mind in a painful way. It isn't that he doesn't want another kid since Quinn unlocked possibilities he never allowed himself to think of. Simply, not again until Angel swears to him that whatever a mostly absent career soldier has to offer will be enough.

As she works her arm free, she exposes a small, fresh puncture on the inside of her upper arm. Just above, a rice sized bulge in her skin can only be a contraceptive implant.

"Giselle took care of it," Angel explains.

Her damaged body shouldn't have to bear another scar, even a tiny and particularly because of him. Unable to hold back, he covers the wound with his lips and seals moist warmth around the mark as he traces the little bump with his tongue. She responds by squirming her legs free, knocking his knees aside and securing his thighs between hers. The rough long underwear dangles from one foot and she raises it higher, waking the skin of his backside with the coarse weave.

She used to be strong, lean and muscled, and eager to be rough when he needed it. Equally able to offer tenderness when they'd fucked each other into exhaustion and had nothing left to share but slow comfort. Now, she's pure softness though with what she's been through she's a hell of a lot stronger than she was then.

When Rye meets her eyes again, she stares back, reassuring him she's still okay. He hoped for something a little more old-fashioned like condoms to avoid injuring her any further.

"Damn, you're warm. I'm gonna sweat."

"Yes, you are," he agrees as he draws his knees up, spreading hers, then shifts upward so she's directly below him.

Although Rye knows how ready he is to have her, he still reaches between them to wrap his fingers around his cock and check. Stupid ritual but she never minds. Angel bites at her lip

134

while she watches to make sure he's pleased with what he finds. When her fingers join his, he rocks them together and swallows her moans as he claims her anew, a little at a time until there's no room for their hands between them.

Angel shudders, squeezing him deep inside so he takes her breast in his hand and finds her nipple. His calloused thumb rakes over the tip and he gets the response he wants. Angel tosses her head back so Rye can bite at her neck then he moves, a little at first to gauge her response. When she sinks her fingernails into his arms he hooks an elbow under her knee, giving himself room to take all of her he can.

"Rye," she moans as he relaxes his hold on her leg. The pressure to climax almost wins as moisture springs from her skin. Then she comes, burying her mouth in his shoulder to keep quiet. Rye doesn't let up, doesn't change his angle or the weight behind his thrusts. All he can do is count out the wait for her second orgasm in order to keep some control of himself until he can let go with her.

"Stop," she begs although she rocks her hips just as hard as before. Her first orgasm hasn't let go and it will be a long minute until he finishes her off. An eternity for him but worth the wait.

"No," Rye buries his face in her blonde hair piled around her head. "Not ever going to stop."

Damn, he loses count but even after six years he knows her well enough. With each thrust she tightens around him. Unbearable, sweet pressure he fights as long as he can.

"Look," he growls and her eyes snap open. "Give it to me."

As Rye finally loses the battle with his self control, she cries out and he shudders and pours himself deep inside her. Every muscle in his body burns as he whispers grateful words until they fall silent, lost in peaceful exhaustion.

CHAPTER 21

Quinn giggles somewhere down the hall, maybe in the main room. It wouldn't surprise Angel if the child lined up the ingredients for breakfast on the kitchen counter. She knows better than to touch the stove but with Rye here, Quinn may be planning to cook for him herself.

"Okay, sshhh," Quinn whispers and Angel pulls her head free from the warm cocoon between the pillow and Rye's arm. Before she can move further, Rye presses her to the mattress from above and covers her mouth with his hand. He uses just enough pressure to urge silence.

Through the fog of waking, the blood drains from Angel's cheeks and pools in a tight knot deep in her gut. Something sounds wrong, very wrong, but she can't place it. Footsteps of more than just her barefoot little girl come from all directions.

"Rye?" She mouths knowing he feels the movement and it doesn't matter what she says, he knows she has questions.

"I'm so fucking sorry," he mutters in her ear, his body even more tense. He shifts his weight on to one elbow and holds her shoulder with the other. "Angel, so sorry."

"Oh?" Quinn says. "Of course Daddy's friends can stay for breakfast. I love my Daddy and his friends are nice."

136

Angel struggles to get up but Rye slides an arm around her shoulders, straddling her legs with his knees and keeping her down.

"No," he chokes out. "Don't make this any harder than it has to be. Think of her."

"Bastard," she growls and lets her head fall to the pillow. He's a complete bastard for using Quinn to ensure her cooperation. She has no chance of getting out from under him and getting Quinn away from whichever of her Daddy's nice friends waits in the hallway.

Quinn's sleep tousled head pokes around the door and her eyes light when she sees Angel and Rye.

"See?" She says as she steps in then she looks up the big Core-gray arm holding her hand. "It's okay, they're awake."

"Perfect," Denman says as he pushes the door all the way open. Behind him, Atom won't look up. He buries his attention in his tablet. "We thought everyone left, with the alarms going off all over. Everywhere but here that is."

"In here," Rye's commander elbows Atom.

"Sir," Atom mutters and steps in, sweeping the room with his tablet before homing in on Angel's hoodie where she left it crumpled on top of her dresser.

Giselle's trinket. Inside, Angel collapses in understanding why she didn't get the warning Core had descended on them. The standard Core alarm system operates on standard Core frequencies, the same ones as Rye's tablet. The device in her hood not only blocked Rye from communicating with *Titan*, it also kept her own alarm receiver from picking up the evacuation order.

"Don't turn it off," Angel begs as Atom retrieves the device. The alarm will scare Quinn as it echoes through the stone rooms of their home. "It's really loud."

"It's quite disabled," Denman says. He gives Quinn's small hand a squeeze and pushes her in Angel's direction. The commander hasn't changed since Angel last saw him and though she never like him much, at least he treated everyone with courtesy, unless you really fucked up. She can only hope he's considerate of Quinn.

Rye doesn't hold Angel back when she slips from the bed. His spare t-shirt dangles to her knees and stiffness makes her wince as she pulls her little girl up into her arms.

"Breakfast?" Angel asks with as much fake cheer as she can muster but her hot tears don't escape Quinn's notice. She pokes Angel's cheek with her thumb and tries to rub a tear away.

"You said you weren't hurt," she accuses, brows knit together before her lips form an exaggerated pucker and seal on the side of Angel's neck.

"I didn't think I'd wake up to pain today," Angel glares at Rye. He hasn't moved, alone in her bed and tumbled up in the blankets. "Bet mom needs her teeth brushed."

Angel sticks a finger in Quinn's side and the girl laughs, makes a face and pinches her nose shut. Once Angel grabs clean clothes from the dresser, she pushes past Denman and stomps into the bathroom. She doesn't recognize the female Core officer who gets a boot in the way to prevent her closing the door.

Angel gets ready as Quinn perches on the counter and brushes her teeth. She doesn't bother with clothes for Quinn. Not yet anyway. She'll need an excuse to get her back in the bathroom, alone, before Denman tries to take them off planet. Quinn's shins and knees show patches of dirt and little scrapes from the brush so Angel will have an excuse.

Once they make it out to the main room, she finds fewer Core soldiers than expected. Rye, back in uniform, sits at the table. Atom has gone and with the exception of two guards at the door the only other person there is a female in the unadorned gray uniform of Core Intelligence. Her raven black hair nestles in a regulation bun and her pale yellow skin displays thick, brown spots in clusters at the side of her neck.

Vaguely familiar with the species and its deadly reputation for firmly following orders, Angel tightens her hold on Quinn.

The T*kit female can't be here for Quinn, that job doesn't belong to Intelligence, but she could be here to take Angel.

Quinn's strength doesn't surprise Angel very often but today it does. Numbness with the reality of her impending separation from her daughter lets Quinn drop to the ground before Angel even feels her absence. She dodges around the table and grabs the T*kit's hands.

"G'na tw rek*k ni?" Quinn asks.

She probably speaks T*kit. It will be the yellow woman's first language, the one she knows best and still thinks in, just like Giselle's German. Keeping Quinn's most remarkable skill quiet is all but impossible.

"Sesia," the Intelligence Officer says with a wide-mouthed laugh that exposes the complex net of speech and breathing gills in the back of her throat. She has eight sets of vocal cords she can use individually or in various combination to create impossible and beautiful sounds. "G'na tw rek*k ni?"

"Quinn," she points to herself.

"How does she speak T*kit?" Denman says from behind Angel. He says it as 'shit' which is about all a non-native can hope for though they hear the difference between shit and T*kit. Denman's mouth, and that of anybody else in the room except Sesia and apparently Quinn, is incapable of pronouncing it properly.

Angel shrugs.

"I haven't heard it spoken since I left my home world," Sesia says. The spots on her wide neck darken in what must be puzzlement.

"Ke tig rek*a pord reh, tiy?" Quinn tries.

"Mh, Quinn?" She lets Quinn drag her to the small kitchen.

"Sesia will help cook breakfast," Quinn announces before she climbs up on the counter and waits for Sesia to do the work.

"T*kit, Angel," Denman tries again.

"She only knows it because Sesia does," Angel whispers.

"Don't," Quinn shouts holding a palm up then drops to a whisper. "Don't talk about my secret language."

"Secret indeed," Denman takes Angel's elbow and guides her to the table, seating her across from Rye. Rye must have packed his crisp Core uniform in anticipation of his superior showing up.

Denman turns enough in his own chair to lean over Angel and have her full attention.

"She couldn't speak it to you at all or to Sesia if she couldn't see her," Angel lets her voice fail. Giselle's research two years earlier found the ability to be undocumented in Genetics' records. Quinn learned English at the same rate as a regular child but it seemed she could pick a person's first language right from their head, even when her English wasn't advanced enough to speak the equivalent.

"I'll inquire with Genetics," Denman finally says.

"Don't bother," Angel mumbles. "They've never seen it."

"Any reason you were blocking my comms?" Rye speaks up. Judging by his stare, he's found something to be mad about even though Denman being here on Helm-Dent is his fault.

"Didn't want our location accidentally noted in *Titan's* logs," she mutters and he shrugs as if her answer doesn't matter.

"Ah, thank you, Quinn," Denman accepts a bowl of granola, hot, nutrient rich milk made from local tree-nuts and the pink berries picked the day before. Angel eats her berries first to please Quinn then pushes the soggy grains around.

"Rye, I appreciate the need to co-operate with the locals," he nods at Angel. "In order to get her home. As we get to know the people here, I'm sure we'll come to fully understand the wonderful things they've done."

"Before the trip to the A.L." Angel snorts. If Denman prefers to be circumspect about what he's really doing here, she will too. Core will see Giselle and her body snatchers as traitors worthy of a quick trip out the airlock. There's no need for Quinn to hear that.

"Indeed," Denman crunches another mouthful of cereal before he continues. "But you'll have a chance to debrief in a while."

From her seat between Rye and Denman, Sesia pushes her empty bowl away. "Perhaps we could take a tour of your lab, Angel? I only got a brief look, but I've studied tech from your old lab for several years. Your work now appears to have evolved significantly since then though I'm afraid I'm at an even greater loss to understand it."

"Of course," Angel says. As if she'll be given a choice. "Quinn, hun? Time for your bath then Daddy's friends are going to take us on a trip."

"Where?" Quinn shoots up from her chair, sending her half empty bowl over sideways into her mug.

"Up," Angel points to the sky. "Come."

She doesn't wait for permission or an escort. Likely, Atom's already been over every centimeter of her small home and found nothing but rock walls. He would have focused on electronics and tech, not weighted stone levers and almost non-existent extra bits of ceramic circuitry hidden in the veins of Helm-Dent's utility grade marble.

Denman stands as Angel does but Rye remains glowering into his bowl. At least he could be man enough to look her in the eye after turning her in. Denman, while every inch the dick required to run Core's largest Sol based station, is at least gentleman enough to get to his feet.

"Something pink, hm?" Angel asks and Quinn nods. It doesn't take long to gather one of the child's favourite dresses, panties and a thick pair of brown socks. Once in the bathroom, Angel signals silence and danger, a communication system everyone on Helm-Dent knew and hoped they'd never have to use. Quinn goes to speak but then dips her chin in a tiny nod and snaps her mouth shut. In her place, Angel would worry about Rye. If there is danger, Daddy and his friends might be in trouble to.

"Pajamas off," Angel says but shakes her head and Quinn remains still. She seats the stopper in the bathtub drain and starts running water then drops to her knees.

"Daddy will be okay," she smiles and spends precious seconds holding Quinn's trembling hands until she nods. She loves so much and so easily. Each insect in her collection has a name and a story in her journal and she remembers them all. Even now, after Rye brought Core down on their little home, Angel wants to get on with forgiving him for Quinn's sake. To get her to safety and bargain to keep her there.

"I love you," Angel whispers, kissing her brave little girl once on each cheek.

"Love you, Mama."

"Ready?" With the tub half full, a few noisy seconds remain to cover their disappearance.

Angel finds the two finger-sized pressure plates, one inside where the water comes from the sink faucet and the other just under the edge of the smooth, marble counter top. It has the appearance of a bluish whorl against white, nothing more. She holds both down for a count of three and waits. The floor movement starts subtly, only a hint of vertigo as her brain denies the movement then speeds up, lowering them into a dark tunnel beneath their home. Angel picks Quinn up and as she steps off. The floor rises though it doesn't slow as it's supposed to. Instead, two tons of marble crash into place.

Angel waits, allowing her eyes to adjust to the dim glowing strips Giselle's father laid down years ago to mark their escape route. Before she takes a step, muffled shouts above sound then the crash of the bathroom door collapsing under someone's weight.

"Daddy's good, hun," Angel whispers as Quinn clings so tightly she feels a joint pop. She isn't sure if it's hers or her daughters. If Quinn could see her face, she'd see the lie. "So are his friends but not everyone from Core is, remember?"

"Yes," she sniffs.

"Some think children should go learn to fight."

"I don't want to fight."

"No, baby," Angel moves, at first a stiff walk since she's unaccustomed to Quinn's weight but after a minute she finds herself in a run and moving too fast to dodge the occasional sharp stone. One foot in front of the other in the hope she hasn't missed the rail car that will take Quinn to Giselle's transport. "You won't."

She isn't in the kind of shape she was before she died and no amount of training will get her there but she's quick enough to get through the seven minute run without doubling over at the end. As she rounds the last corner, Opal and Max turn in surprise. Opal pulls her leg from the transport as Max hits the stop button to keep it from leaving.

"Mink," Quinn exclaims as the little brown face pokes out from Opal's veil.

Angel hugs Quinn hard, drinking in the scent of her hair and skin one last time before handing her over to Max.

"I'm staying," she says and Quinn shakes her head. "I have information they want and they won't get it if they even try and look for you. Giselle can tell me where you are."

Max nods, understanding. "Mom will catch up, Quinn."

"Opal and Max will take good care of you, baby," Angel pulls Quinn's face close. "And I'll see you soon."

CHAPTER 22

"Soldier," Denman leans back in his chair, wiping his mouth with a cloth napkin. His hands dwarf the bright pink slip of fabric he took from Quinn's place mat.

"Had to be real for her," Rye says as he falls back on the plan they hid from Angel. In case they were caught, there had to be a story to keep them all out of the brig since they couldn't help anyone if they were all locked up together. "There's no way she'd betray the people here or give Quinn up. My people were damned surprised to see her and I let them think we really were going to drop her off and walk away until they came to me to question what we were doing with her. Until then, I had to let them think we were helping her. They're too honest to pull it off."

Denman shrugs. "It was a big risk. You might have tried giving orders."

Rye doesn't relax much. Any new looseness to his muscles threatens to turn into a squirm since Denman doesn't let his gaze wander from Rye.

"I don't receive a lot of orders," Rye emphasizes the last word but he doesn't smile. Though he wants to know, he'll look like he might have considered keeping Angel quiet if he asks Denman what tipped him off. Instead, he doesn't blink as he continues. "My commander taught me it's better for your

144

people to come around on their own when it comes to making emotional decisions, Sir."

"Didn't stop you from taking my subject to bed again, did it?" Sesia mutters.

The T*kit interrogated Rye personally in the months following Angel's death. Nothing she did left marks but Rye knew little about Angel's work and it took several painful days for her to figure it out. Other than a few comments Angel made about the promise of better interface with Aphid computers, he knew nothing about what she did in the labs aboard *The Barrington*. Silence regarding his relationship with Angel left him seated in a hard chair with his joints on fire. Sesia's touch took the place of the suitcase full of wires a non T*kit Investigator would place around his body and she didn't let up until he'd admitted to his relationship with Angel. Only then did she seem satisfied he had nothing more to say.

"What the fuck?"

All three jump to their feet as the entire apartment trembles with the impact of stone on stone. It comes from the direction of the bathroom and only the sound of running water remains when the tremor stops.

"Angel?" Rye gets to the door first.

"Step aside," Denman orders and though Rye is capable of taking the door down he backs away and lets his commander knock. The third blow on the flimsy door pops the lock and it flies open, cracking when it bounces off the overflowing bathtub.

"Damn it," Denman growls.

Stone crumbs surround the edge of the empty room and those at the base of the bath form a line at the leading edge of the advancing water.

"Secure your CN2."

Extricating Angel and Quinn from his transport after she's wedged it sideways in the narrow tunnel would be a feat. Secretly though, Rye hopes they've made good on their escape. As Rye bursts out her front door and into the early morning darkness, he tunes his implanted eye to the overhead starlight so he can make his way to the landing cavern. The purple lichen no longer grants the soft glow it had the night before.

Denman must have ordered a search since behind him, in the direction of the central square, urgent instructions and the movement of boots dog his steps.

Rye finds the cavern empty except for the CN2, sitting as he left it on the gravel floor. After pressing his face to the windows, he decides nobody hides inside and proceeds to search the walls for any sign of a hidden door. It looks like Angel dropped out of her bathroom so more passages could be anywhere.

Rye closes his eyes and slows his heart and breathing to increase the sensitivity of his other senses. He woke her twice during the night so he was sure he'd had her enough for the moment. After pulling his spare t-shirt over her head and checking on Quinn, he fell asleep indulging himself in the comfort of Angel's bed. It takes a few more minutes to clear himself of those fresh memories as well until there's nothing but silence around him. He loses track of time, a dormant sensor, waiting for any intrusion to reach him.

The noise starts as a weak, rhythmic vibration he feels in his shins rather than his booted feet. As it grows in strength, the slap of skin on stone accompanies each pulse. Angel wasn't wearing anything on her feet when she left. Several steps come in irregular, quick succession followed by the heavier impact of a fall but by then Rye begins to come up from his trance.

As his heightened sense of smell fades, it picks up Atom and the pressure of his boots on the gravel-floored tunnel leading to the chamber. The other man waits silently at the top of the stairs for Rye to open his eyes rather than speak and give Rye a five-alarm migraine as his voice ravages his wide open senses. Rye's a damned good tracker but still only half as good as Atom.

"Angel," Atom whispers. "Denman has her in custody, alone."

Rye nods and joins his friend to hurry through the tunnel. If Angel got Quinn to an underground hideout it's only a matter of time until Denman has her and she'll be removed from everyone she's ever known.

"Sorry," Atom says. "Damn, I just wanted to find you in case anything went wrong. Just to have your back but then Denman showed up—"

"My responsibility now," Rye lowers his voice even further. "We can't do anything for her if we're locked up. I doubt I'll get a chance to explain for a while."

"Got it," Atom nods as they step out under the orange predawn sky. "I'd kill you too, if I were her. We've uploaded what we can from the computers we can't take with us. The computers in medical, that is. Everything else appears to be Angel's lab and Sesia said to leave it alone."

Atom punches Rye in the shoulder before leaving him at Angel's door.

Rye hesitates before opening up and letting himself in. Wooden chair legs drag across the floor as it sounds like another chair rocks in place. He pushes the door in to find Denman straddling one chair to face Angel, his nose less than a foot from hers. In profile, Rye makes out a bloody scuff on her cheek and the bruise forming under her left eye. If he hadn't heard her stumble in the tunnel below it would be hard not to think she'd been roughed up. Shackles secure both her wrists and elbows behind her back. As Angel presses her bare feet to the ground, her sideways chair rocks and Denman grabs it, slamming the raised legs down. She pulls her feet in, leaving a red smear on the floor. Shit, maybe parts of the tunnel weren't as smooth as they sounded.

"Doubt it," Angel spits. "If they're not already off planet they will be soon and you won't see them go."

"Unlikely," Denman sounds unconcerned.

"Giselle Keller," Angel turns to Rye. "Sound familiar?"

Rye shrugs. He has no place in Denman's interrogation. Even Sesia remains quiet on the other side of the table.

"No? Maybe Gustav Keller?"

Rye recognizes the name moments before Denman does and the older man taps his jaw with his thumb nail as he thinks.

"Gustav Keller designed most of Core's defensive and scanning software," Denman muses before his smile broadens in what Rye recognizes as anticipation of tripping up Angel's story. "Killed nearly fifty years ago, if I recall, testing a new, undetectable propulsion system. An accident that took almost a dozen of his best people with it."

Angel smirks. "Gustav Keller has been in the cemetery on the other side of the village for the past ten years along side his best people and several others who deserted to join him. He'd been ordered to release proprietary information on his tech and disappeared, taking it with him, rather than see it used for genocide of the Aphids. Core uses his research but they don't understand why it works and don't understand it enough to advance it any further."

"And the others here?"

"His daughter Giselle and people like me, saved from a century of cold storage. Only Gustav and the computer aboard the escape vehicle know where they're going. It could be right off *Titan's* bow and the sensors would never pick it up."

Denman's cheeks colour, a clear sign Angel's arrogance pisses him off but he leans away from her until he speaks again.

"I'm quite certain you know more about this place than the whereabouts of the great Gustav Keller," Denman speaks each word with an equal amount of tense emotion. "You're not the first piece of Core property to disappear from cryo. Not the last either. Thousands have gone missing, their implants appearing in first gen soldiers though they have a valid path from manufacture through the supply chain.

"Places like this," Denman spits. "Fucking body snatchers. Hundreds missing since you disappeared."

"No," Angel exclaims, her attitude gone. "Anything I didn't need or want went back to Core, but nobody's been brought here since me. If people went missing, it wasn't us."

"That remains to be determined. Let me tell you how we came to be here in your kitchen, Angel.

"Twenty four hours after you left Earth, smuggled aboard *Titan,* I received Rye's report on his cargo. He didn't mention you, of course. That information we got from Scarlet's eyes-only journal. She isn't aware that I see all reports, private or otherwise. A detailed report on Patient A, five years out of cryo and the mother of a very advanced third gen fathered by him," Denman nods toward Rye.

"I followed up with Acquisitions. Their report on your former roommate in Whistler stated he'd assisted a Core soldier named Angel by neutralizing an Aphid threat before Rye recruited him, at your insistence."

Angel lets her head fall forward, her blonde hair obscuring the bruise. She'd never been safe.

"Rye kept his investigation of you quiet to me, his prerogative, and as long as it didn't hinder my own investigation into the thefts from cryo I wasn't about to interfere.

"When you arrived on *The Barrington* I ordered him to Toll. Our best intelligence suggested this place was near the route to that planet which made it easy for him to accommodate your directions. There was no mission to Toll. It was just the excuse he needed to be in this sector.

"Then we got the labs back on the Aphids Rye delivered, the initial assessment Sesia ordered while she was still on route. When the results came in, I couldn't wait for his official report on this place because you know what I found? The Aphid's contain human DNA, as we suspected but even more surprising is whose."

Sesia leans forward watching Angel's reaction. Her eyes flick to Denman and she waits with the intent look Rye faced for days back on the *Barrington*. The female didn't love her work, didn't even seem to like tormenting others to get to the truth. To Rye, she seemed to suffer through a near religious mission for the truth right along with him. For the T*kit, truth, integrity and giving one's word from the depth of their soul bears the weight of every action they will ever undertake. No wonder so many find homes in Intelligence; always seeking the truth.

"Your DNA," Denman whispers. "Yours, Angel. One in one point one billion is good enough for me."

Angel turns white and shakes her head refusing to believe. She tries to stand, to turn away from Denman and instead falls from her chair. With her hands bound behind her, she collapses face first on a thick rug as she glances off the end of the sofa.

"This place," he continues, "is responsible for Aphid's having free run on Earth."

CHAPTER 23

"He's alive," Angel breathes against the thick carpet she and Giselle made to give Quinn something softer than stone to use as a play place.

Every bit of acceptance drives her back to the day on the family farm when she lost Allen, her brother, to a brutal attack by the Aphids. Either he's alive or he lived long enough for the Aphids to get what they needed.

Nobody tries to help as she struggles on the floor and she chokes back a rough sob.

"Who's alive?" Denman asks from his chair. On the other side of the table, across from his big boots, Sesia's much smaller ones rest side by side.

Damn it, betrayed all round. Civilian life, Core... Rye.

She gets on her side in an effort to get up and cries out with sharp pain in her neck and shoulder before rolling back on her stomach. When she opens her eyes again, Sesia's feet disappear from sight then the Intelligence Officer gets her sitting. Once Angel is back in her chair, Denman tries again. This time the predator in him backs off.

"Who's alive?"

"My brother, Allen," Angel blinks back tears at the sound of the name she hasn't spoken in seventeen years. Her older brother and best friend and all she had left until the day he was taken from her.

Out of Denman's sight, Sesia's fingers wrap around Angel's. Her warm, soft grip soothes and for a moment Angel's joints burn one at a time from the tips of her fingers to her shoulders before spreading up her neck and slowly down her body. Sesia completes her connection to Angel's nervous system and the heat fades, tightening Angel's muscles until they relieve the pressure with a shiver.

"I read Scarlet's report as well, Sir," Sesia says. "She's losing heat and the restraints put painful stress on her injuries."

Removal of the shackles and a blanket over her shoulders follow Denman's nod though Sesia doesn't allow a break in contact with Angel's skin.

"Tell me about your brother," Sesia asks. Although switching up interrogators is standard practice, having the woman ask the questions comes as a relief. The very thought of refusing to answer Sesia's inquiries causes a small discomfort, a general ache starting in her lower back.

"Allen was a year older. We lived with our grandparents on their farm in the Fraser Valley east of Vancouver. Our parents disappeared when we were small. I never understood where they'd gone other than it wasn't to do anything legal. Allen and I always believed it was some kind of eco-terrorism but our grandparents would never say. They spent nearly every dollar on a mercenary, hoping to find them but she strung them along until the money was gone."

"And your brother?" Denman asks.

"I'm getting to it," Angel says. "You have to understand what it was like for two teenagers to suddenly become the adults of the house when our grandparents got ill. There was little money. Nothing left to borrow against for new equipment and barely enough for seed. Allen and I spent our spare time on computers; planning, forecasting and trying to get through another season before the bank took our home but it wasn't enough."

Sesia's hand slips into Angel's, her thumb massages the inside of Angel's wrist. The effect of the interrogator's additional contact takes a moment to build. Angel finds it easy to ignore Rye's presence and the knot in her stomach caused by his deception eases. Given the chance, however, Angel would prefer a few minutes to destroy him in return.

"When I was seventeen, my grandparents passed within a month of each other leaving Allen and me alone. In less than a week the bank would take the farm and Allen planned to work until I finished high school then I'd earn what I could to get him started in college—"

Burning pain interrupts Angel's lie and she collapses forward, folded over double, crying out between gasps for breath. The agony doesn't let up. In the shadow of the door, Rye crosses his arms and through the blur of tears clouding her eyes, Angel sees the coward look away. If he didn't have the stomach for this, he shouldn't have turned her in.

"The truth," Sesia says as her grip tightens enough that Angel can't shake her free.

"We were going to steal," Angel grinds her teeth. "Illegal money transfer, tuition. Allen and I had backdoors into a number of banks and other places."

Angel draws a pain-free breath and allows Sesia to pull her upright. God damn, Angel had no idea a T*kit could do that with just her fingers.

"Why didn't you just steal the money to buy back the farm?" Denman asks.

"You must be kidding," Angel laughs. "With food shortages all over the place you'd think the government gave a shit and would keep the farms in the hands of the people who knew them best but instead, they let the bank take it and let the land lay fallow for months until it could be sold.

"The bank knew we had nothing. Showing up with the millions our grandparents owed would have been all kinds of suspicious. But we could start over. Didn't you ever wonder what kind of computer skills a seventeen-year-old girl could sell to Acquisitions?"

"Get to the point," Denman orders. "*Arsenal* will leave orbit in a few hours."

"We were only a few days from leaving," Angel continues, still weak from lying to Sesia and more than eager to get past reliving the difficult memories and on to bargaining for Quinn's future.

"I was cleaning up from breakfast. It was hot already, no wind, and through the open kitchen window I heard a scream. Then another. Then my name. It was Allen. When I looked up, I saw him running towards the house. The corn only came to his hips and slowed him down but even then I never saw him run so fast. Behind him I caught a glimpse of one or two Aphids.

"We'd skirted around Core computers enough to learn something about them but we didn't know they were so damn fast on all fours. I ran to my grandfather's cupboard and had both shotguns loaded before the sink overflowed. I got to the door and raised one gun but two Aphids had Allen on the ground as a third burst from the edge of the field. There were three more nearby and they came for me when I called Allen's name."

Sesia rubs Angel's wrist and rests her other hand on the small of Angel's back. Angel hardly notices.

"I've always been better than Allen with the shotgun. Better than my grandfather even. The first went down with a clean hit to the throat. I'd never fired at anything other than cans, you know. When my grandfather was young, his grandfather talked about coyotes in the livestock but there hadn't been one on our farm for a hundred years. I didn't squirm or hesitate like I thought I would but my hands shook more from Allen's screams than for taking any sort of life.

"My next shot missed, disappearing into the corn. My third didn't. They were closer and I put two in the next Aphid, one in the belly and one in the chest. I didn't see it hit the ground because I dropped the shotgun, grabbed the second and stepped back into the kitchen. It didn't slow down. I swear

I felt its hands on me as I pulled the trigger then closed my eyes expecting it to have me too.

"When I opened them, I thought the Aphid was gone but it was on the floor. Green blood pumped from where its head had been. The sound of it spraying against the wall sounded just like the dishwater running on the floor.

"Allen.

"He was still shouting my name over and over and I ran for the door, slipped but I got back up. When I stepped out they were too close to him. I couldn't shoot but I kept the gun up. I cried for him. There was nothing I could do. They took him into the corn.

"A few minutes later," Angel stares at the floor, ashamed she couldn't protect her brother. "He stopped screaming and their transport left, low over the fields."

Denman holds a hand up as he studies his tablet.

"Allen registered for university that day. He wasn't with you."

"Aphids don't take people alive. You find one, it kills you," Angel whispers. "There was no point in telling the Core clean-up crew. I knew enough to ask for Acquisitions. Put the gun to my head until they gave in. All I asked for was thirty minutes to get undetected as far as I could into Core systems. Getting into Core was my only chance to find Allen alive or get my revenge.

"I think they just wanted me to put the gun down so they gave in. It took four minutes to show Allen registered in person at Tokyo University. Twenty minutes after that I made the cleanup crew's transport lift off, flip over and land on its roof—"

"Son of a bitch," Rye exclaims before a wave from Denman shuts him up.

"Rye and Tong were in that transport," Denman stifles a laugh. "I'd accompanied them for a month of assistance with Earth based operations. You did that?"

"No more crap, Denman," Angel slumps sideways against her chair and Sesia lets her go so she can stand. Instead of facing Denman, she turns to the Intelligence Officer and hopes her knowledge of the T*kit is accurate.

"I know what you want from me, Investigator," Angel bows until her back lays parallel to the floor. "It would be the greatest honour to promise you the full extent of my knowledge in exchange for your word nobody will seek Quinn, ever. I am at your disposal."

She stands in time to see Sesia's brows draw back together from their wide position of surprise. Then her neck swells further.

"My word," Sesia bows. "Should these dr*np SS-s even consider interfering with our arrangement they will be most sorry."

Angel doesn't look back at Denman or spare Rye a glance.

"Drunken pissbums?" She whispers as she leaves her tiny home for good. The way Sesia said it was so vulgar with the vibrations coming from her throat Angel figures she just issued a pretty vile insult toward the two men.

"Close enough, my new friend," Sesia puts an arm around Angel's shoulders. There's no need for either to direct the other to Angel's lab. "Close enough."

CHAPTER 24

"You're running low, brother," Tong drops into the seat on the other side of Rye's small table. He holds a bottle of low-end whiskey, all Tong will relinquish his credits for. He stands and spins the chair around before straddling it and leaning over the dented, metal backrest.

Rye grunts and pushes his glass across the table before picking up his own bottle and knocking back the half-inch at the bottom. *Barrington's* off duty bar, The Gin Palace, resonates with as much noise as a hangar during emergency deployment. Bad lighting, a mixed bag of tasteless and seedy decorations and centuries-old Earth dance music ricocheting around the metal interior make Rye's head hurt. He doesn't need to wait for morning to feel like shit, just stepping through the beaded curtain covering the door is enough to make him regret his choice to go inside.

"Drunken pissbums," Rye toasts and Tong shares a moustache splitting grin as they touch the rims of their shot glasses.

"A month at Genetics," Tong empties his glass and coughs the burn from his chest. He holds his right hand up and rotates it at the wrist. "I did something to myself."

Rye shakes his head. He doesn't feel the whiskey burn any more though he pretends he does in the hopes a bout of forced coughing will give Tong time to move on to another topic.

"I mean," Tong adds. "A man needs to be sure he's made a sufficient contribution to the next generation. Might have hurt my wrist."

Then he makes a big show of massaging the tendons, letting his eyes half close as he works his thumb around his wrist.

"At least going to Toll didn't happen," he adds, leaning in. "Atom sure made friends quick when we got back. Says the T*kit does amazing things with the gills in her throat."

Rye stopped looking at Atom's table when Tong sat down. The tracker sits close to Sesia across from Scarlet. Neither woman has said a word to Rye in the week they've been back and come to think of it, Scarlet didn't talk to Rye while they were at Genetics either. At the time, he thought it to be a combination of fighting with Tong again and the fact they were housed in different wings of the building. He doesn't blame her anger for Angel being caught. It's all his fault anyway. As an analyst, he should have planned for Todd talking to Acquisitions, forbade Scarlet from documenting Angel anywhere and left Angel behind on Helm-Dent with a simple drop and run instead of sticking around.

In a way, he was relieved to get caught since it kept her close though it's small comfort for the loss of his daughter. Quinn could be any where by now and nothing in the computers on Helm-Dent yielded any clues. Angel was right, only the transport knew the destination.

Angel hasn't been around much, only attending briefings and other meetings with Sesia so Rye hasn't had a chance to speak with her. Maybe it's better he doesn't. This morning her lab coat was on inside out and she'd put her hair up on the left, leaving the right side unbrushed. She spent the hour staring at Denman as if daring him to say something and though the angry colour in the man's throat suggested he was close to coming down on her, he managed to hold his tongue.

"Might want to go see the doc," Rye tilts his head toward Scarlet, though she's more likely to hurt him than help. Angel's capture on Helm-Dent and presence aboard *The Barrington* ripped the old wound that divided Tong and Scarlet back on Constant wide open.

"Nah," Tong says but he waves to the other table just the same, twisting the wrist he claimed to be overworked and showing no sign of discomfort.

Atom waves but Scarlet glares at Tong until Rye wants to sweat for him.

"You're a dick, you know," Tong refills their glasses.

"Ouch," Rye cups himself. "You know how to grab my short ones."

"I have enormous dick recognition skills and you're a dick," Tong repeats. "Plus, since we're genetically identical yours look like mine so I have a good idea where to grab you. Talk to Angel yet?"

"I would if I could get her alone."

"Liar. She'll be alone for the next few hours if Atom gets the Investigator in his quarters."

Rye waggles his empty glass at Tong but instead of pouring, his older brother gives him the bottle.

"Suit yourself, ass-wig," Tong lurches his chair forward. The grind of metal on metal gets Rye's attention as the angry, vibrating scrape invades his body starting with his ass. "I'll tell you what I'm going to do and if I don't get killed in the next five minutes swear you'll do the same."

Nothing to do but shrug. The whiskey makes Tong's voice grind more like an annoying bug to swat than a sober man giving a drunk good advice.

"I'm going over to Scarlet," Tong lowers his voice. "I will ask, very nicely, if she'll go with me to speak in private. If she doesn't gut me, I'm going to find somewhere quiet and tell her something I should have said a long time ago."

"You're an ass-wig?" Rye slurs.

"You got it. I'll tell her I love her and I pissed her off after Angel died because I'm a selfish bastard who couldn't face losing her the way you lost Angel. I tried to forget her with other women even when it hurt her. I was an idiot and I'm more scared of losing her than ever."

Before Rye can spit out any astonishment, Tong gets to his feet and marches straight across the room, dodging a drunk second gen female with another in a none too friendly headlock. Rye loses sight of the pair, their gray uniforms a blur against the steel surroundings. The two roll under a table as laughter erupts around them.

Tong doesn't look back and Rye can't shake the feeling he could be watching his brother take his last few steps. As he reaches the table, Scarlet turns to face the wall and Tong shifts his weight as his lips start to move. She ignores him and he tries again, clutching his pant leg over and over in one unsteady hand.

Then he speaks a third time.

Rye can't make out Sesia's words but she stands to smack Scarlet in the side of the head, hard enough to knock her bun loose. Then she elbows Atom to shut him up but not before his laughter carries over the noise of the bar.

"You have a problem," Denman announces, turning Tong's chair around before sitting down. He sniffs the contents of Tong's bottle and shakes his head to knock the cheap smell loose. Then he puts it as far away as he can, perching it on the edge of the table.

Rye stares ahead, seeking Denman's icy gray eyes. The second gen implant and natural eye don't have the same colour. He never really noticed since he never really looked but his good buzz makes unusual things appear a hell of a lot more interesting.

"Sober up, Rye," Denman continues. "We have a major discipline issue with a member of your team."

"Not my team," Rye argues then bites his tongue. Denman leans closer, bumping the table and sending Tong's bottle to the floor. A quick glance to see if his brother notices reveals both Tong and Scarlet gone and Atom plays with Sesia's hand as she taps her tablet with the other.

"As of an hour ago, I've assigned Angel to be your problem."

"Sir?" Rye sobers though he'll still need chemical help to shake off the alcohol.

"For the past month, she refuses to adhere to our standard of dress, addresses me as Buddy if she has to call me anything and although she pays lip service to my repeated orders to get her shit together she doesn't. I've confiscated three pink socks, two yellow ones and a few I classified as green in my log though she wore black today so I may have succeeded in limiting her access to the chemicals required to alter her Core issued clothing.

"Last week when I spoke to her about it, she excused herself to collect something she said I'd be interested in and as soon as she sealed herself in another room, she activated the decontamination cycle in the lab."

Rye snorts. The hair and lab coat were bad enough.

"Not funny, mister," Denman orders and Rye tightens his lips. "I was lucky to get out with only a rash on the back of my neck. If I file charges, she leaves with Sesia and I lose any chance to prove her statement Helm-Dent has nothing to do with the trade in stolen implants.

"In spite of her best efforts not to help me out, I'm doing her a favour by verifying Helm-Dent is a dead end. At this point she's confined to her lab or to quarters unless she has an escort. This passive aggressive shit's going to stop and you're going to take care of it. She's your Secondary Comms Officer, on loan to Investigator Sesia for the duration of her visit. She will be limited to station bound duties for the time being and though I doubt seventy percent efficiency will get her back in the field, she's still an asset to Blue Team and to *The Barrington*.

"She will not be permitted to carry on like this. It reflected poorly on me and now it reflects poorly on you. Good night."

CHAPTER 25

Behind Angel, Sesia's recently installed computers whir and slosh, overriding the hum of its massive cooling tower. She figures more of her body fluids move through the gene sequencer than through her own tissues. After spending the day exclaiming over the detailed graphs and tables spilling out onto over a dozen over-sized monitors, Sesia took a break and left for drinks with Atom and Scarlet.

Those two, at least, are as upset as Angel over what happened on Helm-Dent. Unlike Rye whose smug and cold attitude deserves every ugly thought she can come up with.

Scarlet set Angel up with a heating blanket to ease the stiffness and ache in her shoulders. It wasn't too bad until Rye came back from Genetics and she got herself locked up in the lab. Other than required briefings where she sticks close to Sesia, she hasn't spent more than a couple of hours in the tight quarters the two women share.

At first, Angel believed her silver data blocks were the key to unloading Aphid computer code and turning it into something she could at least begin to analyze. Sesia hadn't gotten very far with that same data block as with the other prototypes Angel left behind. Though she followed the same process laid out in Angel's notes, she only succeeded in burning out two of the six prototypes before she gave up. The other four failed in one way or another and Sesia spent the last two years duplicating Angel's manufacturing techniques with the same failed results.

It turned out the DNA in Angel's saliva allowed the data cubes to interface fully with Aphid computers. Other Comms Officers could only unload Aphid databanks with the complicated interaction from their built-in CPUs but all they got was complicated, useless Aphid data.

Angel's devices used a unique mix of pattern matching algorithms to partially pre-digest downloaded Aphid data. Her saliva, she theorized, caused the Aphid devices to believe they connected to other Aphid systems thus removing several layers of encryption Core had previously been unable to break.

Sesia agreed.

The device Angel faces off against tonight arrived several hours earlier in a secure shipment of Aphid tech captured over the past three decades. Sesia went through miles of Intelligence bureaucracy to have them released to her for research. The bulky handheld device sat in stores for more than twenty years and won't give its secrets up to Angel no matter how much spit she shoves in the maintenance port.

Through their quick, initial assessment of all handhelds they received, the women discovered Angel could unlock most devices less than ten years old.

Sesia suspects the timeframe coincides loosely with Allen's capture. She also believed Allen's DNA gave the Aphids the ability to interface on a biological level with hardware, an ability they lacked, but the hardware she removed during autopsies of the bodies Rye brought back from Whistler suggested that was no longer the case.

I can come get you, Sesia's words appear on Angel's tablet. Their private communications channel operates invisibly and undetected by the Core data network. A huge breach in protocol, same as making Scarlet's private log truly private, but Angel knows Sesia won't say a word and it's the only way the two can speak without concern their conversation might be overheard. Sesia discreetly monitors Core communications for word on Quinn and Giselle and promised Angel she would reunite with them.

Is Rye still there? Angel replies.

Just me and Atom. Scarlet left with Tong.

Uh oh.

Angel can almost see her friend shrug, throat puffing up in resignation. There's nothing they can do to stop two adults from settling their differences in private.

I think I'll grab some sleep in the back room, save you coming all this way, Angel answers. *Hint hint.*

Atom says you're the best, Sesia types in response then the channel closes.

There's nothing to do but work, anyway. Might as well leave Sesia to their quarters.

With her back to the lab door, Angel hears the access pad out in the hall hum as it scans a palm. She steels herself for another round with Denman. He hasn't shown his face since the decontamination incident other than to announce the stripping of her station-board privileges.

"Got a minute?" Rye asks.

Angel pretends she doesn't hear and gathers up the Aphid handheld, two of her silver data blocks, a small magnifying lens and Sesia's micro-tool kit. She keeps her back to him as she moves to the lockup and secures the items with the devices she tested earlier.

"For Christ sakes, Angel. I don't have time for attitude, insubordination or any of the bullshit you've given Denman."

"Make it quick," Angel raises her chin. "I have work to do."

Rye glances at her feet before moving across the room, keeping her workbench between them though he stays near the door.

"Denman reassigned you to Blue Team and you know how I run things."

She stops listening since this will be the same talk Denman wouldn't stop giving her. With her independence taken and her daughter gone she isn't going to listen to Rye either. Core used to be her home, her cause and everything else she had to live for. Though she is back in uniform and on *The Barrington*, she won't be Core again. Not in her heart, at least.

Rye rests his knuckles on the bench and opens his mouth, ready to act as her commander again. She recognizes the tightening around his eyes and the way his jaw works, having seen it in his 'welcome to doing things my way' speech he gave her almost seven years earlier. Then, she took in every word, blindly happy to serve with third gens and anxious to prove herself first by making a good impression and later by doing a good job.

His mouth snaps shut and he clears his throat.

"Angel," he starts then although his lips continue to move, no sound comes and he gives up. His hands come off the workbench, one falls to his side and the other plays with something in his pants pocket.

"You've heard it before," he shrugs, defeated. Although his sigh clouds the air with the fresh scent of whiskey, his physical self-control and steady voice suggest he either drank little or had help sobering up after leaving The Gin Palace. "That's not who we are anymore, you and me."

Rye pulls his hand from his pocket. A disc about the size of his palm hides in his grip. From what Angel can see, it appears to be clear with something embedded inside.

"I made it," Rye explains with reverence, revealing a reluctance to let the thing go. He places it on the workbench and slides it toward her. "I only knew Quinn a day and miss her like hell. I don't even want to imagine how difficult this must be for you. Your strength, Angel. Inside. Is the most amazing thing."

The clear disk holds the picture of Angel and Quinn she found Rye looking at back on Helm-Dent. Quinn's short, dark hair covered her still-elongated head and was taken no more than a few minutes after her birth. Several small butterflies native to the planet and coated in clumpy pink paint by four-year-old hands cluster about the perimeter.

Angel studies Rye before sliding on to her work stool and wrapping her hands around the picture. No sharp edges mark the outside, in fact no seam or flaw remains to suggest how it was formed. She holds it to her lips and inhales, imagining the scents of little girls, hidden fields and fresh air. It's nearly enough to hide the lingering hint of resin.

"You turned us in," Angel holds the picture over her heart. Although Denman's explanation of how he caught her sounds plausible, she still feels betrayed by Rye and blames him, in part, for what happened on Helm-Dent. "In the end, what you wanted meant nothing. Or maybe it did, I don't know. Maybe, by the time Denman arrived it was too late to prevent it. Doesn't matter now."

"Angel," Rye speaks, sharpening his tone. "What the hell else was I supposed to do? Admit to Denman we smuggled you aboard *Titan*, hid you from *The Barrington* and diverted course to secretly deposit you on Helm-Dent where they, by the way, steal Core soldiers and also have hidden one of the most advanced third gen, maybe fourth gen soldiers Genetics has ever seen?

"Once Denman caught up to us, how were we supposed to stay close to you without claiming we planned to turn you in all along? To try and find a way to get you off the station and back to Quinn?"

She knew that already, from both Scarlet and Atom, but needed Rye to admit it.

"That's all I needed to hear."

Angel's breath catches as Denman appears behind Rye. She didn't hear him palm in or the movement of the door. Backing up against Sesia's computers, she steps sideways to stay between Denman and Rye though she doesn't miss Denman's drawn weapon and deep scowl.

"Over there," Denman looks at Rye and nods toward Angel. "As I suspected. Traitors."

Both remain silent. Angel presses her face into Rye's shoulder, yielding control of his fate to the base commander even though there's nothing he can say to undo the words Denman overheard.

Rye swallows Angel's hand in one of his. Pressed between, the picture warms through the minutes it takes for Denman to speak again. Angel's other hand clings to his bicep and wrinkles his fresh shirt.

"To be quite honest, Rye," Denman says, holstering his sidearm though his hand remains relaxed and too near the gun for Rye to stop worrying. "I've known you for many years and expected this from you."

Expected what? Until he found Angel alive in Whistler, he's been an exemplary third gen and has the service record to prove it.

Denman raises a hand as if to silence Rye's internal indignation.

"Hear me out, soldier. I suspect when I finish speaking your opinion of me will change. What I'm going to tell you has nothing to do with what happened on Helm-Dent and you'd be hearing it anyway. Even if I hadn't walked in on your admission."

Angel lifts her chin but Rye only spares her a glance. Denman just overheard him admit to treason and walked in, gun drawn. Now, an expedited trial will wait at least a few minutes. Still on edge, Rye slips an arm around Angel's shoulder. After his confession, there is no point hiding anymore. He can't be in any more trouble for a simple public act of affection than he is already.

Treason carries a swift sentence of death.

Denman removes his sidearm and takes Sesia's stool then leans over, placing the gun out of reach.

"I was only eighteen, when I was called to Genetics. I'm not just barely a second gen, in some areas I rival a third gen;

language abilities in particular. But you know how we're rated. Lowest aptitude. So I'm a good second gen," he shrugs.

"I didn't give my contribution, or legacy as they called it then, any further thought until six years later. I woke up in what I guessed to be a six person transport with one hell of a headache and a very pretty and apologetic pilot. I assumed it was she who tied me up.

"This does not go beyond your ears," Denman pauses. "Not even to Tong."

At a loss to understand where the commander's story is headed, Rye can only listen. The longer the man talks, the more time Rye has to avoid facing charges. For the moment, keeping quiet to Tong doesn't make sense.

"I don't have time for a long explanation."

"Okay," Angel answers, her confidential tone matches Denman's and she seems to get what he wants much better than Rye. Rye turns, wrapping his arms around Angel to feel her close for the few minutes he believes remain before Denman takes him away.

"She is first gen," Denman explains. "Somehow she found out her legacy and mine produced two sons and, as she described it, she went a little nuts. When she joined Core, she had no interest in children but when she learned she had two she struggled. Her grief became too much and before she knew it she was AWOL in a stolen transport with a kidnapped soldier hogtied in the cargo hold."

He raises his hand to indicate who that soldier was although he already said it was him.

Denman grabs at his trousers as he continues, a gesture both Rye and his brother use to redirect nervousness. "I have to admit, I shared her joy about our boys though I quickly angered for her. I wanted to find them and give them to her. We never understood why we connected so easily and it was hard to back down about stealing them. In the end, I relented, agreeing that since they were already two and a half and didn't know us, taking them from their surrogate parents would be a terrible thing.

"We broke the rules. Not only had she kidnapped me, she'd stolen enough fertility drugs to overpower our implants. I left her two months later, pregnant and as in love with me as I was with her. There were some tough questions, upon my return, but in the end they believed I escaped. When our daughter was three, my girl and I contacted Core and made a bargain.

"She returned to service on the condition she raise our child and I be involved as well. Core agreed our daughter's emotional stability was paramount over all other considerations. Our boys have two sisters now. Both serve with their mother and stay silent regarding the bargain that allowed them to remain together."

"Rye," Angel tugs at his sleeve.

"You can be so damned dense," Denman mutters. "It's taken a month for me to make a similar arrangement for Quinn. It wasn't easy, Genetics will come to her. Placing her with a surrogate family would be devastating. Should she turn up, she'll be returned to Angel."

"You're Rye's father, aren't you?" Angel asks and Rye finds himself clinging to her as a rush of thought overwhelms him. It explains so damn much. "Your bargain, placed Rye and Tong with you when they came to Core, didn't it?"

"Indeed."

"And if not for Quinn?" Rye stammers out an unclear question before losing it in a wash of less clear questions and bitter accusations. Adrenaline pumps through his system, a powerful charge, and without realizing when he let go of Angel, he feels the edge of the table flex under his grip. His own sense of family connects him with feelings for his sisters and resentment they'd been kept apart.

"You never would have known," Denman speaks softly as if aware of how close Rye is to losing control. Everything they've gone through in the past month, grief and guilt and anger, focuses to a sharp point. "That was part of the bargain as well. Although if Quinn comes to live on *The Barrington* it may become a difficult secret to keep. She's a beautiful child and there's no doubt who her father is."

Angel keeps an arm around Rye's middle as he bends his knees, considering getting over the table and to Denman.

"Son?" Denman tries as Angel rubs a hand in firm circles on his back.

"Sshhh," she whispers. "This is good, Rye. Relax."

He does, in stages, de-escalating his temper so he can start to process Denman's words.

"As I said," Denman continues. "I don't have much time. We've received a distress communication from Giselle Keller —"

"What?" Rye demands as the fading adrenaline leaves him aching and nauseous.

"Other than coordinates and the fact it was sent to your attention, I have little to go on. The message degraded significantly from the time it was sent several days ago. It appears that where they landed, Aphids were waiting for them. *Titan* and *Arsenal* will mobilize with full assault crews. You have fifteen minutes to gear up and board."

"Where are we going?" Rye demands, stepping around the table to face Denman.

As he waits for an answer, Angel presses herself in between, an arm around them both. She trembles and Denman pulls her close and places his other hand on Rye's shoulder. With Denman's gentle squeeze, Rye experiences something he hasn't felt from a parent in a long time. Reassurance.

"Constant."

The single word scares him more than any other planet Denman could name.

"We're going to get my grand-daughter from Constant."

CHAPTER 26

Angel shifts her weight. She found a quiet niche between the gangways leading down to *Titan* and up to *Arsenal* and hugs her duffel as a shield between her and the chaos of anti-grav sleds, loaders and shouts. Trouble is, nobody told her which vessel she's supposed to board. *Titan,* she figures, but the wrong choice will leave her stuck with strangers for the nine days of nausea and disorientation caused by overdriving the engines.

"Angel?"

She turns to see Denman a few steps behind her as he makes his way down the gangway from *Arsenal.*

"Sir," she draws her hands up to make sure her quick bun stayed put. Once she finds her quarters she'll make use of a brush and tidy it up. "I, um."

Denman raises a brow. There's so much of him in Rye and Tong. She used to think it was because they served together for nearly two decades but now she knows the real reason, their similarity is nearly complete.

"I won't need my socks back," she shrugs, not sure what else to say. Sorry doesn't cover the bad example she's been or the embarrassment her behaviour caused Denman.

"I hope not," he steps closer. Near enough to loom over her and grimaces as though she's in shit. Angel cringes until she hears his gentle voice. "We're doing everything we can, understand?"

"Sir," Rye interrupts. "Blue Team has boarded *Titan*, we have the helm."

"Red has the helm, Rye," Denman takes his elbow and leads him to *Titan's* gangway, leaving Angel behind. On Rye's part, at least, their outward relationship hasn't changed but then Denman hasn't had the chance to explain the rules for their relationship when not speaking in private. "We've uploaded recents on Constant, though there isn't much considering Core abandoned the system to Aphid hands six years ago. Your team was there last and you're going to get up to speed and brief me. Then the real work starts. We have a delicate assault and rescue to pull off and I won't allow any mistakes."

"No, Sir," Rye answers.

Angel tries to hold her bag but it slips from her arms, hitting the floor with a thud. She leans against a roped down pallet of rations rather than drop to the floor with her gear. Granted, she lost her weapons privileges after running the decon protocol on Denman but she grabbed her clutch of custom data blocks, got to her quarters, packed and onto the lift to *Titan's* docking pylon with minutes to spare. With the round picture tight in her fist, she focuses, daring to keep her spirit intact until the ships leave.

"Angel," Rye shouts and she looks up, expecting she'll be told to step back before the gangway shuts down. "You're holding us up. Get aboard."

Her duffle slows her first two steps then she stumbles while picking it up from the deck. The gangway doesn't sway beneath her as it did when Denman and Rye walked down it and as much as she wants to hurry, a few extra seconds might allow the heat to fade from her cheeks and the sting in her eyes to ease. Halfway through, her stomach lurches with the switch from *Barrington's* gravity to *Titan's*.

When she reaches the airlock and the door seals behind them, Denman contacts the command deck to order disconnection of the umbilicals and immediate launch for Constant. The rattle of clamps releasing resonates with a deep thud and Angel has to brace a hand on the wall since the pilot starts to turn them from *The Barrington* before activating the inertial fields.

Angel holds her chin high in an effort to rise above another hopeless moment, one in which she can't see herself being of any use at all. Before she has a chance to decide if she should ask what she can do or if she should simply find her quarters, the pilot on the command deck punches the engines. The stars outside blur with gray walls and Angel sucks in a deep breath, fighting to remain conscious as she slams into Rye. Departure coincides with full involvement of the inertial fields and gives the sickening sensation of standing both inside and outside the ship at the same time.

Rye doesn't seem affected by the sudden acceleration though he grunts with her impact into his chest. Of course, he's bred to respond to jolts and anything else as they happen. With a nervous system capable of detecting the most subtle movement and reacting before the most human parts of his brain are aware, he'll never find himself on his ass or in the arms of someone with whom he was furious only fifteen minutes earlier.

At least she didn't start this trip flat out on the deck. Even with chemical enhancements, Angel preferred to experience expedited launches in a chair.

"We're moving," Rye says and she doesn't fight the hand cradling her head or strong fingers pressing into her back. Even though the inertial field's full strength holds things together, Angel's stomach senses the conflict between the velocity of the ship and the field's task of keeping her place in it. Once they reach travel speed, the sensation will ease but not by much and will ramp up again with deceleration into Constant's orbit.

"I'll be in my quarters," Angel takes a step back, nervous she's lost too much of her inner soldier to get there without vomit on her boots and those of anyone unlucky enough to be nearby. Seventy percent. The number defines her now. The last trip out, she sat with Atom on *Titan's* command deck and interpreted the signals he tracked. Now they have Officer Glass and their team isn't in command.

"Report to me in the strategy room, Angel," Denman orders. Before she can wobble sideways to avoid another dangerous lurch of her stomach, he takes her elbow as if sensing her vertigo before she does.

"I don't really remember Constant," she argues while making her best effort to sound like she isn't about to be sick. Even before, she'd never been included in a strategy meeting. She'd never even been privy to the big pranks unless they were pulled on her then she found out.

"You know the people of Helm-Dent and have more information than anyone on Gustav Keller," Denman walks away. "Ten minutes."

"I forgot," Rye offers a tight smile. "First gens tell me this sucks."

"Civilian here," Angel raises a hand. "Never liked this much before. I still don't understand why Denman wants me in the briefing."

Rye guides her down the tunnel, taking his hand from the small of her back when a couple of grunts from Red Team pass the other way.

"He said why. You're the expert on Keller."

"Okay," she concedes though she didn't know Keller other than regular visits to the escape pods he built and designed or her use of his lab. "I'm keeping my mouth shut about us and Quinn unless he says something about us first. The last thing I need is Core to come down on us and go back on their word. I don't trust them, too many years of the way I thought things were done."

"I feel the same way," Rye agrees as they reach the main deck and he tilts his head toward the hall leading to female quarters. "See you in the briefing."

Rye waits at the end of the corridor for Angel. All she had to do was drop off her bag though she might be gabbing with Scarlet. In the minutes he spent waiting he's had time to review the cabin assignments and found they were put together. Also, to his consternation, Red has the helm for the entire flight meaning each team member will rotate through time at the controls. Their lead will only take over in the event of an emergency otherwise she'll be involved in briefings with the other leads; four on *Titan* and another four on *Arsenal* for a total force of more than two hundred. Denman doesn't screw around. Eight units with full orbital support of two expedition class starships and their bays jammed with ten-man strikers, each capable of advanced scanning, independent tactical analysis and unloading enough on-foot firepower to make a damned good dent in any surface resistance.

A glance at his tablet shows only thirty seconds until Denman's briefing starts so Rye gives up waiting. Like a fool, he supposes. Angel knows the way to the strategy room and doesn't need a tour guide but after watching the colour flee from her face he worries.

The noise from the strategy room reaches Rye's ears as soon as he finishes his elbows and ankles slide down the smooth steel handrails paralleling the seventy degree pitch of the stairs to the third deck. As he rounds the corner to step in, he's assaulted by several loud conversations between a semi-circle of visual images of the leads on *Arsenal* facing the four already present on *Titan* and Rye's primary team; Tong, Scarlet, Glass and Atom. Most of the talk is banter and under normal circumstances Rye would let it go for another minute but with Denman present, he palms the door shut and sits.

He expects one empty seat, his, but there's a second next to Scarlet.

Angel hasn't made it on time.

Rye does a double take at the pink moustache burn above Scarlet's fair, freckled top lip. The redness grows nearly as intense as the wolfish stare in Tong's eyes. No doubting whose moustache burned the medic. Whatever he said to her seemed to have worked since Tong still breathes.

"We ready?" Denman stands, clearing his throat. The last of the talk dies out around the table. "Rye, where is your Secondary Comms Officer?"

"Sir," Rye shifts. "I can—"

Thankfully, the door whisks open, interrupting his offer to look for her.

"Sorry," Angel says as the door closes behind her. Her pale skin is marked by tiny purple bruises around her eyes and there's no mistaking the evidence she's been throwing up.

"Take a seat," he gestures to the empty one next to Scarlet. The medic gives Angel a worried nod and when Angel shakes her head, a derisive snort comes from one of the monitors. Forge, leader of Gold Team doesn't hide her dislike of anything not third gen.

"Comment, Forge?" Denman invites.

"This isn't a training run, Sir," her image seems to glare at Angel even though the four leads on *Arsenal* face a bank of monitors. "I do believe this first gen was unqualified when we last met and is even less so now. Seventy percent when she isn't too busy hurling to get to briefings on time? This liability will get my men killed."

Rye debates jumping the table and going at the monitor and Angel flushes, two rough pink ovals against her pale skin. Denman seems to sense his growing anger and holds a palm up to Rye, low enough below the table that Forge can't see. The elitist bitch knocked Angel aside on the stairs once that Rye witnessed, bruising her up in the resulting fall to the bottom. Angel ignored her, got up, straightened her uniform and walked away until Forge accused her of sleeping her way up through the ranks. The brief fight left Angel unconscious in the Med Bay and Forge stripped of all credits and denied shore leave for six months. Forge ignored her after that but never let go of her dislike for Angel.

As much as it rankles, Denman has to get opinions like Forge's out in the open and turned around.

"You've read the initial briefing?" Denman asks, eyes on Forge.

"Yes, Sir," she answers, even more self assured than before.

"I thought so," Denman sighs in disappointment and Forge's smile falters. "Blue Team's Secondary Comms Officer single handedly took out two Aphids to save the life of a third gen before she was killed on Constant. You're an idiot if you don't want that kind of fight on your side. Seventy percent or no, she's earned her place."

"Yes, Sir," Forge doesn't even try and hide her surprise. The background data provided by Denman contains the details of Angel's actions on Constant and it's apparent the Gold Lead's prejudice made her skip the first gen's role.

"As you're aware," Denman continues as if Forge hadn't spoken. "One of my tasks is the investigation of disappearances from cryo and subsequent appearance of implants on the black market and in Core's very stores. Tracing these items back through inventory has yielded little and I believed to have found the cause in the group that stole Angel's body from cryo.

"While the people on Helm-Dent were stealing from cryo, I am satisfied it was not for the merciless harvesting of implants. They only took bodies of those with no chance of reanimation and inspection of their records shows only implants these people no longer required or wanted were returned to Core to support our efforts against the Aphids."

Angel allows a nod to Denman as he continues.

"As pointed out in my initial briefing, the people of Helm-Dent fled when I arrived in orbit and we have since received a distress call from them. They evacuated to Constant and report Aphid forces present on the planet. As long as they've avoided the greens we have some hope there will be survivors."

"Sir?" Dice, on the monitor next to Forge speaks. "Why would they evacuate to Constant? It's been in Aphid hands for half a decade. If they're involved with Core, albeit secretly as your briefing states, would they not have known?"

"Angel?" Denman sits, handing the briefing over to her.

With a thick swallow, Angel stands, swaying in spite of her hold on the table and loses a little more colour.

"Sir," she says. "Truth is, we didn't know our evacuation point. He never said and took that information to the grave. Yes, we knew Constant wasn't a good place for humans—"

"If I may?" Dice speaks again. Nothing short of banning him from the strategy session would prevent the Gray Team lead from interrupting. "Who? Who never said?"

Angel hesitates, looking to Denman for guidance. She's smart and used to keeping Helm-Dent quiet. The smallest incline of his head tells Angel to continue.

"Gustav Keller," Angel says. "Our colony was founded fifty years ago by Gustav Keller."

"He's dead," Dice exclaims then the voices of the other leads drown him out.

Angel waits for the outburst to subside before she continues.

"Keller's reasons for disappearing aren't anything I can share," she continues then talks over Dice as he opens his mouth again. "He designed the facilities on Helm-Dent including the evacuation tunnels and ships. When he died ten years ago, Constant was safe. There was no way to check or change the destination. We tried."

Denman rises and gestures for Angel to sit.

"Our last intelligence on Constant suggests several Aphid outposts in and around the original human colony so if the people of Helm-Dent have encountered them, it's a good place to start. I don't have to tell you our comms are useless near their tech and making visual confirmation of their facilities will tell them we've arrived.

"Additionally, the escape vehicle we're looking for has the ability to remain invisible to our scanners, no surprise since it was designed by Keller. It left Helm-Dent orbit undetected by *Titan*.

"Among the people we're out to rescue are Giselle Keller, daughter of Gustav and a four-year-old girl. Preliminary assessment of the child places her as fourth gen—"

The table explodes again and questions for Denman quickly turn to arguments among the leads over whether such a thing is even possible.

"Enough," Denman shouts. "The child in question is Angel's. She's been through cryo so talk to your medic if you aren't clear on how it can happen. The child's father is a third gen."

Rye's too focused on Angel to notice Denman points at him. She doesn't look up until the room quiets again.

"Genetics has agreed it's in Quinn's best interest she remain with her parents on *The Barrington*," Denman continues. "There is no doubt you and the entire station will figure it out upon our return so to minimize gossip and distraction I've told you now. I suggest you take some time to review all the data. I want a mistake proof plan in six hours.

"Dismissed."

The grinding of chairs on deck plates and the shuffle of people around the table goes on until Angel, Rye and Denman remain.

"Rye," Denman starts. "Core instructed me to keep you, Angel and Quinn quiet but as I told our team it isn't reasonable to think that will happen. I do ask you keep your personal relationship as discreet as possible. We're still at war. Private fraternization is fine, that goes for everyone aboard, but in public we're all soldiers."

"Sir," Angel mutters and crosses her arms around her stomach.

"And us?" Rye asks, still angry that so much was kept from him for so long.

"We missed a lot. The same reasoning that brings Quinn to us kept you with your surrogates and if yours mean as much to you as mine do to me," Denman gathers his thoughts. "They're your parents. I'm your commander. I haven't earned any more than that.

"I believe Core is beginning to come around on their policies regarding reproduction and families. Mine was the first arrangement I made with Core and Genetics but yours was not my second. There are a lot more families like ours around. Not all surrogate parents on Vix are actual surrogates. Either by accident or taking things into their own hands, we find ways to do what the civilians do.

"I know I have more to share with you about my wife and your sisters."

"Wife?"

Denman smiles. "No other word for her, is there? Nobody for me but her, not in all the galaxies.

"Look, I know what it feels like to see your children in danger. Mine are trained and seasoned soldiers with Core resources behind them. I believe Quinn won't be harmed, nor will the others. I have to. Take some time, you two."

CHAPTER 27

"Sshhh, sshhh," Rye's weight on the mattress sends Angel's stomach rolling and she reaches out to press a palm to the cool metal bulkhead inches from her nose. After the initial briefing, they walked to his cabin and without any exchange of words, curled up in his bunk until she fell asleep. There had been whispers between Rye and Tong while she threw up in his head, and since then the upper bunk remains empty and Tong hasn't returned. "I brought you something to drink, if you think you can handle it."

When Forge spoke up, Angel expected it would be the beginning of the teasing but there'd been no such thing. Not that it didn't feel good to hear Denman tell her to stow it. She'd feel even better if she didn't feel so damned sick although she doesn't expect to get used to high speed travel where the excessive velocity doesn't feel precisely constant.

With a sigh, she rolls into Rye and makes a quiet prayer the return trip will be more manageable.

"Did you sleep okay?"

"I shouldn't have but I want to be there, now. Every hour..."

"Sit," Rye sits and offers a bottle of green liquid. "Electrolytes, mostly. Scarlet says there's nothing in it you don't eat anyway so shouldn't make you feel worse."

"You've seen Scarlet?" Angel feels relief the medic knows where she is since she didn't return to their shared quarters.

Rye shrugs and rests a palm on her forehead then her cheek as she eases herself upright.

"What?"

"Drink. You don't feel warm."

The first sip goes down a little too easily and Angel pauses, certain it's going to bounce right back up.

"I missed the strategy session," she slumps over in disappointment with herself.

"That was ten hours ago."

"Damn. I guess I've still got time to get up to speed."

Rye looks away and she knows his tight nod. He doesn't want to talk about it.

"Rye? Who do I deploy with?"

"You don't," he stands, turning his back on her and paces into the head before turning around and taking a seat at the desk.

"Son of a bitch, Rye," Angel snaps around a mouthful of electrolytes jammed in her throat. "You need everyone. We can't leave the secondaries stuck on the ship."

"We're not, Angel."

"Just me?"

Another stupid nod.

"My daughter is down there," she starts with the unfair and obvious remark since she can always ease up on him later. "I wouldn't leave you behind."

"That's not your call," he grumbles, colour rising in his cheeks.

"I won't be held back," Angel gets to her feet and wobbles back onto the mattress. "Denman said—"

"You can't even walk on your own. That's my daughter down there too and if I have half my attention on keeping her mother alive I'm not going to be any good for her or my unit."

"I'm not asking you to do that," Angel crosses her arms. "We need all hands."

"This isn't a debate, soldier," Rye stands and stalks to the door, his face a hard mask.

"One person made all the difference the last time we were on Constant," she blurts out though it sounds more like a sob. "To Tong. That person was me. You think it's fair to bring me so close then expect me to do nothing?"

"Angel—"

"Don't bother. I'll find my own way there," Angel slaps her palm on the panel next to his door. When nothing happens she hits it again then presses her stinging hand under her arm before trying the other. She turns on him. "You going to lock me in or let me out?"

Rye stares at her through his brows.

"I'm not untrained and I'm not careless and I certainly won't wait up here. You heard Denman, he said I can do it."

Rye's eyes narrow even further. "You going over my head on this?"

"I shouldn't have to," Angel lowers her shoulders but not her stare. "If all eyes are on the planet I'm in even more danger up here. *Titan* and *Arsenal* will have their hands full if a unit from their support fleet shows up. I'm not stupid. Or reckless. I never have been."

Then she sees it, the moment he surrenders. He drops into the chair, closed eyes toward the ceiling.

Titan shudders, stirring her stomach with a tremor only her civilian body can feel and she chances the few steps to Rye. After bracing her hip on the desk, she crooks her finger under his chin and tilts his face to hers.

"I'm sure we can make this work."

Rye drops his chin and uses it to lift her fingers then brushes them with his lips.

"I told Denman," he murmurs. "Until Tong knows. I don't want to change anything with Denman until my brother knows. It's right we figure it out together."

"Of course." It's too easy to forget Rye got an extra dose of surprises. He used to deploy with the reassurance Tong knew his shit as well as he did. Now he needs to manage a lot more distraction.

"I'll put you down with Glass in the D-10 we have designated to hold comms with *Titan* and *Arsenal*. The other D-10's have been earmarked to set down within possible comm blackout areas. Tong will be aboard coordinating whatever we can gather through the interference and overseeing the grunts designated to protect our lifeline to orbital support. You manage local sensors."

"I can do that."

The lashes under Rye's left eye twitch as he jams his hands further under his thighs.

The shakes.

Angel doesn't try and still the vibration in his hands like she did the last time.

"I need to lay down," she says, putting the focus on herself instead.

"I'll join you. Denman ordered everyone get a minimum four hours a day for the duration."

Rye squeezes in against the wall and Angel folds his pillow behind her shoulders so she can keep herself upright and finish the drink Scarlet sent. The pressure of Rye's head on her shoulder isn't likely to set her stomach off so she sips and runs her fingers through his hair until his deep, even breathing nearly puts her out as well.

Without moving enough to wake him, she retrieves her tablet from under the mattress and opens a private comm line like the one she set up with Sesia.

Scarlet? I need to ask a favour.

184

CHAPTER 28

"No Aphid comms detected on this side of the planet and no Aphid orbitals; satellites, gunships or otherwise," Atom says. He doesn't take his eyes off the complex readout on the table-sized display. Rye, Denman and the other team leads and their primary trackers crowd around as he makes his assessment. *Arsenal* links via audio only. Nobody offers an alternative to Atom's interpretation. At least it's mostly good news since the likelihood they've been detected is small but the D-10's need to go in low and blind to keep it that way.

Rye keeps an eye on Angel as she musters near her assigned D-10; full battle armour including a plasteel helmet, of which he approves, but she damned well better not take a single step from her ship unless it's about to destruct. Her bag hangs unevenly in her hand. Something heavy sits in one corner and the tough, camouflage fabric stretches into a tight crease where the broad straps connect. She glances up to make sure she isn't watched and adjusts how it sits on the ground to hide the uneven fold.

Son of a bitch.

She concealed something and Rye is fairly certain he knows what.

Angel doesn't touch it again as he goes over the general landing plan with the rest of the team. Atom's D-10 with Angel will land close to what their old intel says is the only Aphid settlement on Constant. Close enough they can still communicate with *Titan* and *Arsenal*. Ground comms will be limited by Aphid interference though if their compound is the loose network of clusters of buildings they think it is then they should have some, albeit intermittent, ground communication. The other D-10's will land around the perimeter to allow ship-to-ship communication on the ground. In theory, they'll be able to relay commands. Whether those orders reach the soldiers inside the perimeter remains to be seen.

"Load up," Denman orders. "We decompress the landing bays in ten minutes. If you're not aboard, you'll be the first off the ship when the airlock opens."

Before heading to his own D-10, earmarked for debarking his squad of six grunts to head into the northern section of the Aphid zone, he checks on Angel.

"Hey," she says as he approaches, then her eyes drop with a nervous look at the bag.

"Hey, yourself. How you feeling?"

"Better now we're sub-light."

"Ah," Rye nudges her bag with his booted toe and connects with something solid. "What did you pack?"

"Something I'm working on with Sesia," she shrugs. "Homework. I've felt too sick to get much done so I thought if it turns out I'm not needed I can get caught up."

"Uh huh," Rye squats, the bending of his knees punctuated by the groan of his body armour pieces rubbing against each other, and unzips her bag.

"Hey," she exclaims as Rye holds up a small pistol. The thigh holster also contains a double edged dagger.

"Thought so. It went missing from the armoury a few days ago. How'd you get it out?" Rye puts the weapons on a nearby bench.

Her nose flares with indignation.

186

"What do you expect me to do if Aphids breach the D-10? Show a little skin and promise them a good time if they just put their weapons down? Nobody bothered to clear me for weapons after Denman took that privilege away and I didn't bother asking because I figured the answer would be no."

"Uh huh," Rye stands and straightens his armour. "This could see you in the brig for the duration of the mission and up on some pretty stiff charges."

"Then do it."

"No," he sighs and tosses the weapons into the open top of her bag. "But damn it, Angel. You never used to be this much trouble."

"No?" She laughs. "I guess not."

Rye turns and heads to his own D-10 as he replays their quiet, private words of good luck. Failing to reinstate her was an oversight. He figured Denman restored her privileges since he took them away. He didn't even check and almost sent her to the planet unable to defend herself.

Inside, Rye groans. If he had time then he'd issue her something bigger but he doesn't. Rotating red lights fill the crowded landing bay signaling three minutes to zero atmosphere inside.

Before he steps aboard, he turns to see Tong and Scarlet with Angel. The medic has overburdened herself with supplies as usual but a look around the room shows all other medical personnel have done the same. With more than two hundred Core soldiers and twenty-some civilians to look after they need to be prepared for heavy casualties.

After Scarlet rearranges her bags, she hustles off to Rye's D-10 and Tong follows Angel aboard hers, giving Rye a wave.

Two minutes later, the D-10 vibrates with the main door opening and seconds later they lift off. Rye's display shows the D-10's separate on their planned routes, each approaching the Aphid settlement from a different direction. He pays particular attention to Angel's dot as he pilots them down through the day-side atmosphere and into the dark of Constant's night.

High cloud conceals the peaks of the mountains lining the east side of the big continent and Rye uses his location relative to *Titan* and elevation maps stored in the D-10's memory bank to avoid them. Minutes later, as the glow of re-entry fades from the hull, they descend into the foothills and eventually reach the lowlands where the original Constant settlers first founded their agricultural community.

"Rye," Atom crackles over the comms and Rye delays his descent so the curve of the planet doesn't cut them off completely. "Visual on a ship. Not Core and not Aphid, in your landing sector."

"Affirmative," Rye acknowledges as the curve of Constant cuts off narrow beam communications. "Estimated time to land three minutes."

With an hour of night left, he sets the D-10 down in a sheltered river bend. A steep rock face covered in thick trees rises above, cutting off most of the starlight and giving him a respectable hiding place. According to the map, the dark, fast-moving water is only three klicks downstream from their evacuation point six years earlier.

"Last chance to pee," he announces and earns a couple of snorts from the men and women behind him.

A burst of heavy static chokes free of the comms and he curses he doesn't have Glass or Angel aboard to fine-tune the signal. Instead, he has to waste precious seconds waiting as the onboard comms A.I. does it for him.

"Rye?" a woman's choppy voice demands. "Forge."

"I'm here, Forge," he replies.

"Rye? Damn it, no," another pause. "I hope you can hear me. Atom sent coordinates for the ship he spotted and I'm forwarding them now. We'll meet you there but I think we're further away and have a fuck of a lot of uneven ground to cover. Do you copy?"

"Copy, Forge, copy," Rye jams the talk pad down harder than he should but some days it's the only thing that works.

"I think I heard you. See you at the party, Rye. Forge out."

Rye transfers the coordinates to his tablet and waits for nods all round to make sure the grunts have them too.

"Backup's coming," he says as he goes over the route, comparing it to where the Aphid hotspots were two years ago when they last had a successful survey. Maybe he should have put them down on the opposite bank of the river but judging by how bad comms are already, he may never have heard from Forge. "Looks like we're going to get wet."

"Bugger," Angel mutters. She forgot Tong flies like a yahoo and clings to her seat to keep from rolling off it and under someone else's. The D-10 holds ten; two up front, Atom and Tong, and a crowded rear cabin with two bulkhead facing seats behind the main cabin and six others facing inward for the rest of the crew. Angel has one of the seats behind the main cabin where the console has been configured for secondary comms and her assigned task of monitoring the immediate area.

As soon as they land, six Blue Team grunts gather at the rear hatch with Tong as Glass moves to the front with Atom to coordinate comms with *Titan* and any of their ground force they can reach.

When Angel signals there's no movement outside, they step out and take station in a circle a hundred meters out around the D-10.

Angel draws one of her data units from her pocket and connects it to the ports under her cramped work station. With the unit tucked away out of sight, she uses her data tablet to record a full twenty minute patrol cycle. Tong and the grunts are nothing if not punctual. It doesn't take her long to initiate a script to alert Atom if there's any movement outside other than the patrols. The only modification to the automated sensor is that it temporarily ignores her movements through a narrow strip of taller brush. She has to take the chance no Aphid will use that exact route and if they do, they'll be her problem.

After she leaves the scanned area, her silver data tab will switch back to fully automated scanning, showing a live feed of the soldiers. As long as Atom and Glass don't look up from their trance-like stares at the command console she should be able to escape them.

She wasn't even sure she'd do it, not until Tong created their perimeter and she had everything ready to go. Now, with nothing to do but sit, stare at the screen and feel useless, Angel moves. Sitting and watching seven dots on the display asks too much of her patience.

Atom and Glass don't notice as she slides the pocket door from the bulkhead just enough to block their view of the rear door. Once out of her seat, Angel pulls her heavy duffle over her shoulders and secures the secondary straps around her hips and across her chest. It weighs a fraction of what she used to carry, but with a five kilometer run into the town of Constant or anywhere else, it's more than enough to tire her.

"Son of a bitch," Atom exclaims and Angel freezes, preparing her excuses as she slinks back to her console.

"On it," Glass mutters. "Comms to *Titan* restored... shit. No, gimme a second."

Before they get a handle on the distraction, Angel opens the rear hatch and jumps over the three steps to the ground. The unexpected weight of her duffle tries to bring her to her knees and she staggers to the edge of her safe zone, catching her balance before she sets off the alarm inside the D-10.

The moon highlights stone and the silvery bark of native trees surrounding their landing site but the D-10 reflects nothing, just a dark shadow in the tight confines of the clearing. Angel verifies her bearings and sets off into the trees, hoping for a glance or two of the low mountains to her left to keep her on track. Through her condensing breath, she doesn't see the pit ahead of her until she tumbles in. The small blast crater is only a meter or so deep but her landing knocks the wind from her lungs and she clutches at her ribs for several minutes before pushing to her feet and clambering up the other side.

What the hell have I got myself into? I'm a mother, not a soldier.

A soldier would do as she's told. A mother goes on.

Angel checks her tablet. Since she's now outside the D-10's ground scanner range it will pick her up if she turns around. She sits on the edge of the crater to catch her breath and activate the thermal suit she wears under her camouflage uniform and plasteel armour. It doesn't take long to heat up.

Maybe a little further. The last time she was here she'd have run five times the distance by now carrying three times the weight and wouldn't be massaging her cramping thighs.

After tilting her head aside to work out a knot in her neck, she shrugs off her duffle and opens it up. The small pistol she took to *Titan's* landing bay is with Scarlet. The medic had swapped bags with her after Rye's search. In this bag, two of Tong's smaller arc-guns nestle among two-days supply of food and water, a med bag, cold weather gear and a few pounds of explosives. Tong doesn't know the weapons are missing from his locker in the cabin he shares with Rye.

She modifies a thigh holster to carry her knife under her left arm then straps the larger guns to her thighs. With the weight off her back, she makes better time but not much. If she'd eaten on *Titan* then she'd have more strength. As it is, she's half giddy with hunger.

Breaking open a protein bar, Angel grimaces at the taste then stuffs it in her pocket at the sound of an Aphid patrol. The low hum of their ground transport stirs the pre-dawn glow and Angel eases herself down and out of sight.

When the transport stops, Angel holds her breath. Two sets of Aphid boots hit the dirt only three meters ahead and Angel hugs the ground, not even bothering to get a weapon ready. The movement will bring them down on her and pressed between the narrow trunks, she'd never get them all anyway. One speaks, a long series of clustered clicks before it's cut off by the sharp squeal of another. One inhales several deep breaths and Angel wants to inhale in sympathy.

Her belly spasms and she fights to keep her air in and the only relief is to dig her nails into the dirt as she presses the side of her head hard into a tree.

Before she can concede a breath, they step aboard the transport and power it up.

She waits until the only sound is her breathing and the chill breeze through the branches overhead.

With the coming of dawn, Constant's hybridized Earth plants open to the light. Heat will come quickly, just as quickly as their fragrance. Already the large, white lilac reaches her. A cooling breeze carries the scent and for a moment Angel remembers the midday sun in Constant, the explosions and the blood.

Then, the breeze brings something else.

Angel closes her eyes and tilts her head until she's sure what she heard. Voices. Human voices. A man, perhaps, and something higher pitched.

A child.

She frees the arc-gun from her right thigh and checks the charge, the safety and the steadiness of her hands. Six years ago, tremors would have been cause for a med disk to get her through and a message to her commander to say she was close to being useless. Today, nothing shakes and for a moment nothing moves but her pounding heart as she catches the music of Quinn's voice.

With a running leap, Angel clears the worn, dusty path taken by the Aphid transport and disappears into deeper brush.

CHAPTER 29

The river moved quick enough to pull one of Rye's soldiers under and he's lucky he didn't lose any more to the deep, swift flow. The woman came up a few dozen meters downstream before regaining her footing and slogging the rest of the way across. With a grace the rest lacked in comparison, Scarlet keeps her over-stuffed bag held high over her head and avoids slipping on a single stone. Once they regroup on the other side, they climb the slope up the other bank. Under the partially frozen top layer, the mud remains soft and a firm step digs in enough to slip.

Rye pauses just before the top and pulls out his tablet. Somehow his pocket scooped up a load of dirt so he wipes the device off on a patch of Constant's tough grass.

"Lost touch with our D-10 already," he whispers into his built-in mic. Interference at their pre-arranged landing site is much worse than predicted.

"No shit," Webber replies.

Rye shrugs. He can count on his secondary tracker to use that reply for pretty much anything.

"You're such a yes-man."

"No shit," he snorts and drops next to Rye.

193

Constant's cold night seeps in around the team as they gather just under the crest of the hill. Peering over, Rye studies the trees about thirty meters away. More knee-high coarse grass fills the space between. Cold air finds every icy drop of river water in his clothes and the chill sinks through even into his wet shorts. It also brings a familiar smell.

Webber inhales, filling his second gen implants with the scent of Aphid. The greens are either numerous or very close. The presence of an unexpected Aphid installation would explain their lack of comms.

"Need your ear for a minute, Rye," Scarlet whispers into his implanted earpiece. Her voice chops in and out even from a meter away.

"Sec," he mutters and uses his tablet to make the channel private.

"How are you doing?"

"Fine," though he spits it like a curse. As if he has time for smalltalk when he has to get the team through or past a pile of Aphids. He scans the tree line on the other side of the field but his irritation with Scarlet interferes with the focus needed to mentally control his implanted eye. The cold dark shadows give away nothing.

"Your heart rate is up, adrenaline spiking pretty bad for climbing a hill."

"Uh huh."

"We're all doing our part, Rye," she continues. "Each and every one of us. We've been friends a long time. If you don't calm down you'll fuck up and lead us into hell, understand?"

"Son of a bitch, Scarlet," he grunts and squishes his eyes shut to try again. She doesn't answer though he hears her swallow. "Sorry. Keep having my back, okay?"

"You got it."

Rye closes the private channel and slows his breathing. She's right. His bad mood isn't her fault. When he looks around again, his implant reveals three almost still humanoids in the trees. Webber tilts his head to the left and nine more move closer, weapons scanning in all directions.

"We can wait for the patrol but the greens across the way will bring them down on us before we can get to them," Webber observes.

"Unless we nail them from here," Rye replies and shoulders his arc-gun. "I've got the one on the right."

"Middle," Webber calls his mark as a third soldier finds space on his other side and calls the green on the left. The rest of the team gets in close behind with Scarlet in the center. Without her, anyone hit could be in a ton of trouble.

"Now we wait."

The nine Aphids don't hurry and Rye has time to take his eyes from his target and inspect the patrol. Though they carry the usual types of weapons, their clothes are much lighter than he'd expect for a sub-zero Constant night. Patches of armour and gear cover their thin, brown clothing. Gone are the days when Aphids were sluggish and easy targets in the cold.

"D-10," someone whispers from behind and Rye turns. An Aphid emerges from around the rear of the vehicle, fingers trailing over the side as it makes its way to the sealed rear hatch. It scans both up and down the river before finding the wet path Rye's group couldn't help but leave on the bank below.

The Aphid emits two, short chirps and scans up the hill as two more appear at its side. The rush of the fast moving water between the Aphids and soldiers swallows any echo the Aphid call makes.

Rye only has a moment to think.

"Webber," he orders as they're spotted. Webber cuts the trill of Aphid alarm short with a faintly glowing orange round from his arc-gun. The other two Aphids bring their weapons around and he puts down a second as an Aphid round buries itself in the mud several meters away. Although they're sloppy shooters, it's unlikely the next shot will miss the cluster of humans.

The rest of the team is already on the move, Rye cresting the hill first. The patrol of nine Aphids doesn't notice Rye. When they turn to investigate the sound from the D-10, he has several seconds to clear the ledge. One more shot from Webber and the man's head breaches the hill, then he takes his place with Rye.

Two grunts move on the trees, focused on the three hidden there and Scarlet shelters in Rye's six. With her med bag secured on her back, she draws her smaller arc-gun and crouches ready to stay with him.

The air around the team erupts in fire.

Explosions behind and in the direction of the D-10 vie for attention and blind Rye's biological eye. As he tunes out the input, his implant registers movement in the trees and ahead in the direction of the larger Aphid patrol. To his right, Webber scrambles forward on his elbows and knees. Thick grass doesn't slow him. One Aphid goes down under his fire, a leg missing just above the knee. Its wailing seems to trigger the remaining eight to disappear in all directions.

"Back up," Scarlet shouts from behind and Rye takes a step toward her. Over his armour, he feels the weight of her hand on his back while a slug from her arc-gun races skyward, leaving an orange trail through the thickening smoke. She's like a third arm in combat. Although she's his best medic she'd have made a hell of a grunt. Rye takes a quick mental snapshot of the degenerating situation around them as he gets his own gun up. One Aphid, six meters above them, is missing half its head. They both tag a second leaping green in the chest before he takes them a few steps to the left to avoid the falling bodies.

"Damn, Rye," she mutters as they take a knee. "They should be catatonic in this cold."

"No shit," Rye replies and shelters over Scarlet in a subconscious reaction to the start of a massive movement of air. As he gets his head down another blast knocks them over.

A pained, human grunt cuts Scarlet's laugh short.

"Down," he orders and she drops flat in the grass, nearly hidden in a tire rut. The bulk of the Aphid rounds come from the trees and Rye has a good idea where the rest of the patrol went.

"Scarlet, need ya, darling," Webber's tight voice makes it through the interference.

Rye looks over at Webber. He crouches over another man. One hand puts pressure on what could be the man's shoulder and the other tears at his smaller triage kit. Webber would only call Scarlet out if it can't wait.

"Go," Rye orders and she takes off, keeping low in the grass. One Aphid stupid enough to think it's invisible in the trees takes aim at her and Rye makes sure it doesn't get the round off.

As Rye moves on the trees, he releases his short knife with his left hand. The one legged Aphid stops screaming, much to Rye's relief. The sharp keening never fails to set his teeth on edge.

Let's make this quick, he prays more to himself than to anyone else.

"I see one outside the transport," Webber says. Only his lips move. Rye hears him through his internal ear piece.

The twenty meter long craft seems thick enough for two levels. With the exception of the folded open stairs, hidden with the lone figure on the far side of the ship, the sides give no evidence of window ports, hatches or storage.

The blackened hull and ground below tells another story.

Three elegant, tapered legs press a third of a meter into what was once Constant's sandy soil. The charred surface reflects the dawn light in all directions off thousands of tiny, smooth mirrors. Worst around the legs, the damage to the ground appears in ripples and waves progressing outward, large at first then smoothing out as they intersect with the rings around the other legs.

The underside of the ship appears undamaged in spite of reflective bits of melted ground stuck all over the surface.

It must have been a hell of a blast. The only thing that would have caused it was an emergency discharge of the ship's power core.

"Human or Aphid?" Rye asks.

Scarlet's head comes up, waiting for the answer. If the person outside Gustav Keller's unusually sleek escape vehicle is human, he or she could be the first of many injured.

"Human."

"Got it," Rye mutters and moves to the right. He rubs at a set of three scratches under his left eye, earned by not getting out of the way of a branch Webber pulled out of place. At least their silent sprint through overgrown berry bushes allowed them to avoid another delay taking on more greens. On the ground forty minutes and they have a firefight under their belts. Their D-10 took the injured soldier on an automated trip back to *Arsenal* for treatment by the stand-by medical team.

Rye's route around the clearing brings him closer to the ship. When he's certain the figure is human, he slows, boots finding only quiet, bare dirt until he places a foot on the black, crystallized ground.

The figure sniffles and when she turns her head, Rye recognizes her veil. She sits on the second to bottom step, leaning against the side rail, eyes closed as if asleep.

"Opal?" Rye whispers and she stiffens, eyes flaring wide as she drops her head and gives all her attention to both knees.

"Opal, honey?" He tries again, lowering his voice. She ignores him, so Rye adjusts his implant to scan what he can see of the inside of the transport. No Aphid waits inside. Opal's bare feet stick out from a pair of baggy trousers. He recognizes her apparent fear for what it is, shyness.

"Scan the perimeter again," he orders through his mic. "Target is friendly."

No acknowledgement reaches him. He doesn't expect any unless there's a problem. Their built in comms seem unencumbered by Aphid static here though they still can't raise anyone else.

"Opal? It's Rye. Any Aphids around?"

She shakes her head and turns in his direction. Tears wet her red eyes. A dirty bandage appears under the hairline behind her right ear.

"You okay?"

Again, the head shakes but Rye doesn't expect her to speak since she can't.

He steps free of the bush, eyes on everything but nothing moves but him. With a hand up, he signals for the others to break cover and move in. They do, weapons away from the ship as they keep watch for trouble. As they get closer, the loose crunch of the ground shattering beneath their boots deepens as the shards underfoot get bigger. At the stairs, the glass spikes stand as high as knives, row upon row of deadly blades.

Opal reaches for Rye and for a moment it looks like she'll take a step but she waits.

"Opal," he gets an arm around the woman and she clings. Reigning in a tight sob, she grabs Rye's hand to pull him aboard.

"Boots off," Rye orders. "We're not tracking this crap in."

"Rye?"

He lifts his eyes from his laces to see Giselle, hugging her slight frame. Her drawn-back hair reveals a bandage behind the same ear as Opal.

What are the chances of that?

Some kind of altercation went on and if Giselle resorted to discharging the power core to defend the ship it must have been ugly.

"Giselle," Rye gives in to Opal's impatience and lets her haul him up the stairs. "Where's Quinn?"

"She's unharmed," Giselle glances away when she says it and he can imagine why. A four-year-old doesn't need to see combat. Then Giselle glances past Rye. "Thank God, you have a medic."

"What's going on?" Scarlet demands and steps one socked foot on the inside heel of her boot then gives a rough yank, pitching herself forward. The momentum gets her up the stairs faster than Opal dragged Rye.

"Last door on the right," Giselle points and Scarlet hurries down the hall, followed by Opal.

"Giselle," Rye says as he gives in to another hug. The old woman trembles and when she steps back Rye takes her small hands in his own. Only a step into the ship and he's already assailed by the stink of unwashed bodies and iffy sanitation.

"They stumbled on us, I think," Giselle rambles in relief. "Two days after we landed. My father's route took us everywhere before we set down. Barely got the door shut to keep them out. Two teams of nine. Quinn said they didn't see us come in to land. I guess we're hidden from the Aphids, too.

"Started to force the door. Quinn said they wanted to take the ship apart for my father's stealth tech. I know enough about it that they won't learn anything without power and the only place to charge it is back on Helm-Dent. We didn't have enough power left to lift off anyway so I dumped the power core and cooked the little bastards. Couldn't let the Aphids get their hands on it."

Giselle shudders.

"Then all they had to do was wait us out. No life support or water. Light. We hid Quinn in a cupboard with an oxygen bottle when the air failed and opened the door.

"Then they took us, a couple at a time," Giselle grips Rye's hand and leads him toward the rear of the ship. Each berth he passes holds one or two people, clustered around small, utilitarian tables or curled up on their beds. After looking in a few rooms he realizes everyone is as barefoot as Opal. Damn, no need for guards when the ground outside is a field of broken glass.

Then he notices a third has a bandage in the same spot as Giselle and Opal.

A fourth.

Rough nausea wakes in Rye's stomach though he's not so sure he wants to know why they all have a similar injury. The whole scene aboard the ship is wrong, starting with the fact that everyone is alive.

"Gone a day and a half then back. I thought we'd all be dead," Giselle echoes Rye's thought.

"Then why did they take you?" Rye asks. The Aphids' actions don't make any sense.

Noise outside interrupts the question. He rests his hand on his weapon and moves to the hatch. Only human voices make their way into the dank interior but Rye still keeps Giselle behind him. Forge and her medic confer with Webber at the base of the stairs. She gives her team a few hand signals and her grunts split up to reinforce Blue Team's perimeter.

"Forge," Rye says. "You made it."

"Heck of a walk in," she mutters and wipes at a thick patch of blood on her thigh. "Sent two back to *Arsenal* after a steep walk back to the D-10 with them. What the fuck."

Rye thinks the same thing about the skirmish they had when they landed. Forge eyes the boots at the bottom of the stairs and adds her own before she leads her sock-footed medic aboard. Good woman, doesn't wrinkle her nose at the stink. Rye teamed with her on more than one long and unwashed mission.

"Bring rations for these folks," she orders and starts going through her pockets.

"We have injured," Giselle points and Forge gives the medic a shove.

"Giselle Keller," Rye introduces. Forge holds out a hand. "Forge, Team Lead. Giselle says the greens have been taking them away a few at a time."

"Why?" Forge asks. She pulls a couple of protein bars from her pocket and gives them to Giselle. The old woman opens one and accepts a pouch of water.

"Genetic testing," Giselle chews. "Best I can gather."

"Fuck me sideways, Rye," Forge exclaims.

"Makes sense considering..."

"Fill me in, please," Giselle says as she pulls her hair back to show the dressing. "Tell me why they have pieces of my brain, my seventy-year-old ovaries and every other organ I've got."

Forge glances at Rye.

"Compatibility, I think," Rye admits. "We've captured Aphids with human DNA incorporated into their own."

"Wait, whose DNA?" Giselle holds up a hand to interrupt.

"Angel's," Rye's voice rasps out as the gnawing feeling in his gut turns in to something frightened and violent.

The old woman pales and her bar slips from her fingers. In a flash, Forge catches it as Rye keeps Giselle from going over.

"This way," Giselle leans and Rye holds her up as they make their way down the hall and into the ship's Med Bay. The sweet smell of infection mixed with the sharp, dusty stink of Aphid assaults them. Giselle doesn't react but Rye turns his head aside for all the good it will do. Even unflappable Forge puts a hand over her nose to stifle a wet retch.

"Rye?" Scarlet doesn't look up. She's at the head of a gurney adding a fifth small bag to the I.V. in Max's central line. Foil packets from over a dozen little thumb-sized med disks litter the ground around her feet and black, pus-soaked bandages cover Max's right arm. "This man's in deep shit. I need him in *Titan's* hyperbaric chamber now or he won't make it to sundown."

Opal backs away into a corner. Only the two walls at her shoulders keep her from crumpling. Damn, Aphid bite. Under the dressing, Aphid saliva eats away at his arm.

"Sweetheart?" Scarlet looks up at the distraught woman in the corner.

"Opal," Rye whispers.

"Opal, honey," the medic tries. "He knows you're here. Come closer. His vitals are better when you touch him."

"Four days ago," Giselle whispers. Opal tugs a chair closer and wraps her hands around the fingers of Max's good hand. A small movement of the blanket reveals Quinn's little mink tucked in the corner of his elbow. Like Max's face, his fingers and the rest of his body have already started to swell. A sure sign the Aphid infection has spread through his blood. Most of his vitals go back into the yellow, still poor but at least red isn't winning.

"They came for the last time. Took everything but food, water and some medical supplies. When they were going through the cupboards in here they found Quinn."

"No," he hisses.

"Max fought them until they knocked him out cold and they took her. They took our shoes, hover chairs and prosthetics, anything we could use to get across the ground outside."

Giselle finally breaks down and Rye crushes her into his chest.

"They haven't been back."

"Fuck," he shouts then seals his lips shut.

"Rye," Forge orders. "I have solid coordinates on Atom's D-10. We need to evac these people. We'll get *Titan* overhead for visual surveillance."

"Yeah," he gulps. Forge makes sense. They can't afford to operate blind anymore and Max needs more help than Scarlet can give him here. "Get everyone ready."

"I'll coordinate the evacuation," Forge takes Rye's elbow and leads him to the stairs.

Rye nods and hurries to get his boots on as Forge transfers the coordinates to his tablet. He doesn't bother looking, rather, he studies the terrain on her display and memorizes the path.

"Rye?" Giselle calls from the top of the stairs. "Allen is with them."

"Who?" Forge asks.

"Angel's brother," Rye finds his mouth dry. "Abducted by Aphids more than a decade and a half ago." And the whole reason Angel pushed her way in to Core.

"He took Quinn," Giselle nods. "Be careful, Rye. He isn't human anymore."

Jesus, Rye nods as he forces his fear and worry deep into his gut where it won't slow him down. *Get to Atom, put the green assholes under a microscope and figure out where the hell they have my daughter.*

Rye doesn't look back as he sprints the three kilometres to Atom. Only sheer luck prevents him from crossing paths with any Aphid patrols. The little green fuckers have been busy and through the seven minute run, he crosses several roads and skirts clusters of closely-packed, domed Aphid buildings. Atom's D-10 rests between two small hills. Surrounded by thick, flowered trees and native scrub, it's invisible.

A hundred meters away from the D-10, Rye's noisy passage gives one of his grunts plenty of warning though with ground comms still poor, he doesn't hear the request for ID on his internal ear piece.

"Shit," he skids to a stop, hands in the air as he faces down a fully charged arc-rifle nestled in the soldier's shoulder.

"Fuck, boss," she curses. "You just about lost your damned head."

"With me," Rye gets his feet under him and bounds forward, not caring if she follows.

The D-10 sits undisturbed and nearly invisible overhead due to the flowering branches above. The breeze doesn't reach down this far into the small valley and the sweet flowers make the air sticky with both their scent and their pollen.

"Boss," Atom shoves the door open. "We have—"

"Inside," Rye barges in. "Get word to *Arsenal* and *Titan.* Confirmed coordinates on Keller's ship. Medical emergency aboard and they've been low on food and water for days. All aboard but Quinn and I need orbital support overhead with eyes on the ground."

"Sure, but—" Atom tries.

"Better yet, get to Keller's ship and pick up Max. Four-day-old Aphid bite and Scarlet needs him on *Titan.*"

"On it," Glass shouts from up front.

Rye drops to the bench seat and not because the run took it out of him. He's got nothing to do now but wait for intel from above and pray they spot the blonde man and the dark haired little girl.

"Where's Angel?" Rye asks though the knot in his belly tightens again.

"She ditched us," Atom frowns. "Tong's gone after her."

CHAPTER 30

Angel shelters in the shade of a towering purple wisteria. The gnarled roots provide a rough seat and clusters of blossoms the size of her duffle loom overhead. Never thought she'd need to switch her thermal suit from heat to cooling but after downing three packs of water in three kilometres she's ready to strip the thing off and leave it behind.

The voices she heard continue to tease, just far enough away she can't make out the words and never in the same place twice.

Maybe the D-10 fell apart on re-entry and I'm really dead.

With a silent laugh, Angel shrugs off the thought but she can't shake the feeling something plays with her. Chasing Quinn across the surface of Constant would be hell but at least hell smells good. The sweet floral cloy was a distant memory, absent from her nightmares so she's free to find some peace inhaling it.

Ahead, Angel faces low, pale green hills. Hidden between those hills and the flowering trees before her, the colony of Constant sits a kilometre away. The two year old orbital survey showed a few domed Aphid buildings clustered on the south side, past the devastated schoolhouse. No sign of space vehicles though Atom suspected the large, nearby metal platform could conceal an underground hangar.

For the moment, the air around fills with the low whistles of Constant's plain, small, arboreal animals calling out for a mate. No bigger than her fist, they expand to the size and shape of dinner plates when they glide high above. Their squirrel-tailed bodies have startling large, blue, forward-facing eyes. The little creatures aren't docile like Quinn's faux-mink. Instead, the carnivores hunt in packs.

Safety from them relies on staying out of the trees.

No problem.

As soon as their song crescendos, a heavy crash shakes the high, distant leaves and their calls disappear in a fast moving wave. Angel holds her breath, mesmerized by the advancing stillness then slides to her knees and crouches down near the wisteria root.

The voices come again. Quinn speaks, only a few syllables but enough to be sure she's near. The male worries her. At first Angel assumed it to be Max but now she doubts the voice belongs to him or anyone else she knows.

She waits to see what the voices will do. Too many times she's run after Quinn only to have her appear in the distance behind her. This time, they move away, closer to the town and Angel gets to her feet and follows.

An old, human paved road leads her down hill and Angel jogs, sticking to the low brush at the side. Nobody follows and nothing leads her forward but Quinn. Above, the trees have succeeded in overgrowing the aged and broken pavement and although no sun reaches down, the shade offers little relief from the heat.

A final turn brings her to the outskirts of town.

No colour remains in Constant's buildings since the sun bleached everything man-made to a shabby yellow before the tree cover began to move in. Brilliant purples, blues, pinks and blinding whites fill the gaps and overflow onto patches of rubble. The town hall rests in pieces, partially visible under ropes of a native yellow-flowered vine. In a few years one would have to look hard for evidence humans ever lived here. By then, the floral canopy will be complete.

Stepping from the shadows, Angel takes a moment to inhale the hot scent of flowering trees then crouches as she gets her weapon to her shoulder. Each building could hide a nine-pack of Aphids and Angel checks every corner. With the exception of branches blowing together, there's nothing but the distant sound of Quinn's voice. The residential building where Angel spent her last rack time with Rye bravely holds up more yellow-flowered vines.

She risks crossing the street to the schoolhouse. In spite of damage from the explosion that killed her, the first floor stands and much of the second. The building slumps sideways in deference to gravity and thousands of kilos of vines swim up the exterior. Maybe they're the only thing holding the building together. Angel takes a step in and looks down the long hall to the stairs. Sunlight brightens the steps to the second level and she moves forward, intent on just looking and giving herself some peace of mind. The open door to the classroom where she hacked the Aphid computer reveals the contents even more broken than before and she imagines Tong there, looking but pretending to not see her. A ghost.

Although no sound comes from the street, small scratching noises come from overhead. The shuffle of a child's feet? Angel makes her way down the hall, arc-gun snug to her shoulder. A tiny thud follows, back in the direction of the door from which she entered. At the bottom of the stairs, she pushes her back into the wall and turns enough to keep the gun on both the top and bottom floors. Brilliant light finds its way through the canopy above and catches in the grooves and ridges of the gun. Black and deep rust of aged Aphid and human blood crusts the surface.

She didn't notice it earlier but for the past half hour her eyes have been on her surroundings and not her weapon. It must be why Tong had these stashed in his semi-permanent quarters aboard *Titan*. The blood belongs to Angel and the Aphids she and Tong killed.

Only blackness waits past the top of the stairs, deepening into the far end of the room ahead. Angel flips the visor of her plasteel helm down over her eyes and fingers the control buttons until it shows her what her bare eyes can't see.

The room remains cluttered. The Aphid bodies have been removed and Tong doesn't lay in a pool of blood. The wooden floor darkens in places. She lets herself indulge in a few seconds of staring, taking it in, and hopes it will be enough to ease the memories.

Angel keeps moving, her training kicking in, as she becomes aware she's been in the same place too long. She starts around the perimeter, moving the gun around as her eyes track in the corners but freezes when a chunk of fallen roof begins a slow, raspy slide down the wall.

Tracking in the direction of the sound, Angel pivots and brings her arc-gun around. The slow fall pauses and she waits. It can't be a coincidence it moved now but even with her helmet enhanced vision she doesn't have a clear view.

Two steps closer and the rubble falls, shaking the room and stirring up blinding dust. Movement everywhere should trigger panic but the gun in her hands keeps her steady, focused. As Angel withdraws, two large shapes coalesce no more than three meters away. Each curls low to the ground.

"Shit," she hisses. Aphids only jump one way, up, and there's no way they'd get through the remains of the ceiling to come down on her. The purr of threat comes from many tiny throats, not two green ones.

Angel snaps her arc-gun down into the clips on her thigh and draws her dagger with the other as she backs up for the stairs. With the gun secured, she draws the helmet's protective throat panels closed. The constricting semi-solid panels annoy under normal conditions but she'd rather not have to risk getting her knife near her neck. At least her plasteel armour will minimize the damage she does to the rest of her body as she slashes them away.

Two gangs of squirrel-monkeys advance faster than she can retreat as they skitter around in a confusing knot of hungry bodies. Angel's hip hits the jagged remains of the hand rail and she misses a step, coming down hard two stairs down. Hard enough to buckle the fatigued wood. She sinks hip deep into the hole only stopping when her thigh holster proves too large to follow her leg in and wedges painfully up under her butt.

Her other leg bends sideways, straining her groin as she braces to take on the eye-level pack of carnivores.

In less time than it took to drop through the stairs and into the stairwell, they're on her. Tiny razor sharp teeth scrape at her armour without doing more than scuff the surface but a couple of the little beasts find purchase on the cloth in between.

Angel tries to knock one loose. Its teeth haven't worked their way through the blade resistant fabric of her camouflage pants but the thing squeals. Their collective weight grows as more climb her, scrabbling for purchase and piling on top of each other. She still swings the knife but has more success grabbing them in her gloved hand and tearing them free.

Then tiny, cold feet find their way in between her throat guard and the collar of her shirt, followed by the sharp sting of its fangs. Angel bites at her lip to silence a pained cry as she seeks the beast's jaw in an attempt to pry it loose without doing more damage.

As the warmth of blood soaks inside her shirt and the coppery smell fills her visor, the squirrel-monkey screeches and lets go. Angel tosses the creature aside and it disappears.

It doesn't return to bite her again.

As quickly as they swarmed, she's free as the band of little attackers echoes the cry and as one, they flee into the darkness.

Angel presses a hand to her wound as she holds the knife out at the ready but no second wave comes. Only a soft chorus of alarmed chirps reaches her ears.

Unwilling to wait for the frightened animals to change their minds, Angel secures her knife and reaches up for what's left of the railing. It takes both arms to pull herself up enough to get her free foot under her butt and work her leg out of the hole.

Fresh pain accompanies standing and blood trails down the inside of her pants from several cuts. The worst soaks the fabric beneath the piece of plasteel armour covering the back of her thigh.

Great, cut my ass. Scarlet's gonna laugh hers off.

Angel frees her arc-gun and limps backward to the landing, more aware of the creaks and groans of the old building around her than before. At the bottom, she drops her duffel and pulls out a palm sized adhesive med patch to deal with the heaviest bleeding over her collar bone.

She lets the adrenaline work through her system and keeps her chin up to hold her stomach down until it passes.

Quinn's voice reaches her from the street, too far away to be just outside, but Angel has to follow. By now, she can only hold out hope it's her daughter and not some cruel prank. She can't take the chance so she moves to follow.

Each step causes her armour plate to dig into the bruised cut the thigh holster made when she fell and jammed it into her backside. Overhead, nothing moves and even Quinn's voice has gone silent. Step by pained step, she makes her way down the street and watches for ground level movement. The morning breezes weaken then fail as she spots the pure white side of an Aphid dome.

Angel slows and groans as she crouches down behind a pile of rubble. The Aphid domes nestle together just beyond the last human building. Six-sided and white, the roads between form a honey comb so she can't see what lays past the first few though one several times taller looms in the background.

The scope on her arc-gun shows nothing and as she scans the compound an Aphid crosses her field of vision on her second pass. She lowers the gun to see more than just a small circle of its body. It watches her but when it sees her looking back it lowers its eyes, presses its lips shut and lets its hands fall limply to its sides.

Submission? Surely not to her. It only wears the simple beige tunic and trousers common to Aphids not dressed for combat.

After another minute a second joins it and takes the same position.

Angel doesn't dare breathe. Since they both face her, there's no possibility they surrender to anyone else. The arc-gun still carries a full charge. No point in hiding so she turns on the red laser sight and lights up a tiny red dot. The Aphid doesn't react as she moves it up its body and places the marker square in the center of its forehead, just below the start of its green crest.

"No," Quinn giggles from the other side of the Aphid huts, in the direction of the big dome.

Angel eases off the release plate on the arc-gun before she can remove the top of the Aphid's head. Her daughter's laugh pitches higher than it should and cuts short. Angel doesn't take a breath and Quinn releases a second torrent of laughter like she would if she were honestly amused.

The man's voice follows, cool and unemotional.

"Of course you want to be a Regent," he says. Is he trying to keep her calm? Angel doesn't know him. A soldier? The idea Core could already be in the compound gives a brief flash of hope since there's no reason for the Aphids to keep any of them alive.

They kept Allen alive.

Angel steps clear of the mass of stones and vines, wincing at the pain in her butt. The movement releases a fresh trickle of blood down the back of her leg. The Aphids before her don't react and she takes a step forward, then another, toward the narrow path between their buildings. She steps between two domes, then has to choose, left or right but a submissive Aphid blocks each route. Shreds of little brown bodies litter the sides of the paths. Nothing left of dozens of squirrel-monkeys but patches of fur, bones and the thickest leather of their flight membranes. Similar debris litters all the paths she can see.

The Aphid on her right makes her choice for her, retreating. It inhales, thin nostrils flaring at her scent before hurrying out of her way. Its booted feet crunch the small bones as it deviates from the path.

With her gun up, she follows as it back-tracks, leading her through the honeycomb of paths. Other Aphids appear, immobile in submission, sealing off other routes leaving her no route but the one leading to the big dome. Angel assesses each and covers them for a few seconds with her gun before returning her attention to the one she follows. It slips into place next to another guarding the rounded opening at the side of the large dome. Two flaps have been drawn back and rolled up at the sides giving the appearance of an old fashioned Earth camping tent and not an Aphid scented building.

Inside, Quinn and the man speak in unclear whispers. Angel waits until the Aphid guards withdraw another step then she walks in, stepping sideways to cover the door incase they follow.

Angel blinks in response to the unexpected brightness inside. The dome seems to take the limited light filtering through the trees and increases it tenfold. As her watering eyes adjust, she makes out low tables around the perimeter and shelves containing what she knows to be Aphid medical equipment. Each table has an Aphid computer with its long, rectangular keypad and many of the white tables are smeared with red human blood.

A man sits on one of four curved benches arranged in a circle in the center of the room, his back to Angel. He wears Aphid clothing, the light tan fabric appears warm against what she can see of his sallow skin. Tangled blonde hair exposes patches of bare scalp beneath but not in the normal pattern of thinning on top. Just over his shoulder, a smaller bunch of dark curls rises and Quinn jumps to her feet.

"Mama," she squeaks.

Though Angel holds her hand out to summon her daughter, the child remains still. Her oversized Aphid tunic hangs well past her knees.

"Come," she tries but instead the man stands, blocking Quinn from her sight as he turns to face Angel.

The material covering the dome turns out to be softer than it looks and Angel staggers backward, stretching a deep, Angel-sized dent in it before she catches her balance. The section recovers, returning to its usual brightness as it returns to its previous shape.

"Allen?"

He smiles and tilts his head then reaches an arm around Quinn, digging his fingers into her shoulder. She squishes her eyes closed as her breathing races, each exhalation a tiny mewl of fear. Damn, why is she so scared? Angel brings her arc-gun up but doesn't point it at her brother. Not until she's sure what's going on.

"It's okay now," Angel forces a smile. She speaks to Quinn and hopes to reassure Allen as well. After years in Aphid captivity she doesn't know what to expect from him.

"Angela," he smiles, exposing jagged sharp Aphid teeth. If he's responsible for some of the small carcasses outside then it's no wonder the animals abandoned their attack on Angel.

"Oh," she gasps. Putting Allen DNA in the Aphids appears to have been an exchange, not a one-way donation. Not only have his teeth changed but a modest Aphid crest starts under the pale skin of his forehead. From behind, his straggly hair covered it. Her grandfather's eyes, the same startling deep blue Angel vaguely remembers on her father, have lost their pupils and Allen centers his gaze on her.

"You should have taken the shot, Angela," Allen says. "All those years ago, you should have taken the shot. You couldn't do it then and you won't do it now.

"It's too late."

CHAPTER 31

Too long.

Seven minutes.

Ten.

Rye estimates Atom's D-10 should be in contact with Giselle and ferrying their first load to *Titan*.

I'm gonna buy that kid a drink. He kicks at a clump of grass and sends more dirt flying than yellow blades. At least he stops scratching at the plasteel plate covering his pant leg. Max threw down to protect Quinn and will probably pay with his life. They beat him until he couldn't get back up, then they took his legs and left him to die of a rancid bite.

Anger swells in him, building on the low rage he already struggles to contain.

The grunts with him pretend they don't notice as they wait for *Titan* to move and Denman's D-10 to get planet side.

Fourteen minutes.

Rye steps to the edge of the small clearing but doesn't take his eyes from the direction in which Keller's ship sits. Then he glances up into Constant's pale blue sky, still waking with early light but well on its way to the near-white of the planet's day. A tiny silver flash high above blinks twice more and then stays solid, growing until it's as large as he remembers Earth's moon appeared from Whistler.

Damn, *Titan* won't miss a thing from there.

It's also a major target if the Aphids decide to take it on. Something tells Rye they won't, not if they hold Quinn as some kind of prize. If Allen's DNA is in the Aphids, he guesses Quinn is full of whatever it is they've been looking for and they won't take a chance on getting fired on. Or they're using her as a shield.

And the way she could talk to the T*kit and understood her. Rye wouldn't be surprised if she can speak to the green fuckers.

Denman's silent D-10 appears overhead and settles in the clearing. Rye and his men stay back as the hull cools, popping and cracking, and its runners burn a pair of scorching lines in the short grass. The old man doesn't wait for it to cool. The rear hatch wheels open and he ducks to jump out as soon as he'll fit.

"Rye," Denman growls. The man doesn't usually look so rough but then this fight is as personal to him as it is to Rye. Denman grinds the bottoms of his boots into the ground as if making sure he's really here and not stuck on the ship. Even Rye's seasoned men hang back. *Barrington's* boss's displays of quiet anger move men and ships with a word and sometimes much, much less. He leans close and keeps his voice low.

"This is still your show," he says. "I'm here because I'll put a round through my own ass if I have to spend another minute waiting for you to finish this thing up."

"Sir," Rye allows a tight smile.

"We should have stills coming in from *Titan* by now. Atmospheric distortion will limit our clarity for the next couple of minutes but then I expect Atom to be able to send us live vid of my grays."

Denman shoves Rye toward the hatch, follows him in then slams the door shut. He doesn't speak. Instead, he holds Rye's stare until Rye nods, getting it.

"Focused a hundred percent," Rye mutters. "I'm good."

Denman palms the door open and the grunts come in, filling the seats for a break from the growing heat.

Rye is already up front, scanning the stills from *Titan*.

"Where's Angel?" Denman asks.

"Tong's gone after her," Rye shrugs. She's as safe with Tong as she'd be with him and Rye tunes out further questions as he finishes with the first set of pictures. The second set is much better quality and Rye zooms in as far as he can, scanning section by section.

"There," he says as he centers on a nondescript patch of Constant's yellow grass. The clump forces its way up through a widening seam in a patch of human pavement. Blurred above, a cluster of yellow flowers obscures much of the frame.

"I don't see it," Denman comments and Rye brushes his fingers across the screen.

"The shadow."

Denman takes three tries to get a signal through to Atom to bring the video feed in for the area.

"Arc-rifle," Rye explains as they wait for the feed to go live. "Narrow barrel. Tong."

"Take your word for it," Denman says. As an analyst, finding this kind of order in a photo is something Rye does best.

When the video comes up, the shadow is gone.

"Bring up the Aphid buildings, entire compound."

After another minute, Atom complies. Several smaller domes surround the main dome, most of them sit between it and the town. Humanoids between the buildings move away and disappear in the trees as Rye's implant picks out the difference between the foliage and the green of Tong's combat gear.

"There," he says.

"You sure?"

Denman isn't asking if he's sure he sees Tong. He wants to know if they're moving in on the town.

Rye lets his vision blur as he sorts out his feelings. He embraces the agitation dogging him since leaving Keller's ship and sees it for what it really is. His worrisome connection to his twin brother. It's Tong who feels anxious, not Rye, but the unsettled caution is now offset by heavy relief and far more than locating Angel explains. Something else, as well.

Danger.

"Yeah," he sighs.

The Aphids disappear from view and the camera aboard *Titan* pans out so they can watch as they keep moving toward the huge metal doors half a klick away. In fast groups of three, the greens cover the space in under a minute. The camouflaged figure moves, taking cautious steps into the open and toward the Aphid compound. No mistaking the man for anyone other than Tong.

Rye's anxiety rises with each step Tong takes as he senses his brother move closer and closer to trouble.

"We don't have much time."

"What if—"

"Yes, what if," Allen purrs in threat. From his human throat, the unnatural grinding makes her skin crawl and continues in the background as he speaks. "You could have killed me."

It might have been better than whatever he is now. He sneers, cold and unemotional, and twists his fingers in Quinn's long hair. Damn, having Quinn forced Angel to accept her life belonged to the living family she was blessed with. Not those for whom there was no hope.

Angel shifts her weight, considering. He could be coerced, unable to do any more than keep Quinn in line for the Aphids in order to protect himself but then, maybe not.

The dome's rear panel opens, revealing an invisible door and Quinn tries to dodge around behind Allen only to be pushed toward the hole and a trio of Aphids. These don't wear regular Aphid clothing. Toughened leathery armour covers them leaving only hands and heads exposed. Angel brings her short arc-gun over on the group, sighting on the leader. These three belong to a dangerous class of Aphid killers, comprising about fifty-five percent of any battle force they've encountered.

"What do they want?" Allen asks. "Speak."

His voice echoes from the first Aphid. It touches a small device on its belt and the echo ceases. Angel swallows as she gets sicker with the situation. She'd been following the Aphid, not her daughter.

Quinn draws in a frightened breath before letting loose several high pitched clicks. She follows with a purr. Other than her little girl voice she sounds completely fluent.

The lead answers, the only one to raise his eyes to Quinn.

"They say my father is here," Quinn starts with no more than a rush of air. Her voice finds strength at the word father.

"Tell them their Regent wishes they leave him a clear path to us and prepare to depart the planet. We'll be underway in a few minutes."

Quinn glances to Angel before issuing the instruction. Once they click their assent and turn away, Allen pulls Quinn to him, his arm around her shoulder.

"Many years ago our parents found their way into Aphid hands," Allen explains. "A weak faction took them in when they should have been killed. The history isn't clear since they were eventually eradicated. Several years later only mother survived and participated in our genetic experiments."

Our? Angel thinks.

"Twenty or so years ago she killed herself when she set off an explosion, destroying the lab and research. Our scientific losses were devastating, all the samples and subjects destroyed so they came for us."

He shrugs since there's nothing more to say. They took Allen and Angel devoted the next years of her life to Core and the hope she'd find him again. And their parents? How hard had their life been as DNA experiments? The blood marked tables around her would only be a start and Angel forces out thoughts of her people on Helm-Dent.

"Your blood was all over the schoolhouse," he waves in the direction of the town. "But then you disappeared from cryo. Every Aphid knows your face, Angela. We almost took you in Whistler. What a surprise to see my niece and now her mother. With her father, our new Regent will be part of her own triad."

"Quinn and I won't be staying," Angel states. Not for a triad, the afternoon or even the next few minutes. Not if she can help it. "Neither will her father."

Although the arc-gun only weighs a couple of pounds, she's had it at her shoulder for a long time considering how prone she is to aching. A knot starts deep in the side of her neck and twists its way up into her temple and down into the small of her back, stopping just short of connecting with the tacky, stickiness of her butt and the pain of pulling away fresh scabs each time she moves.

"You already are," Allen answers. "With her father here? She'll be the first of a new breed of Aphid. I was too old to take full advantage of Aphid DNA but she's so young. Our new Regent will be the envy of all Aphid society."

"No," a man growls over Angel's right shoulder.

Angel doesn't turn to the door to see who it is. He doesn't sound quite like Rye, more like Tong.

"Daddy," Quinn whispers and takes a step forward before Allen pulls her back with a fist full of hair and tunic. The child yelps, then covers her mouth to keep herself silent. Her efforts don't hold back tears and Angel's anger flares. No man treats a kid like that. The Allen she knew never would.

Angel takes a step sideways since she has to do something. If she moves toward Quinn then Allen might do worse than pull hair. When the man takes position near her, she turns enough to look.

Tong presses his cheek tight to the stock of his longer arc-rifle, thin moustache drawn into a tight line. The visor on his plasteel helmet sits back far enough to give him some shade from the glowing dome overhead without covering his eyes.

"Quinn," he says. "How you doing, baby girl?"

Tong would only know Rye called her baby girl if Rye told him. Quinn's brave, little chin comes up. Her lips move but no sound comes.

"Just like old times," Tong says and Angel watches his left hand on the barrel of the arc-rifle.

No backup. Primary is mine.

"Who's this, sweetheart?"

Sweetheart? Rye never called her that.

"Allen," Angel says. "My brother."

Tong doesn't move and the silence stretches.

"Well. Allen, Angel's brother," Tong says. "Come on with us. I'll escort you out."

Allen grins, exposing his sharp Aphid teeth and puts his free hand in his mouth, coating his fingers with saliva then rests them on Quinn's shoulder, much too close to her throat. His nails have grown thick and sharp, not the softer, rounded ends of a human. Just a scratch would be enough to put someone Quinn's size in a lot of trouble.

"You wouldn't hurt your Regent, would you?" Angel asks. "Quinn would tell the others you did."

Allen hesitates then moves his hand closer, touching the skin below her ear.

"With the pair of you in our possession, we'll always have another Regent. The difference is you love *this* one."

Tong tilts his head to his left, releasing a soft pop in the vertebrae. A second later, his Adam's apple bobs, concealed from Allen by the arc-rifle.

They must have comms.

No Aphid sounds come from outside the dome but then the leather armoured trio returns, filling the round opening behind Allen. She hadn't heard Tong's approach either but the man could be damned silent if he set his mind to it, almost as quiet as Atom. Angel would hear the conversation Tong hears if her built in mic and ear piece hadn't been damaged beyond recognition in the explosion six years earlier.

Hold, Tong hand signals then he takes his right from the stalk of his arc-rifle and stretches his fingers. Allen shouldn't know Tong doesn't tire and could hold his position for a very long time but his pupil-less blue eyes narrow.

When Tong replaces his hand on the grip he puts his third finger on the trigger plate.

Two.

One.

At zero, Angel slams her arc-gun to her thigh and launches forward. Before her first step hits the floor, a stunning concussion shatters the air inside the dome, followed quickly by a flash of yellow charged to ten times its brightness by the Aphid fabric overhead.

The last thing Angel sees clearly is her daughter, dangling by her hair in Allen's hand and barely out of reach of his claws then Allen's shoulder opens up. A spray of red-gray blood flares behind him.

Quinn screams, a terrorized wail Angel hopes will never stop. While immersed in light, dark and fire, it's the only beacon she can follow.

CHAPTER 32

"This won't be subtle," Denman mutters as he takes position next to Rye on the shady side of the schoolhouse.

Rye nods his assent as Denman activates the plain, black box in his hand. While it lacks the subtlety of a device like the one Angel used to carry, it makes up for its shortcomings in sheer power. It should cancel out Aphid interference half a klick beyond the domes in the event they need comms as far away as the Aphid underground hangar bay. Also, there's no time to fuss with shaped diffusion matrices, enhanced echoing barriers or anything else requiring an internal hardware interface.

The rest of his team is out of sight, in a semi-circle advancing around the Aphid domes. He hopes. While they still don't have direct comms with *Titan*, he knows where Tong went. The box does its work. Rye watches the display on his tablet. Two brilliant green dots represent Denman and Rye in the center of the display. Rye uses two fingers to expand his view and the grunts on either side of him light up, one at a time, as the device cancels Aphid interference.

Last to appear are two green dots in the large dome; Tong and the Core transmitter Scarlett implanted in Angel the night before.

"Move," Rye says as Denman buries the box under rubble and vines. Not much of a disguise but the thing will last longer hidden if the Aphids have to look for it.

Tong? Rye sends. If he can see his brother on the tablet then he should be able to communicate with him. A final glance at the overhead video on his display shows all but three of the Aphids have disappeared into their bunker. The broad doors begin their slide open and Rye drives forward, certain he's running out of time.

In the big dome. Have Quinn, Angel and some messed up half-Aphid. Quinn's not safe.

Affirmative, Rye acknowledges.

Denman keeps up, staying in tight to Rye's left shoulder as they pass the last building in Constant and approach the cluster of domes.

Three more Aphids entering the building.

Secure Quinn, Rye doesn't say the rest of his order, to keep Angel safe too. He has to trust her training now. If they spread themselves too thin then they could lose everyone. *In three.*

Rye and Denman approach the main entrance from the side, out of sight, and crouch with their arc-rifles ready.

Two.

Sharp, dusty Aphid stink overlays traces of human blood as Rye checks the charge on his rifle. At the same time, he lets the slowing of time focus him as he feels the weight of his smaller arc-gun on his left thigh and the tightness of the straps holding his dagger across his back.

One.

Together, Rye and Denman pivot and push forward, low to the ground. A crouched, sprinter's start propels them around the corner and into the building as the interior lights up with a disorienting flash none of his soldiers caused.

The room fills with white smoke, obscuring the blinding white ceiling and for a moment the orange of a Core arc-rifle tints everything. Rye's sensitive sense of smell recoils at the overwhelming smoke overlaid by a mix of coppery human and earthy Aphid.

Straight ahead, Tong calls.

To Rye's left, Angel cries out. Her shout briefly drowns out Quinn's screams. In spite of the sense of bodies all around, the smoke and light don't let up and Rye runs ahead, tripping on a knee level bench and stumbling over a second. A body stops him, rife with the scent of Aphid and encased in hard leather. Rye takes a blow to his ribs and goes for his knife. With Quinn somewhere nearby he won't risk firing.

The Aphid withdraws, tugging at Rye's chest piece as it frees its knife from the plasteel and tries again, probing for a soft spot.

Left, Tong orders and Rye moves more in response to a feeling Tong is right than any wonder about how he knows. The Aphid knife whispers by his throat and catches on his collar before passing by with the vibration of the green's knuckles on his helmet. The attack came hard and Rye's sure the Aphid will be off balance for the moment it takes to follow through so he brings his knife around and slashes it deep in the Aphid's throat. It screeches, giving away the location of its head. Rye finishes it off, putting all his strength behind the blade to drive it up into the roof of the green's mouth.

The Aphid tenses, then goes limp in stages as its body shudders in response to steel in its brain. Rye can't pull his blade free and chooses to not hold the Aphid up so he lets it drop.

Then he senses something very wrong from Tong. Their twin connection overwhelms everything and Rye shouts, certain he's too late.

Fire, Tong. Take cover.

Rye's built in earpiece comes to life with a barrage of acknowledgments from the rest of his team though there's confusion as some have made it to the hanger and engage the departing Aphids there.

Got it, Tong replies.

Only then, Rye takes his own advice and drops to the ground next to the dead Aphid.

The shock of explosion knocks him flat on his stomach and drives the air from his lungs. A second blast rolls him over more times than he can count and he comes to rest, face up, under Constant's sky. As the first bits of debris fall, Rye turns on his side and covers his head in his arms.

Status? He orders but his built-in seems dead. He'll have to wait for the ringing in his right ear to subside in order to know for certain. As the rain of pebble sized rock passes over, larger pieces impact. One strikes his thigh hard enough to make him swear in spite of his armour.

Where is my helmet?

"That was hell," Denman mutters from behind and Rye rolls over to see the man push himself up and dust himself off.

There's no sign of the Aphid Rye killed and little remains of the large dome. Shreds of the smaller surrounding domes stand and Rye gets to his feet. He turns, scanning the thinning smoke. No Core soldiers appear down and no Aphid bodies either but he still can't see more than a few meters away.

He pushes forward into what he thinks was once the large dome. Heavier medical equipment and Aphid computer parts remain. One arc shaped bench shattered, its shards driven into the underside of another. Rye leans forward to rub at his shin but can't remember if the growing lump was from tripping or if he was hit by something during the blast. Under the broken pieces, Rye spots the top half of the Aphid he killed and plants a boot on its head so he can work his knife free. Then he wipes it on his pants and returns it to the place on his back.

As he straightens, the wind shifts and reveals blood covered camouflage pants. The soldier lays on her side, knees bent and tangled blonde hair covers her face.

Small, dirty bare feet peek out from between her knees. Fresh blood covers the back of Angel's leg and coats Quinn's toes.

"Oh, damn," he mutters. Rye can't look away and staggers forward afraid of what he'll find. The thought of Angel dying twice in this place and Quinn with her becomes a lead weight.

"Medic," Rye calls both out loud and into his internal mic. Someone has to hear. Denman appears behind Rye, startling him out of the numbing seconds and guiding him forward.

Quinn's little bare arm comes up and pushes Angel's hair aside.

"Mama?"

There's no answer and Quinn tries again, angry her mother doesn't listen.

"Baby girl," Rye takes Quinn's hand and presses his fingers to the side of Angel's neck. Even through the thick scars, he feels her heart beat strong and even. Angel stirs, groaning, as she gets a hand to a bloody lump on the side of her head.

"Quinn, baby?"

"Here, Mama."

"Okay," Angel rolls to her back and gets her eyes open then mashes her lids shut several times to focus. "Rye? I couldn't take the shot."

She pulls Quinn closer and Rye leans forward to kiss his daughter's cheek, then Angel's. So damned lucky.

"Where's Tong? He took the shot, went after Allen."

"I know," Rye says and pulls Quinn into his arms. Angel tries to get up but Denman's there, pressing her back down.

"Tong," she coughs.

"Hey, baby girl," Rye wraps his daughter up, covering her in as much of his body armour as he can. The simple, sweetness of his little girl rises above the sharp dust of Aphid and lingering sweat of others from Keller's ship. Under the shapeless Aphid garment, Rye feels her thinness and the fatigue brought on by days of fear. "You know who else is going to be happy to see you?"

"Who?" In spite of her sleepy yawn, she still fists what she can reach of his shirt.

"Your mink."

"Yes? I was so scared they'd eat him," she frowns. "Is Max okay?"

"Mm hm," Rye says. "My friends are looking after him, everyone's okay."

"Here," Denman orders, taking Quinn as he starts scanning Angel with his tablet. Quinn resists for a moment then smiles when she sees who it is.

"I couldn't take the shot, Rye," Angel repeats. "Where's Tong?"

"Concussion. No fractures," Denman says then turns the tablet on Quinn who leans over to watch the display. "How you feeling, Quinn?"

She doesn't answer and slides one of her little hands into Denman's much bigger one.

"I want Forge in command of *Arsenal* and her teams," Rye says as he starts removing Angel's body armour to get a better look at the wounds by her neck and thigh. "The Aphids want the stealth tech on Keller's ship and apparently the only place we can recharge the power core is on Helm-Dent. Forge needs to get it aboard *Arsenal* and bring it to *The Barrington* with all haste."

"Agreed," Denman says. He peels back the dressing on Angel's collar bone to expose a deep tear in her skin then presses it back in place. "My D-10 is en route via remote. Quinn and Angel will be off planet in a few minutes."

Rye squeezes Angel's hand and moves toward the Aphid underground bunker as Angel repeats her self again. Tong, the shot, Allen. The pops of small arms fire reach him from the old style projectile weapons favoured by many Aphids and some Core soldiers as well. One door on the hanger has been peeled back, blackened and charred from an explosion inside. The other door remains hidden from view.

Core soldiers running from the bunker precede a ground rattling rumble as Rye's internal earpiece wakes up. The soldiers get clear just before an Aphid transport rises from the hole in Constant. Rye raises a hand to keep the heat from its engines off his face. The bulky, black ship rotates, fortunately turning so the engines face away, before rising to make a quick escape from orbit.

228

Titan doesn't fire since the chance of dropping wreckage on the soldiers below is far too high.

As the heat becomes bearable, Rye steps over the uneven ground and tries to feel Tong. The anxiety in the minutes before the explosions grows crushing in its absence. Guilt, inadequacy and a deep sense of failure he believed were simple grief and anger about losing Angel appeared to be much more and now Rye feels hollow without his irrational fear of losing his brother.

Tong has been cut from his senses.

"Tong?" Rye calls as he works his way past the sparse, heavy, tilting trees. The open spaces still provide a clear view of the bunker and behind him, the remains of the Aphid domes. Denman's broad back faces Rye, his arm around Quinn as he stays with Angel.

Rye tunes everything out, seeking his brother. As he gets up on a small rise, he catches sight of brilliant green Aphid blood, brown leather and the duller green of Core fatigues.

"Tong?" He tries again but there's no answer until he gets near enough to be greeted by a slow snore.

Tong lays on his side, spooned between two dead Aphids. The one in front uses Tong's left bicep as a pillow for what's left of its head. Tong's right hand rests on the other's ass.

Out cold, no wonder it feels like he's gone.

Rye takes out his tablet to contact *Titan* where it floats beyond the range of his internal mic.

"Atom, can you take a high res of a ten by ten right in front of me?"

"On it," is the prompt reply. "That's priceless..."

Atom trails off in laughter before closing the channel.

"Tong," Rye kicks his brother's boot then squats down and tugs on his leg. Only a dozen meters away, movement in a thicker patch of trees gets his attention. Rye keeps his head down and lets the implant swivel toward the trees to investigate. At first, he thinks it's one of the tree dwelling mammals except its big, blue eyes sit too far apart. Pale skin, gray and almost pearly under Constant's sun, draws back into the shadows.

"Hey," Rye tries again, this time Tong presses his eyes shut as his right hand tightens on the Aphid's ass. He makes Atom's job too easy.

"Fuck," Tong tries to sit but the weight of the Aphid on his arm keeps him down and it takes three tries to get upright. He glances at the Aphids and clutches his head in his hands. "Not a fucking word to Atom, understand?"

"Not a word," Rye keeps his face neutral. Allen still waits nearby.

"I got my bell rung," Tong moans.

"Yeah. Scarlet will kill you if she thinks they meant anything to you."

Tong offers a sideways smile as he shields his eyes from the sun.

"Angel and Quinn?" Tong asks and almost goes over as he leans to look around Rye and get a view of the shredded domes.

"Safe," Rye won't say any more with Allen so near.

Gray skin, blue eyes. Anyone you know? Rye says through his built in mic.

Tong nods. *The Allen-thing. I went after him but wound up dating these two before everything blew up.*

Can you get on your feet? Rye asks. *He's behind you.*

Tong puts his hands out and Rye pulls him up. His implant wanders around on its own though the natural eye looks fine. Although he sounds winded, he's steady enough.

"Allen?" Rye moves toward the brush, wary of any other Aphids but it looks like he's alone. A path of red-gray blood leads into the trees.

"Rye?" Allen's soft voice calls then he breaks down into sobs. "I'm hurt, I think. They forced me. I'm so sorry."

"It's okay, Allen," he offers.

Not okay, Tong sends as he moves off to the left.

"I just," Allen lets out a trembling sigh. "You have no idea how scared I've been. They're gone now, right? I'm safe?"

"Come out, Allen."

What the hell did they do to him? Rye asks. The man who appears before him sure isn't Aphid but doesn't look like anything he's ever seen. Scorched and tangled blonde hair clings to one side of his head, the Aphid crest and the other side have no hair. Allen clutches his left arm with his right. Each little movement oozes more blood from his shoulder.

"You can fix me, right? Make me human again?" Allen begs and falls to his knees. "Please, I just want to go home."

Don't, Tong says but Rye can't stop himself. Allen was all Angel had and the reason she joined Core. If any human remains in the half-Aphid, Rye can't just kill him. Not unless he's sure.

Tong chants no, over and over, as Rye reaches around Allen and pulls him up. He feels human enough since he doesn't have the flattened chest of an Aphid but Rye glimpsed the teeth when he spoke and his scent sends shivers of alarm along his spine. Rye forces it down as he urges Allen forward one step, then another.

"He shot me," Allen whispers, leaning his mouth close to Rye. Even though Allen stands a couple of inches taller than Angel, the top of his head only comes to Rye's chin. Not very close to his neck but near enough to his unarmoured shoulder. Rye considers how long it might take Allen to get his sharp teeth through the knife resistant fabric and decides he won't have any trouble pulling the injured half-Aphid away.

"Don't let him hurt me again."

Tong rolls his eyes, having regained control of the implant and rests a hand on the butt of his arc-rifle. In response, Allen cringes closer to Rye.

"Tong," Rye warns but Tong remains wary. Truth be told, Rye's older brother is clearly angry at what he sees as a gross lack of judgment.

Allen stumbles, though Rye can't think what has caught his foot and as he reaches for Allen with his other hand to keep the man upright, he feels the soft click of his knife leaving the holster on his back. Then the pressure of the deadly sharp blade finds a soft spot beneath Rye's back armor and between two vertebrae.

"Leave us," Allen hisses, his eyes settle on Tong. "I'm not leaving empty handed."

Rye curses himself for his mistake but Tong doesn't see the immediate danger from where he stands.

"Neither are we," Tong growls. Rye knows his brother only understands they have a problem and Allen is the cause. Tong raises the arc-rifle and sites Allen's head.

"Are you sure?" Allen goads. "I'll sever his spine before you shoot."

"Try me."

Rye drops a hand to his smaller arc-gun, and hopes Allen's peripheral vision isn't as good as a full-blooded Aphid.

He guesses wrong.

As Rye takes the grip in his palm, Allen tenses and Rye feels the sharp pressure of his own knife pressing into his skin. The fabric isn't good defense against a strong and direct knife attack and Allen's inhuman strength threatens to drive Rye's shirt through his back along with the tip of the serrated blade.

Rye takes two quick steps forward since stepping out of reach only makes sense. He turns in time to see Allen squat then disappear upward, narrowly avoiding two quick rounds from Tong's arc-rifle.

"Son of a bitch," Tong growls and Rye has no choice but to agree. Kicking himself for his mistake can wait. As Tong brings the arc-rifle up and tracks Allen's leap, Rye pushes it down.

"Alive," Rye says though it takes extraordinary restraint for his brother to lower the weapon. Far more than it took Rye to give the order.

"Shit," Tong hisses as they follow Allen's path and run to intercept.

The half-Aphid squeals as Tong takes him down, a split second before he lands. The pair tumble as Rye adds himself to the pile and they both wind up on top of Allen. Even with a shot-through shoulder he struggles, all claws and teeth. Tong lands a gloved fist under Allen's chin, buying them the half second needed to get Allen into a safer position on his stomach.

As Rye secures Allen's hands behind his back, Tong draws his knife and places the point at the base of Allen's skull. He raises his other hand ready to drive it in.

"No," Rye gets a hand over Tong's hold on the knife.

"You didn't see," Tong spits as he keeps a knee on Allen. "He scared Quinn, hurt her. I love our parents, Rye, but other than you she's the only blood family I have. He was going to kill my niece, right in front of her mother."

"I know," Rye says softly, risking his grip on Allen to get a palm on Tong's cheek. Tears spill over Tong's lashes. "Other than Quinn, this is the only blood family Angel has. If there's a chance for him, we have to give it to her."

Tong shakes his head though he looks away.

Soon, Rye swears. Soon he'll tell Tong he has a lot more family; a mother and father and two sisters. Soon they'll figure out what all that means. Together.

"Do you want to tell Angel you killed her brother?"

"No," Tong sits and together they secure Allen.

CHAPTER 33

Rye fists the thigh of his gray Core issued pants then forces his hand to the shelf below the glass pane separating the private observation room from the surgery on the other side. As he considers how many times he moved his hand back to the shelf, it returns to the crease he's already made in the fabric.

The woman on the operating table doesn't notice. Two facial reconstruction surgeons transported to *The Barrington* from Earth, stand on either side of her head and are themselves surrounded by a team of nurses, anesthesiologists and other specialists. A drape conceals their work.

Nearby, Scarlet clasps her gloved and immaculately clean hands before her and stands watch over the green packages holding Opal's new jaw and ear implant. A second team works on Opal's leg, removing sections of muscle to anchor everything in place.

Routine, they assured Rye, but he can't help but worry. Few things have scared him as much as this. They let him stay with Opal until she was asleep since she wouldn't go in without him.

"Hey," Angel whispers as she closes the door behind her. "How's Opal doing?"

"She's in there," Rye answers.

"Yeah," Angel slips an arm around his waist and Rye switches to creasing the shoulder of her shirt.

"I promised Max. I told him I'd be here for her. I know he couldn't hear me but I went to tell him. After what they did to him and what he tried to do for Quinn, it's the very least I could do."

"I know."

The lead surgeon's mask moves as he gives instructions and Scarlet rolls the table within reach of the lead nurse. The serious looking woman earned Rye's trust immediately when she put the whole procedure on hold until Opal was ready. She unwraps the curved metal jaw and it disappears behind the drape. Opal will face more surgeries, dentures, skin grafts and cosmetic work, but Rye told her all he wanted was to one day see her smile.

"No money to wake her up and fix her," Angel shakes her head. "But now she's here, Core's falling all over themselves to make her life as good as she wants it. Same with the others."

Rye doesn't answer. For the moment, his thoughts are with the brave young man still spending time in a hyperbaric chamber. Chances remain positive for his recovery, though he's still unconscious through the painful process of removing the Aphid toxins from his system.

"How's Quinn?"

"Giselle is with her in my quarters. They're arguing in German about the best way to keep the mink hidden. Atom built a ladder so she can get up to her bunk. Denman's working on getting us family quarters aboard *Titan*."

"You sure you don't want to go to Earth?" They'd talked about Earth and even Vix Three but they agreed there would be too much pressure on Quinn to fit in to the Core Advanced Training Program. Rye's daughter wants to be a vet, at least today, and Denman loaned her his full sized med scanner. Having the device also helps her feel less powerless about Max's Aphid infection.

"Our baby girl feels safer here."

"Yeah," Rye pinches the bridge of his nose. No family quarters means more nights on Angel's floor. Quinn doesn't have bad dreams when he's there so it's worth it.

"Max is Giselle's brother, you know."

"Her what?"

"He had a falling out with his father when he accepted Core's offer to become a first gen. Gustav wouldn't hear of bringing him out of cryo since he was so disenchanted with Core. Max had been frozen for forty years when Gustav died and Giselle brought him to Helm-Dent."

"Wow," Rye breathes. The more he hears about Gustav Keller the less he likes. Forty years is a hell of a grudge.

"I know, Quinn doesn't speak German to him," Angel adds. "He grew up with his mother on Mars and moved to Keller's home when she died, he was ten and apparently a big surprise to Gustav and his wife."

"I'll bet," Rye agrees.

"Max Keller is close to deciphering his father's work. They worked together until he joined Core. If anyone can figure out how the ship works, it's him. I know Gustav was bent on sympathizing with the Aphids, making friends, but Max lost faith in his father's vision of peace and signed up. He knows enough about recent history to understand we will lose to them without Gustav's work."

Inside the operating room, the surgeon at Opal's thigh passes another pink strip of muscle over the drape. Rye looks at the clock. Only a few more hours and he can breathe again.

"Have you talked to Sesia?"

What he really asks is if there has been any news about Allen.

Angel nods then drops her eyes to hide her sniffles in Rye's shoulder.

"Tell me, sweetheart," he tries.

"You only call me sweetheart because Tong did," she accuses and though she laughs, the tightness doesn't leave her muscles.

"I always called you sweetheart."

"Uh huh," she says even though it damned well isn't true. "He's, um, the only Aphid we've ever had we could talk to."

"And?" Rye whispers as he presses her cheek to his chest and sways with her until her eyes close.

"Sesia says if there's any chance he can be rehabilitated she'll push for it. She has three layers of superiors coming to *Barrington* but we're not supposed to know about that. She thinks they'll have other plans for him but she'll do what she can."

Rye nods. Another secret to keep.

"You," Rye pulls her chin up and kisses her, then runs his thumb along her jaw before tangling his fingers in her soft blonde hair. "Will come see me in my quarters when Opal's awake. I need you alone for a while. In my shower and on my bunk. I'm going to put a smile on your face and tell you again how much I love you."

"Okay," Angel nibbles at Rye's lip. "What about Tong?"

"Busy," Rye shrugs. Atom has him working on *Titan's* bi-annual overhaul in exchange for keeping a particular picture out of circulation.

"Perfect."

Thank you for reading Constant. Writing it has been an amazing experience and sharing it with others has made the experience even better. Other readers would love to hear your thoughts on this book (or any others you have enjoyed!) Please take a moment to visit your favourite online retailer or website such as www.goodreads.com or www.shelfari.com and share your thoughts. Your support helps small publishers and independent writers continue to provide great and original stories!

Thank you.